THE
WEEKEND
TRIP

BOOKS BY JOANNA BOLOURI

Bootcamp for Broken Hearts

THE
WEEKEND
TRIP

JOANNA BOLOURI

bookouture

Published by Bookouture in 2023

An imprint of Storyfire Ltd.
Carmelite House
50 Victoria Embankment
London EC4Y 0DZ

www.bookouture.com

ISBN: 978-1-83790-100-5
eBook ISBN: 978-1-83790-099-2

This book is dedicated to everyone who has multiple sclerosis. You've got this.

PROLOGUE

2012

'Jeez, can you crank it down a notch? I don't need the neighbours calling the Guards over your sudden love for Katy Perry at five thousand decibels.'

Alexandra Moran frowned. Neighbours? What neighbours? They were in the middle of nowhere, surrounded by nothing, and there wasn't another soul for at least a mile, unless Erin was implying that the local wildlife somehow had the ability to summon the Irish police force.

'I'm certain the County Kerry cops have better things to do than break up the world's tamest party,' Alex said, passing Erin the bottle of bubbly. 'We're all still respectably tipsy. It's hardly a rammy. I mean, Beth hasn't even fallen over yet.'

'Give it time,' Beth interjected, pointing towards her wedge trainers. 'I'm pretty sure there's some fresh air somewhere that needs tripping over. The night is still young.'

Erin grinned. In the midst of their Irish squawking, Beth's pretty Welsh accent was like a musical interlude. Alex was right, however; Beth's clumsiness was legendary as was the impressive bruising it often left behind.

'Fine,' Erin replied, flipping her light brown hair over her shoulder. 'It might not be the wildest shindig we've ever thrown, but I'm still turning it down a smidge for the sake of my own eardrums.'

Tara, currently hunting for her cigarettes, snickered. 'Christ. I hope someone does call the cops and they arrest you for saying "shindig". I mean, in the name of the wee man, Erin, are you twenty-two or eighty-two? I swear if you turn that music down, they'll never find your body.'

This was not the party they had planned for their last weekend together after graduation. A girls' weekend in London had been the frontrunner, somewhere with a fancy spa, a rooftop bar perhaps. Their current location, Loughview House, while hardly a run-down shack, barely had Wi-Fi.

As a child, Erin had stayed there regularly. It was designed by her late grandfather Colm, an architect whose wife, Clodagh, had passed from kidney failure when Erin was three years old. Erin loved Loughview House, often spending summers there while her parents navigated a very rocky relationship. It was a large white brick building with five bedrooms, a beautiful kitchen, a huge living room, three bathrooms and a beach practically at the end of the garden. However, this was her first night staying here as the new owner. Eight months ago, Colm died and four weeks later, his last will and testament was read. Everything went to Erin.

Her dad, Terry, Colm's only son, had contested this of course, even taking his only daughter to court, but Colm's last will and testament had made his wishes perfectly clear. The only stable home Erin had ever had growing up was now hers. She hadn't spoken to either of her parents in months, choosing to put herself first, something that they'd never done. Last she heard, they were on a cruise somewhere, bickering most likely. It's what they did best.

Alex wondered whether inheriting a house automatically came with an irrational fear of noise complaints from invisible neighbours, but she kept her thoughts to herself. Instead, she watched her friend Erin, champagne in hand, manoeuvre her way towards the stereo, sidestepping Beth and Rebecca who were currently dancing as badly as they sang.

'And it's hardly a *sudden love*,' she heard Tara yell from outside, through a cloud of cigarette smoke. 'Beth plays her music all the time and I'm pretty sure "I Kissed a Girl" was Becky's coming-out anthem. She loves a bit of Perry, right, Becks?'

Alex knew that if Becky had been a touch more sober, she might have retorted that not only were the lyrics to the song actually rather problematic but also that she came out as bisexual in 2007, a whole year before Katy Perry developed a taste for cherry ChapStick. But instead, Becky just clinked her champagne flute with Beth, who announced that Katy Perry was a goddess before yelping as the contents sploshed over the side of her glass and onto her bare feet.

'And this is why the good Lord invented shoes,' Tara informed her, shimmying in from the patio in her leather pencil skirt, but unsurprisingly Becky didn't care. She liked to go barefoot whenever possible, even if that meant having wet, slightly sticky feet. She called it 'grounding herself' and it was just one of the many *esoteric, new-age, feckin' witchy-woo-woo* (Tara's words) beliefs that she held dearly, like waving smouldering sage around to promote positive energy flow or (Alexandra's personal favourite) freezing the images of her enemies and detractors in their small fridge-freezer. Not long after they'd all moved in together at university, Beth said she had found a photo of Reese Witherspoon, frozen in a clear, plastic sandwich bag, sitting next to the fish fingers. This was never questioned.

'Does anyone know what any of this does?' Erin bellowed, her hands gesturing wildly at the various buttons and knobs on the stereo in front of her. 'There are spaceships with less confusing interfaces. Alex? Any ideas?'

She watched Alex fix her hair in the mirror, pawing at some dark brown curls which appeared to be going rogue.

'Not a scooby,' Alex replied, trying to flatten one particularly springy coil. 'For feck's sake, I look like Medusa. My Greek roots betray me, no pun intended.'

Alex was the funniest, warmest girl Erin had ever known, and had absolutely no idea just how lovely she really was.

'Beth'll know how it works,' Becky interjected. 'She's been in charge of the music so far.'

Beth took charge of most things to be fair. With a sleek brown, perfectly styled bob, she was like the head girl of their little friendship group – reliable, rational and often hilariously bossy when things weren't going her way.

'It's pretty simple,' Beth said, 'It's a bit like the sound system my Paul has in his bedroom, although his is—'

'Cool story, bro, but can you just turn it down... and put something else on? Please not Kanye West, I still haven't forgiven him for Taylor Swift. Oh God, don't give *me* the remote, I've had far too much wine to navigate *that*!' Erin waved her free hand dismissively.

'Y'know, if you're going to live here, you're going to have to know how things work,' Beth huffed, secretly annoyed at Erin's brutal dismissal of Kanye.

Erin smirked. 'God, you're such a bossy cow! You sound just like my grandpa. It's uncanny! In fact, you're even starting to get the same moustache he had ...'

Alex snorted with laughter watching Beth swat Erin's hand away as it now reached for her top lip. 'At least your eighty-year-old grandpa could work this,' she retorted, taking back the remote control. 'It was full of his CDs.'

'Glen Campbell?' Erin asked, as Beth turned down the music. 'Oh, and let me guess... Frank bloody Sinatra. He loved them.'

'Yep, and someone called Dustin Springfield. Never heard of him.'

'Dusty,' Erin corrected. '*She* was an icon. Well, they all were. They were influential and—'

Erin's insights were quickly drowned out as Tara barged past, restoring the music to the previous volume.

'For the love of God, it's supposed to be a party, remember, not a bloody seminar on forgotten singers of the past century,' she informed them. 'If I wanted to be bored shitless about music, I'd have stayed in Dublin with Keith.'

Tara's latest boyfriend Keith was a twenty-eight-year-old shop-assistant-slash-aspiring-musician. Like Tara, he was very beautiful, very tall and made everyone feel very bad about their own genetic makeup.

'He still only knows that one song on the guitar, then?' Alex asked.

Tara nodded, her heavily lined eyes rolling back so far in her head, she almost looked possessed. 'Wonder-bloody-wall. Even I'm surprised I haven't dumped him yet.'

Everyone in the room was surprised about it, too. Not just because Tara hated Oasis, but because her relationships never lasted longer than eight weeks and this one was almost at the four-month mark. A new record? Unlike Beth who'd been dating Paul Cooper since the first week of university, or Erin who was madly in love with fellow acting graduate Damien, Tara found the whole idea of long-term commitment completely absurd. She couldn't even keep the same hair colour for longer than six months.

She'd once said, '*I mean, sure, love is great and all, but once you get to know everything about the other person, then what? You just sit there, never being surprised again until one of you*

dies? How is that remotely appealing? My parents alone are
proof enough that marriage is the work of Satan himself. Why
can't we just properly ravage each other then move on?'

Alexandra felt a pang of self-pity. At the ripe old age of
twenty-two, she'd never been properly ravaged, not in the way
she'd have liked. She'd never even had a boyfriend, let alone
been in love. Sure, she wasn't as gorgeous as Tara, who'd
inherited her face and figure from her former Miss Ireland
mother, or as breastily gifted as double-D Beth, but she wasn't
exactly a bucket of snots either. She'd just never had that
spark with someone and God knows, she longed for that spark.
That moment when you meet someone and you just know
that—

'Shite, it's almost midnight!'

Alex snapped back to reality to see Becky spring to her feet
in a panic. 'Calm down, Cinderella, there's no curfew here.'

'Let's go, people!' Becky insisted, clapping her hands like a
schoolteacher. 'Everyone outside, bring your notes.'

'Yes, miss.'

Notes? Alexandra's face fell. She'd forgotten about this part
of the evening that Becky had planned. Luckily, she'd scribbled
something down yesterday.

'Oh Christ, she's covering up her feet,' Tara exclaimed. 'She
has shoes on! This is not a drill, people! Rebecca, darling, just
how far are you expecting us to walk?'

Loughview was aptly named as it sat on the banks of Lough
Currane, a sight impressive enough to make up for missing that
rooftop bar. A small, slightly rocky path from the bottom of the
garden led directly to a long stretch of deserted sandy beach
where they found themselves at 11.55pm. It was time for
Becky's plan to unfold.

'I cannot believe we've left that nice warm house to stand on
the beach beside a bin,' Tara mumbled in protest, watching
Becky draw a circle around everyone in the sand with a piece of

driftwood. 'Rebecca Murphy, I love you, but I swear if you start summoning demons or walking on water, I will leave.'

'I mean, *technically*, it's not a bin, it's an incinerator,' Erin offered cheerfully, as if that made the situation any less weird. 'There's some law against open fires and—'

'Anything Could Happen' by Ellie Goulding began drifting down from the house and over the beach.

'Did you play this song on purpose, Becky?' Alex asked, conceding that maybe the noise level had been a tad higher than she first thought.

'Nope,' she replied. 'It's just perfect timing. Now, ladies, have we all written down our intentions?'

Becky's request for their final evening together was a peculiar one. Each person had been asked to write down their goals for the future, in present tense. The plan was to burn the notes, sending them off into the universe where they would become reality, *so mote it be...* or something along those lines, Alexandra wasn't entirely sure.

'I have!' Erin replied excitedly, clutching what looked like a Post-it. Can you even do spells on Post-its?

'Yep,' Beth said, pulling her cardigan around her. 'I have my words.'

Alex nodded, briefly holding up her offering as proof of participation.

Becky smiled, delighted that everyone had made the effort. 'Tara?'

'Um...'

'*Tara?*'

'But what if my intention is to not participate in any of this? Do I still have to write that down? Because I will, it's really no bother—'

'Tara, I swear to...'

'Oh, calm down, Glinda, I'm only messing, It's right here.'

Alex clasped her own piece of folded paper and giggled.

Maybe this was ridiculous, but regardless, she understood Becky's desire to mark the occasion with a ceremony. It was a big deal. This was the last night they would all be together until God knows when. In a couple of days Tara would leave for New York, Beth for Manchester and Becky for Glasgow. Even though Alex and Erin would remain in Ireland, at least for now, they'd be at opposite ends of the country. They had spent the last three years living together and now it was all coming to an end.

Becky lit some twigs she'd already placed in the incinerator and waited for them to burn, waving her hands around to speed up the process. It was like Halloween and Bonfire Night, all rolled into one. Tara leaned in and lit a cigarette.

'Those things stink!' Beth informed her, flapping her arms around.

'Well, I'm not smoking rose petals, am I?' she replied. 'Besides, it'll keep the midges away.'

'Midges don't come out at night.'

Becky cleared her throat, breaking up the squabble. As much as the group would argue individually, it was Tara and Beth who clashed most frequently. Alex often said it was like living with Walt and Jesse from *Breaking Bad*, minus the meth and murder.

'So, I want you to hold your notes in your hands, close your eyes and just repeat your intention in your head. Make it feel as real as possible. Then when you're ready, say your intention and place it in the fire.'

'Wait... we have to say it? Like, out loud?' Beth asked. 'Oh, no thank you, that sounds utterly humiliating.'

Tara began to laugh. 'Well now, I definitely think Beth should go first. Humiliating how? Is it like a weird sex thing or...?'

'This is a safe space here, ladies. I'll go first.' Becky stepped forward and took a deep breath, sweeping her blonde fringe from her eyes before closing them. After a moment she opened them and said, 'I am happy. I am healthy. I am loved.' She dropped her note (blue, star-shaped, probably written in glitter) into the fire and stepped back.

'What. That's it?' Alex asked. 'I thought this was like a wish-type deal. You've just asked to be exactly what you are right now.'

Becky smiled. 'Because that's all I need. You're next.'

'Oh, feck off,' Alex replied. 'That's far too humble. Now I'm going to seem like a big egomaniac.'

She stepped forward regardless and closed her eyes, trying not to cringe. Beth was right; this was excruciating.

'OK... I am a best-selling, millionaire author. My husband loves the very bones of me and he has excellent hair. Oh, and I'm happy and healthy, kind to kittens and all that.' Alex scrunched her note and tossed it into the fire but she could have just as easily held it against her bright red face for the same result. 'Gangnam Style' began playing inside the house. Becky frowned and shook her head at Beth and Tara as they started to dance. This wasn't the time.

Next was Erin's turn, her stomach churning in anticipation of her impending humiliation. For someone who hoped to have a career on the stage, she could be painfully shy at times. Something she'd vowed to work on.

'I am a success... no, I am a *hugely* successful actress with awards and homes all over the world which I share with my husband, Andrew Scott.' Note successfully burned, she retreated.

'Andrew Scott off *Sherlock*?' Beth asked. 'What happened to Damien? You know, your current boyfriend, Damien.'

Erin laughed. 'Oh shite. I forgot about him. He's fine, he was more than happy to step aside. Your turn!'

Beth took a deep breath and stepped forward. Then

stepped back, had a quiet word with herself and stepped forward again.

'Right. Here goes. I'm married to Paul and we have two beautiful children, a boy and a girl. Lilly and William. I lecture part-time, maths or computer science. Maybe both.'

'That's it?' Tara exclaimed. 'Why on earth would that be humiliating?'

'Because you all want big careers and I just want a husband and kids. I thought you'd laugh at me.'

Tara shook her head. 'There's no way we'd laugh at you for that. We have so much else to laugh at you for. However, I will make fun of the fact that you're going to name your kids Lilly and Willie.'

Beth scowled. '*William*. Not Willie.'

'Too late. He's a Willie... ooh, maybe a Billy! Lilly and Billy – all versions are equally funny.' Before Beth could say another word, Tara stepped forward, clearing her throat. 'I successfully made *Dick Thirty* a recognised time, like wine-o'clock but for sex. Unfortunately, I was shunned from my home country but have bought an island with my lottery winnings which softened the blow.' Tara grinned, scrunched up her note, paused, aimed and launched it like she was making a basketball shot.

'You didn't write any of that,' Becky said, laughing. 'What did it actually say?'

'Oh, nothing much,' she replied. 'Just happiness and all that good stuff.'

It said nothing of the sort. In fact, it was a scribbled list of things she'd needed to pack for the weekend.

Becky reached out and held Tara's hand in her right and Alexandra's in her left, gesturing to everyone else to link up too.

As Becky said some *woo-woo witchy shit*, the rest of the group just smiled. Maybe it was the cold or even the booze, but as Alex gripped Becky's hand, she felt the energy and warmth from every one of her friends flow through her. They held onto each other, and that moment, together, until the flames died out.

'Promise me we'll keep in touch,' Alex said as they began walking back to the house, 'No matter what.'

And there on the beach, five girls from Dublin University made a promise to do just that. It would be the easiest promise they'd ever make but the hardest to keep.

Date: 28th July 2022

Venue: Loughview House, Kerry.

So, I know Facebook is entirely outdated but I don't use Instagram so this will have to suffice, I'm afraid. I tried emailing but most got returned (understandable unless you're still using Hotmail in 2022 :-D

I'm selling Loughview House and I thought that it might be fun to have one last weekend together. Just the five of us, plus your significant others of course, for a long weekend break. A reunion, if you will. It's long overdue.

I've missed you all.

Erin x

CHAPTER 1

'If you're going to hang out here, can you at least keep your feet off the couch?' Alex shouted from her bedroom.

Alex didn't have to look at Pete to know that he was rolling his eyes. She didn't even have to be in the same room. After five years together, she could anticipate his every move, even before he made it. He was just so... predictable; it was one of the many reasons she'd broken things off last year.

'You let the dog on the couch!' he replied, 'And he has four feet!'

'Yes, but he takes his shoes off.'

I always make terrible jokes around him. Another reason.

Alex glanced down at Winston, her three-year-old dachshund who was currently sniffing inside her suitcase. 'If he puts his dirty great boots on the couch again, I'll blame you,' she whispered to him, while he buried his nose in her pyjamas. 'Why is he one of the only other humans you'll tolerate, besides me? You're cutting your big long nose off to spite your face, you know. You could have gone into some fancy kennels for the weekend. Had your hair done, maybe one of those doggy pedis... Winston, can you stop sniffing my knickers, it's just creepy.'

Winston was a particularly fussy dog, about everything from where he slept (Alex's bed – middle; the couch – left hand side only; the dog basket – the one by the window in the living room with the weird smell), to what he ate (beef, biscuits, shoes, anything really except that organic shite Alex once tried to fob him off with after a visit to the vet). Who Winston allowed to be within ten feet of him was another contentious issue. Alex was obviously fine, as was Pete and also Geraldine the postwoman. Darren the postman, however, was seemingly the most suspicious-looking motherfucker Winston had ever seen and he made sure everyone knew it.

But when Alex had to work, travel or procrastinate herself into a coma when she knew a deadline was looming, she knew Pete would step in and take the fussy little canine, so that had become routine.

Alex was always proud of how amicable her split with Pete had been, but it was hardly surprising. Since they'd met at a book signing seven years ago, their entire relationship had been without drama, so it'd be pointless to start now things were actually over.

There was no yelling, no fighting and compared to most breakups she'd heard about (her editor, Jasmine, had regaled her with tales of her own divorce where she and her ex had had screaming matches over who got the French coffee press), Alex and Pete had been nothing short of cordial towards each other – friendly even, barring the odd passive aggressive remark about couch hygiene. She'd stayed in the main house and Pete had moved into the granny flat in the garden, while he saved for a deposit. To them it made sense; it was less than two kilometres to the fire station where he worked shifts, so their paths didn't cross as often as they used to (unless to co-parent Winston). However, this living arrangement seemed rather odd to everyone else, especially Pete's girlfriend, Florence, an occupational therapist with a penchant for baseball caps and cute ponytails. Alex didn't see the problem. Pete was her best friend; she couldn't think of anyone she'd rather rent her flat to.

Alex placed the last of her clothes into the case then zipped it closed, much to Winston's disapproval. He waggled his bum out of the bedroom, leaving Alex to finish getting ready. The taxi for the airport would be outside in half an hour and she still hadn't put her face on.

'You looking forward to the weekend?' Pete asked, in between telling Winston what a good boy he was. 'The weather is supposed to be great.'

She paused mid-foundation-blend to ponder this. 'I am,' she replied. 'I mean, I think I am.'

'You think?'

'I haven't seen any of them in years. It feels like a lifetime. It'll be surreal to say the least. And strange... really strange.'

'Aren't you friends with them on Facebook? Instagram? Snapchat?'

'Snapchat? I'm not twelve, Pete, and besides no one bloody posts anything anymore! It's only old photos, old status updates. We've all been horrible at keeping in touch. I'm hardly on Facebook, in fact I nearly missed Erin's invite.'

Alexandra hadn't realised quite how anxious she was feeling until now. 'Oh God, what if I'm the only one who got fat?' she yelled to Pete. 'I swear if they all look exactly the same, I'll throw myself into the sea and sink like the bloody great hippo I am.'

She resumed makeup blending and heard Pete chuckle from the living room.

'What's so funny?'

'Nothing,' he replied. 'It's just that hippos are actually pretty strong swimmers, so...'

'Fine then, Indiana Jones, a different animal altogether.'

Now Pete was laughing loudly. 'Alex, Indiana Jones was an archaeologist, not a zoologist. They're not the same.'

She liked Pete's laugh. It was a laugh that came from the soles of his feet and it was infectious. It was the laugh of a man who'd once been a huge part of her life and despite his ability to annoy her, that still meant something. Sometimes, when she was in bed at night, she could hear him laughing with Florence in his flat. It always nipped at her heart. She was glad he'd found someone to make him happy, she knew that was never meant to be her role long term, but his laugh being carried across the garden and into her bedroom only reminded her that she was still alone.

It wasn't like she hadn't tried to find someone. Once a fan of online dating apps, Alex had now resigned herself to the fact that there were no decent single men in Dublin or indeed on planet earth. Once Pete had started dating Florence (and inadvertently flaunting his happiness in her face), she knew it was probably time for her to get back out there again. Get swept off her feet. Find that elusive spark she'd been chasing for so long. However, unlike Pete, that special someone hadn't magically appeared after just one date.

'They can't all be terrible,' her editor, Jasmine, had said over lunch. Working lunches with Jasmine were three percent book talk and ninety-seven percent an excuse to chat shit and eat steak on company expenses. 'It's Dublin, for God's sake! Men are everywhere, you can literally trip over them on Grafton Street any night of the week. Surely one of them must be good company?'

'You'd think,' Alex replied, picking at her side salad, 'but I've been on seven dates in the past month and only one fella has been worthy of a second.'

'There you go! What about him?'

'Unfortunately, I'm not *his* type apparently. I have a functioning brain or something.'

'Fuck him!'

Alex wasn't sure whether that was an instruction or a dismissal, but she nodded anyway.

'Is it just easier for men?' she asked. 'Pete literally matched with one woman, went for a drink and now she's practically living with him in my granny flat, doing her best to hate me.'

'Nah, he just got lucky,' Jasmine replied, 'and you will too. One day, *BAM*, your perfect person will appear and you'll get married and have babies and—'

Alex grimaced at the B word. The thought of being responsible for another human being was terrifying.

'No thank you,' she muttered. 'It's hard enough looking after a grumpy dachshund.'

'Fine then, maybe not babies, but your time will come. Even after the divorce, I managed to find someone and I'm a complete nightmare, you know this.'

'I do. I'm still stunned.' Alex smiled and sipped her chardonnay, but deep down she wasn't so optimistic. Next birthday she'd be thirty-three and she was still no closer to finding The One. She wasn't sure if she'd ever been in love, not really. She loved Pete, she still did, but it was never in a 'fire in your pants, butterflies in your belly' kind of way. Their relationship was like a warm, fuzzy blanket: enormously comforting but not terribly exciting.

'I dunno, if I never meet anyone... well, maybe it's not the end of the world, is it?' Alex said. 'I have a good life, I have Winston—'

'Pets die, Alex.'

Alex gasped. 'What? For feck's sake, Jasmine, break it to me gently, why don't you?'

Jasmine waggled the empty wine bottle towards the waiter.

Alex continued, 'Look, all I'm saying is that being alone doesn't have to be this tragic story and I'll have you know that Winston and I have an agreement where we're both immortal.'

'Seems reasonable,' Jasmine replied. 'Just promise me you won't give up entirely. You're still young. I truly believe that there is someone for everyone, *even authors who miss deadlines and make my life harder than it needs to be and—*'

Alex coughed. 'Where is that wine...'

As the third bottle of wine appeared, Alex had found herself warming towards Jasmine's advice, albeit with a pinot glow. Maybe there was someone out there for her. She'd rather keep the door open to that possibility than close it forever.

Now, face complete, she dragged her case through to the front door, glancing at the grandfather clock in the hall. She adored that clock; it was one of the first big pieces of furniture she'd bought when she moved in. *Serious writers have serious homes with serious furniture*, she told herself, yet still managed to buy one that bent to the left and also doubled as a wine rack. Close enough.

'Do I look decent?' she asked, standing at the living room door. 'I mean I wanted to make the effort but not go full Kardashian.'

She twirled around so Pete could admire her blue patterned shirt dress. He gave it the once over and nodded. 'You look great. Really nice. Blue suits you.'

'Mm-hmm...and?'

She waited. It was Pete. There was always something.

'I'd maybe rethink the heels though. They can be quite the hazard. I mean, if you need to run or, God forbid, the plane crashes and you need to use an emergency slide then they could puncture—'

'Spoken like a true health and safety guru! Thank you, Mr Connor, I shall take your comments on board... as well as my heels.'

Pete's job as a firefighter meant he had a keen eye for potential hazards, even Alex's extremely amazing – and appropriate for every occasion – Christian Louboutin summer sandals, a gift to herself when she hit number one on the *Sunday Times* best-sellers list.

He shrugs. 'You did ask.'

I was fishing for a compliment, not a hundred ways your shoes can kill you.

'I did,' she acknowledged. 'Thank you. Right, I'm off. Look after my baby boy and give Florence my love, won't you? I'll be back Monday night. I left some fancy bath fragrance out if she wants to have a jacuzzi.'

Both Alex and Pete knew it was unlikely to happen, but she was determined to make Florence like her. It had almost become a mission, a side quest in her pursuit to live a happy, hate-free life. She disliked the fact that it was awkward between them, for no other reason than that she once dated Pete. She always thought that she and Florence could be the best of friends if Florence wasn't such a feckin' po-faced cow.

She was pleased to see that her taxi was right on time and the driver, Patrick, was an elderly man of few words, taking her to Dublin airport in plenty of time to catch her flight. *So far so good*, Alex thought. *No additional stress, no mind-numbing small talk and still time for a glass of wine before I board.*

Alex enjoyed the noise her heels made as she left the check-in desk and crossed Terminal One towards security. They produced a noticeable and expensive-sounding click-clack. Definitely more clicky than clacky, she thought, which made her feel rather sophisticated, feminine even. Magical. She felt like the lead in an arty seventies European film called *The many faces of Chantal* or *l'amour dans un aéroport*. If she'd had a sheer scarf she would have swept it across her neck while she laughed gaily at children playing nearby. Men called Pierre and Hugo would raise their eyebrows in lustful approval.

Going through security was as non-eventful as ever, though for some reason Alex always felt like a master criminal, slipping past undetected and now able to move freely among the duty-free sunglasses shops and kitschy Irish whiskey displays. Not that she'd ever done anything remotely criminal in her life but she liked to think that if she did, they'd never catch her.

The best part about airports, however, were the books. Namely hers. She always got a kick out of seeing her books in the wild, especially those placed beside more famous authors. Today her latest novel, *Midnight*, was displayed between John Grisham and Lisa Jewell, and directly under Stephen King. Delighted, she snapped a photo to share online because this was as close as she'd ever get to any of them in real life.

Her road to success had been a tricky one, getting turned down by almost every publisher until finally getting a deal with only a three-thousand-pound advance to publish her first thriller, *The Forgotten*. No one expected it to sell as well as it did, let alone Alex.

'That one's really good.'

Alex turned towards the voice to see a guy, mid-thirties, in a black hoodie, gesturing towards the shelf. He looked like he had just woken up.

'Really? Which one?' she asked, finding herself transfixed by his messy brown hair. It was bloody awful and somehow, stupidly attractive.

'*Midnight*,' he replied. 'A.S. Moran. It's excellent.' Dear Lord, his accent was charming. American? Canadian maybe? Did Canadians sound like cowboys? Regardless, it was distracting enough that she hadn't even noticed that he'd just said the name of her own novel.

'Great,' she replied. 'Hope you enjoy it.'

'Enjoy what?'

'The book.'

He looked confused. 'I did. I just said it was great.'

Did he? Alex felt her cheeks burning. Actually, she felt her entire body start to burn from the inside out but in a nice way, not like that time when she was seventeen and had a suspected

appendicitis on a school trip to Stratford-upon-Avon. As discon-
certingly exciting as this feeling was, she had learned that glistening red was not her colour.

'My flight,' she managed to say, starting to walk backwards.
'I'd better go.'

He watched in apparent amusement as Alex turned and
scurried off, her shoes making a wonderfully loud click-clack as
she scarpered.

CHAPTER 2

'Mam, can we not do this right now? I'm trying to pack and I'm so behind schedule.'

Louise Walsh heard Tara's request but as usual ignored it in favour of reminding her daughter what a *useless article* her father, Christopher, was. Tara was well aware of this fact, given that she'd cut all contact with him six years ago, but Louise, full of animosity and gin, continued to rant.

'Did you know that, when you were six years old, he bought a burger van? A bloody burger van! I said to him, Tara needs new shoes and you've gone and bought this monstrosity? Is she supposed to—'

'—put burger buns on her feet? Yes, Mam, I did know that. You've mentioned it several thousand times.'

Tara placed her mum on speaker and continued to pack, vowing to switch her phone off after this call, in case her mother remembered any further tales of marital hell while her daughter was away for the weekend. Tara didn't want anything to ruin this trip. She was looking forward to seeing the girls again, so much so that she got butterflies every time she imagined walking into that house and greeting the only real friends she'd ever known.

'I heard the van went on fire and I thought, well, that's karma. You set my life on fire, now the same has happened to you.'

Tara cringed. God, her mother could be so overly dramatic, it was mortifying. She would need nicotine if she was going to have to sit through this shit again.

'When I won Miss Ireland—'

Oh, dear God, not this Miss Ireland anecdote. I do not have time or the energy to go back to the seventies with her.

'—I never thought that out of all the roads that opened up for me, one of those roads would lead directly to that morally bankrupt French Canadian. Thank God I still have my looks because that man literally left me with nothing else. Not one good thing came out of that relationship.'

Not one good thing. Really, Mam? Have we met?

Tara always thought that if her mother had been born with a different, more *ordinary* face, she might have actually become a decent human being. One who considered her daughter to be a blessing from her awful marriage, not an inconvenience It had always bothered Tara that she looked just like her mother. Having grown up with Louise Walsh, she understood just how damaging conceit could be. When her dad remarried someone younger, someone fresher faced, it absolutely broke her mother because youth was the one thing she couldn't compete with.

'Anyway, why are you packing?' Louise asked. 'Are you going on holiday? I haven't had a holiday in years.'

'Didn't you go to Bulgaria with your cronies in March?' Tara responded, scrambling around for her vape. It was only July now, surely she couldn't have forgotten already.

Her mum sighed. 'I wouldn't consider that a holiday. It was more of a mental health emergency. It was life or death, darling.'

'Two secs, Mam.'

Tara put the phone on mute and screamed into a couch cushion. Life or death? Her mother had stayed in a five-star Marriott hotel in Sofia! She had photos of them on the beach and wine-tasting. She even got reiki! Jesus, why couldn't she admit to having a nice holiday, like a normal person? Her mother's histrionics were nothing new. For as long as Tara could remember, she would turn everything (good or bad) into some kind of melodrama. She was the type of woman who would hear a song playing on the radio and swear that it could have been written by her, for her or about her.

'OK, I'm back.'

'I mean, I barely relaxed the entire time,' Louise continued, 'Far too cold to swim. I might have well just have stayed in—'

'San Diego.'

'Pardon?'

Tara found her vape and inhaled, producing a ridiculous amount of vapour, like a walking smoke machine. Six months cigarette-free and she still missed them. 'You asked where I was going. I'm going to San Diego. And no, not a holiday, I'm working.'

She didn't feel bad about lying to her mother because if Louise had even gotten as much of a whiff that her daughter was heading back to Ireland without telling her, her life would not be worth living.

Louise sniffed. 'Must be nice. You've certainly done well for yourself. If it had been up to your father, you wouldn't even have gone to university, you know. That fancy degree you have is no thanks to him.'

Fancy degree? Tara smirked. Business and economics was the least fancy degree she could think of.

'Yes, you're probably right.' Tara found this blanket statement to be incredibly helpful during conversations with her mother. She used it often, along with 'That's really interesting' and 'Oh dear, my phone's about to die.'

Tara batted away another cloud of vape and looked around the room. *Laptop... check. Chargers... check. Urge to cut all contact with my mother... checkcheckcheck.*

'Anyone going with you on this little business trip?'

Tara sighed. Louise had said 'business trip' like it was code for something far more salacious. Like *Secret Sexy Liaison* or *Penis Adventure.*

'No, I'm not seeing anyone, if that's what you're asking.'

Louise huffed. 'You say that like it's a bad thing! Sweetheart, you're almost thirty and—'

'Almost thirty? Mam, I'm already thirty-two.'

'—and time is ticking. I just want you to understand that the options for middle-aged women, especially in this day and age, are sparse and cruel.'

Tara snorted. 'Wow. OK, thanks for letting me know, I'll be sure to lower my expectations to zero and *oh dear, my phone's about to die.* Talk to you later.'

She hung up and vaped again before tossing her phone onto the bed. How Tara's mother could possibly think that her words were remotely helpful or encouraging was beyond her. Tara wanted to tell her that she'd never had any trouble finding quality male company, but it just wasn't the be-all-and-end-all. Opening up her phone again, she began typing on WhatsApp.

Hey you! How was Dublin? My flight gets in an hour after yours. Can't wait to see you xx

In an ideal world she would introduce her boyfriends to her mum but, realistically, that was never going to happen, especially not with this one. Maybe he wasn't the most thrilling man she'd ever met, but he was the only stable thing she had in her life and she wasn't letting anything or anyone ruin that.

CHAPTER 3

'We should have flown. I knew this would happen.'

'Oh, you did, did you? You knew that I'd get seasick, despite never having a single episode of water-induced nausea in my entire life. Well, good for you, *Mysterio*, you'll be happy to see Becky again. Maybe you both can read my tea leaves over breakfast.'

Beth placed her head between her legs and groaned. She felt awful. For someone who normally loved the heat, this weather was too much, making her feel like she'd been left to drip dry after a shower. Even her eyelashes were sweating. Combine this with nausea and right now she'd happily accept the ferry sinking and would use her husband Paul's stupid face as a life raft.

Unaware that Beth was currently dreaming of using him as a floatation aid, Paul sat down beside her, rubbed her back and offered her water. Beth very quickly calmed, feeling somewhat embarrassed by her overreaction.

'Ugh. Sorry, hun,' she whispered, taking the water bottle. 'I know I'm a lot these days.'

'You're not, sweetheart,' he replied, giving her a reassuring smile. Fourteen years together and that smile still soothed her. 'And I don't think it's seasickness, I think it's your meds. One of the side effects is nausea.'

She knew this, having googled the nerve pain medication to death as soon as she was prescribed it. Another side effect was chronic diarrhoea. Small mercies, she thought. Small mercies.

'It's my fault,' Paul insisted, 'I stupidly hoped a little land-and-sea adventure might be fun. Romantic, even.'

It was romantic, she thought. Drive from Pembroke to Fishguard, catch the ferry to Rosslare and then continue all the way to Kerry, maybe stopping for dinner or staying over in a cute little B&B if the journey became too taxing to do all in one day. But now that she was on the deck of a crowded ferry, melting under the blazing afternoon sun and seriously close to saying hello to her breakfast again, she'd probably choose to fly next time.

'It was, no, it *is* a lovely idea,' Beth replied, leaning into his shoulder. 'Kind of reminds me of that road trip we took to France for your thirtieth, only without the car trouble.'

He chuckled. 'RIP that Honda... but it was about as old as me. At least we have a more reliable car now. Our new one is a beast.'

Beth nodded but found it hard to be overly happy about it. The car they currently owned was absolutely more reliable because it was brand new. A beautiful, bright blue, electric Nissan provided by a disability charity which they'd never have been able to afford to lease under normal circumstances. As much as she loved and appreciated it, she'd give it back in a heartbeat just to be well again.

She slowly sipped her water, starting to feel more human. 'It's going to be weird seeing them all again, isn't it?' she remarked. 'Total blast from the past.'

'I'm looking forward to it. Umm... there's going to be other men there, right? Husbands, boyfriends? Swat team?'

Beth smiled. 'Why? Scared, are we?'

'No... maybe. Look, you were all mental back then, I just want to make sure I have some extra testosterone on hand in case you all want to dismantle the patriarchy in a bloody coup or something.'

She laughed. Paul had gotten along remarkably well with her friends back in their uni days and that had always worked massively in his favour. Her girls were as important to her as he was, maybe more so back then. If they hadn't liked him or vice versa, Beth was certain that they wouldn't be sitting on a bench, looking out to sea at this very moment, man and wife.

So important to you that you didn't all get together for ten years? Great friend you were.

Beth didn't like that little voice of reason in her head and resisted the urge to have a full-blown debate with herself in the middle of the Irish Sea. But that voice did have a point.

'You OK?' Paul asked. 'You've gone a bit quiet.'

Beth wearily exhaled. 'Ugh, I'm alright. Just thinking that maybe I should have made more of an effort to keep in touch. Liking a Facebook or Instagram photo occasionally doesn't quite cut it.'

'Perhaps,' he replied. 'But it happens. Life happens. You all scattered across the globe: keeping up with all of that is a very big ask. Don't beat yourself up.'

'Ladies and gentlemen, we will shortly be docking at Rosslare.' A crackly tannoy sprang into life.

'Might need to use the loo again before we get back in the car,' Beth said, closing the lid on her bottle of water. 'Oh, and then every fifteen minutes when we're actually in the car.'

He laughed. 'Whatever you need.'

'Also, my leg's a bit spasmy, can you drive first?'

Paul groaned. 'Gah, I'm such an idiot. I mean, what kind of moron plans a lengthy road trip when their wife has multiple sclerosis? See, we should have flown.'

'Stop it,' Beth insisted. 'I agreed to this too, you know! We'll make it work. We always make it work.'

'I know, I just—'

Beth grabbed his face and kissed him. 'You are a lovely man, Paul Cooper. I don't deserve you and I promise I will never use your face as a raft.'

'Good to know,' he replied, a confused smirk appearing on his face. 'You ready?'

Beth nodded, slipping one hand into his as the other gripped her walking stick. She was as ready as she'd ever be.

CHAPTER 4

The weather forecast for their reunion weekend couldn't have been more perfect, but, for once, Erin begrudged the sunshine. Glaring at the living room window, she quietly cursed the great fiery ball in the sky which happily beamed in, highlighting every streak she'd just inadvertently made with her new window cleaning spray.

'Everyone raved about this product on Instagram,' she shouted towards her phone. 'I'd have been better just spitting on the window and rubbing Jasper's fluffy arse all over it.'

She heard her agent, Nicole, laugh before attempting to steer the conversation away from Erin's cat's backside and back to business. 'Look, Idris really wants you to do this film. Will you at least go in and read with him?'

'Three attempts and this window is still taunting me. Do you think everyone would mind just sitting with the curtains closed?'

'Erin...'

Erin sighed, setting her cloth down on the coffee table. She sat on the couch and picked up her new Samsung flip phone.

'I don't know,' she admitted. 'I mean, as tempting as the

thought of working with Idris Elba again is, I just think it's too soon.'

'At least think about it,' Nicole replied. 'It might be a welcome distraction, you know. Get you back out there, back in the land of the liv... oh shit. Oh shit, shit, I didn't mean—'

'I'll think about it. I'd better go, I still have lots to do. Take care, Nic.'

She flipped her phone closed and placed it on the table. *Breathe, Erin. Just breathe.*

She knew Nicole hadn't meant anything by it, just the wrong turn of phrase, but still it jolted her heart into her throat. *The land of the living.* The one place where Scott couldn't exist and she wasn't ready to go back there without him.

She wiped at a tear. She hadn't noticed it escaping from her eye until it trickled to the corner of her mouth. Even after twelve months of crying, she could still hear Scott in her head, sarcastically telling her that sadness was vastly overrated and only led to uncontrolled clicking of Facebook shopping links at 3am.

Jasper's meow near his food bowl was a welcome distraction. He wasn't a particularly vocal cat so when he did decide to articulate his annoyance over an empty dish, it was adorable as she knew it was a sound reserved solely for her. The long-haired tabby had shown up at Loughview House three years ago and never left, choosing to spend his summers lounging outside and his winters curled up at the foot of Erin's bed.

'No mice this weekend,' she warned him as she squeezed a foil pocket of cat food into his bowl. 'Not everyone appreciates rodent corpses as much as you do.' After three years, when it came to mice, Erin had gone from terrified to ambivalent to sympathetic, even to the point of humanely capturing the ones that Jasper let go and driving them to a field where they didn't have to deal with a spoiled tabby who only ate a particular fish soup but liked to torture mice for pleasure.

She checked her watch. Another couple of hours and the girls would be arriving.

With the windows now officially a lost cause, Erin pottered around making sure the guest rooms had everything she thought they might need. She had considered leaving individual gifts in the rooms, but after ten years of minimal contact, how could she presume to know what they now liked? Would she even know them at all?

Did Becky still have a problem with Reese Witherspoon? She knew that Alex was still writing, but did she still read as voraciously as she once did? Was Beth still into Katy Perry? Did Tara ever dump Keith and his monotonous music?

She pondered these questions as she went room to room, leaving towels on the beds and making sure all the bathrooms had loo roll and fancy hand wash. She had thought about hiring a cleaner to blitz the place before her guests arrived, but she had not had anyone in the house since the funeral last year and the last thing she needed were stories appearing in the *Daily Mail* about how grief had turned actress Erin Flynn into someone incapable of taking care of herself and her home. Besides, cleaning gave her something to do. Something to focus on.

The house had been renovated since the girls were last here. Nothing major structurally but now it was much more their home now than her grandpa's. *Their* home. Her home.

She found it to be a tad more modern than she'd have liked, but Scott was very much into contemporary design and she wanted it to be as much his home as it was hers. He coveted helpful gadgets, minimalist rooms and shiny white surfaces whereas Erin preferred a home by the sea to be more shipwreck than shipshape. Erin preferred her memories and keepsakes to be dotted everywhere, despite Scott's protests. To begin with, Erin was grateful that she had stuck to her guns and displayed their life together for all to see. It was proof that Scott had lived here and that he had been happy. They had been happy. But now... now it was just a reminder that the world had moved on and she was completely alone. A few months after Scott died, her agent had broached the subject of selling Loughview House, an idea that Erin initially dismissed. It was still too raw, too painful to even consider. She needed time to grieve. But now, eight months later, while time hadn't exactly healed her wounds, it had given her an understanding of just how fleeting time itself was. Much to her dismay, life carried on and no matter how much Erin wanted the world to stop, it just kept spinning regardless.

Contacting the estate agent wasn't as hard as Erin had anticipated. As much as she knew she knew it was the right thing to do, she wasn't so sure she would ever convince her heart to leave it all behind. Of all the memories Erin held dear from Loughview, from her and Scott drinking beer by the firepit, to playing with her grandpa on the beach as a child, the one that hit the hardest was a memory from a decade ago. Graduation night with her best friends. Those women weren't lost to her, not in the way Scott and her grandpa were.

Erin realised that while Scott might have been her greatest love, he certainly wasn't her first and she was not ready to lose all of her soulmates entirely. Erin knew that in order to move on, she needed her past friends to help her see a future.

She just hoped it wasn't too late.

CHAPTER 5

At the end of the road, turn right.

'Of course I'm looking forward to it! Why wouldn't I be? These women were my entire life back then!'

'You seem a little on edge, Rebecca, that's all. I just wondered if there was something else going on. Maybe something a little deeper that perhaps you haven't acknowledged yet.'

'Like what?'

Christine flipped the indicator to the right and sat at the junction, despite the road being clear enough to proceed. 'Hmm, I think you'll find that's a question only you can answer.'

Becky grimaced. That tone of voice. That accent. It never used to be as grating.

When she'd first heard Christine speak at a mindfulness retreat two years ago, she'd been positively captivated. That soft English accent, soothing yet commanding. She thought she'd never tire of hearing it.

Hmm, I think you'll find that's a question only you can answer.

She'd thought wrong.

Becky pursed her lips and bobbed her head like she was contemplating her girlfriend's words. It was almost like appeasing her. Recently, she found herself doing that a lot but considered it par for the course when dating a psychologist. They needed that, right? To have their thoughts and opinions taken seriously, regardless of whether those thoughts and opinions were actually solicited or not.

Becky sat quietly, reminding herself that everything would be OK. That they would continue to work through their issues with *mutual love and respect*. Becky thought that two years was an awfully short time to already be having relationship issues, but Christine had assured her that it was quite normal, especially when one party (Becky) had come into that relationship with unresolved issues, issues she wasn't aware of until Christine informed her that they existed.

Continuing to sit at the empty junction, Christine removed a bobble from her wrist and began sweeping her hair back, forming a sleek, brown ponytail. Unlike Becky's wavy blonde, unruly mop, her hair was straight and thin and always sat perfectly. She was wearing it like that the night they first met, when Christine had approached her and said:

'So, you're the massage maestro? I've been hearing great things.'

Becky had looked up from her phone and smiled. It was the first genuine smile she'd given that day, a day in which she'd been run off her feet promoting her new massage training courses to guests who'd paid ridiculous amounts of money to try and live in the moment. Still, the hotel they were staying in was gorgeous and now it seemed like Becky's evening might be far more interesting that she first thought.

'Christine, right?' she replied, feeling her cheeks flush a little. It was the woman with the gorgeous voice from earlier. 'Rebecca... well, Becky. Nice to meet you.'

'Rebecca is a beautiful name. May I join you?'

So, there is a God. Sister Harvey from St. Mary's was right all along.

'Sure, that would be nice,' Becky replied. 'I hate to drink alone and I intend to have several.'

As Christine held her gaze, Becky felt her heart leap against her chest wall. 'Great,' she replied, to an increasingly red-faced Becky, 'Let me just grab a wine list.'

It had been eight months since Becky had had her heart broken by Stephen, and while her self-confidence was pretty much in the toilet, she knew a big old dirty flirt when she saw it. However, it was the first time in a while she'd been hit on by someone who didn't have facial piercings, a sleeve tattoo or a PhD in applying unnecessarily thick black eyeliner. She was flattered if somewhat confused. Maybe, just maybe she'd finally met someone who had their shit together.

Relax, for God's sake. You're just having a drink with the woman, it's really not that deep.

Christine returned with the wine list and handed it to Becky. 'They do a wonderful chablis. The merlot is also fine, but it needs to be decanted.'

Becky knew nothing about wine, generally choosing a bottle based on the discount the supermarket happened to be offering. 'Chablis is good,' she replied, briefly browsing the list. Christine smiled and returned to the bar to order.

Two hours and one bottle of overpriced chablis later, and the bar was filling up quickly with guests from the conference. But Becky found herself absolutely enthralled by Christine. She'd never met anyone like her.

'So, both of your parents are doctors? That's impressive.'

Christine bobbed her head while she poured the last of the wine. 'Surgeons actually. They were a little disappointed I didn't follow suit. I prefer to look inside someone's head without actually cutting it open.'

Becky laughed. 'I think my folks wanted me to be either a nun or a teacher. Something faith based at least. They live in Valencia now, probably within polishing distance of Holy Grail.'

'Ah,' Christine replied. 'Religious, huh?'

'Paragons of virtue,' Becky said with a smile. 'My ma especially. Way back, her side of the family were travellers, some not so morally upright as she discovered. I think she's trying to repent on their behalf.'

Becky couldn't remember the last time she'd felt so comfortable with someone. Christine was beautiful, intelligent and listened intently to every word Becky said.

'It's fascinating to me,' Christine said, her fingers stroking the stem of the wine glass. 'My family were very much secular. To me, the whole concept of religion is... oh God, here come the wackadoos. They cornered me earlier.'

Even the way she insults people is adorable. Wait, who is she insulting...

'Sorry?'

Christine motioned towards a group of women being seated by the window. 'They're all crystals and metaphysics and bogus concepts that have no place in modern, science-based mental health practices.'

Becky was a little unsure how to respond to this given that she had a degree in philosophy, which included metaphysics. She also had an in-depth knowledge of all things Wicca and carried polished tumble stones in her bag for good luck.

'Oh... right. So, you don't consider all forms of healing to be valid? I mean, if it helps people...'

'Not as far as *they're* concerned. They might as well just cast spells and dance around a bonfire for all the good it does. Now, where were we? Oh yes, I think we need more wine!'

As Christine walked towards the bar, Becky felt her heart sink. Her ex, Stephen, had felt the same way about her lifestyle, although he'd strung her along for months before telling her, 'This whole voodoo thing. It's ridiculous and embarrassing. Grow up.'

Becky had never practised voodoo, but she'd figured that explaining the differences and nuances of magic-based religions and beliefs would be pointless at that moment. Instead, she'd made a mental note to put his picture in her freezer and began packing her things.

His words had stuck with her, however. She was thirty. Maybe it was time to grow up. Becky slipped her rose quartz rings and pentagram bracelet into her bag. It wasn't often that she clicked with anyone, and she really liked this woman. Maybe her *wackadoo* tendencies could have the night off. They hadn't exactly been helping her lately anyway.

That was two years ago and she hadn't worn her pentagram since.

Finally, the car moved off again and before long they were passing nothing but lush green fields, sheep and the occasional farmhouse, a sight Becky welcomed after living in London for the past six years. She'd lived in Scotland before then, a country which made her little Celtic heart happy, but then that same heart fell for a masseur from Croydon and off she followed.

If she had family left in Ireland, she might have come back more often, but her deeply religious parents had moved to Spain and no doubt were still trying to *pray away the gay* from their home in Valencia.

After what seemed like a reasonable amount of time for the consideration of Christine's question, Becky finally replied. 'I think I'm just a tad nervous, but I'll be fine. I imagine that everyone else will be feeling the same, right?'

'Hmm,' Christine replied. 'It'll be fascinating to say the least. I imagine that partners were invited to take some of the pressure off. After ten years, who knows whether you'll actually have anything in common anymore!'

True, Becky thought. She was no longer running around barefoot and pulling Tarot cards out of her arse. She'd grown up.

Becky smirked. 'Actually, it's the strangest thing. We really didn't have *that* much in common to begin but—'

'Can you pass me some chewing gum?'

'Sorry? Oh, right. Sure.' Becky reached into her bag and obliged, handing Christine two pieces of gum from the packet. *She rarely chews gum*, Becky thought. *Wait, is this her round-about way of telling me that my breath stinks so I'll take some too?*

She quickly slipped a piece into her mouth. Better safe than sorry. No one wanted to be stuck in a car with the halitosis queen.

'You were saying?'

Becky paused, mid-chew, like a cow who'd just been asked to solve a maths problem. Her mind went blank.

'About not having much in common?' Christine reminded her.

The chewing recommenced. 'Ah yes. It's nothing really, just that we were all very different girls back then. We all attended the same uni, but our interests were quite diverse. It's surprising we became as close as we were.'

She smiled to herself at the thought of their old apartment in Clondalkin. A miserable three-bedroomed dump that the five of them could just about afford if they shared bedrooms and kept their fingers crossed that the landlord wasn't jailed for housing standards violations. She'd been the last to move in, and she remembered that moment she'd first met them all together.

'Everyone, this is Becky.'

Becky Murphy had smiled at the group of girls who were all in various states of slouching throughout the living room. She hadn't thought that meeting her new housemates would feel quite so intimidating, but now that she was here, it was all rather daunting. Looking around, she recognised the tall girl, Tara, from when she'd viewed the house a week earlier, and Erin, the girl who'd placed the advert at the uni coffee shop.

'Nice to meet you all,' Becky said, noticing how much smaller the living room looked with everyone in it. Erin motioned for her to sit on the well-worn couch. 'You remember Tara, and this is Alex and Beth. Alex moved in last week, the rest of us have been here about a month.'

'Welcome to the madhouse,' Alex said. 'Ooh, I like your necklace, it's so pretty!'

Becky thanked her, not mentioning that she'd worn this particular black tourmaline pendant to shield her from any weird or unwanted energy. For all she knew, she'd just agreed to share a house with four energy vampires; a little grounding and protection was necessary.

'So, you'll be sharing with Beth, this week,' Erin informed her. 'I'll help you up with your bags in a sec.'

'Sorry? This week?'

'We move rooms,' Erin replied, grinning. 'It's a little unconventional, but it works. Also, you'll buy your own food, but we all split washing powder, Fairy Liquid, etc. No point having five of the same things. Fiver a week in the jar on top of the fridge.'

'Sure, makes sense.'

'We keep the same wardrobes but get a basket for your toiletries and makeup. Makes it easier when moving rooms.' Tara added. 'Although we end up just sharing each other's shit.'

'And by *sharing*,' Beth interjected, 'Tara actually means breaking the third house rule and just helping herself without asking.'

'Jesus, it was a bit of perfume,' Tara whined. 'You'd think I'd borrowed your boyfriend.'

Everyone laughed as Beth threw a pillow at Tara. 'It was Chanel! I'd rather you borrowed Paul, he costs less. Oh, house rules are on the fridge by the way, as well as the bathroom rota. Don't worry, you'll get the hang of it.'

'Beth is like our house matron,' Erin said. 'She'll keep you right... are you OK? You look a little bewildered.'

Becky nodded. She'd spent a year in student accommodation before this, so she'd been used to sharing. However, hardly anyone spoke to each other in halls, and the friends from her course were all happily flat sharing already. But this setup was an entirely different ballgame. This was like a rather chaotic family gathering.

'Sorry, I'm good,' she replied, 'It's just, you're all so relaxed with each other! Did you know each other beforehand?'

'Nope,' Alex replied. 'We all met here. Tell us about yourself then! Any arrests we need to know about?'

Becky laughed. 'Nothing they could charge me with, and there isn't much to tell, to be honest! I'm from Derry, studying philosophy and I'm a Taurus.'

Tara started to giggle. 'Philosophy, horoscopes and crystals,' she said, her eyes fixed back on Becky's pendant. 'I bet you're vegan, too.'

'Vegetarian,' Becky corrected.

'Then you'll get on well with Alex; she's a new-ager.'

Alex rolled her eyes. 'Ignore her, I bought some incense cones last week and she's convinced I'm now about to whip out a headscarf and a crystal ball.'

'Crystal balls are overrated,' Becky replied. 'Mirrors are much better for scrying. I have one with me if anyone wants their fortune told?'

The room fell silent.

'You're kidding, right?' Beth said.

Becky laughed. 'Maybe a little. OK, I think I'll get settled in,' she said, looking over at Erin. 'This Ouija board won't unpack itself.'

Alex started to laugh while Erin helped her upstairs with

her cases. As she reached the top landing, she heard Tara say, 'She's obviously mental and I for one am fucking delighted.'

It took Becky exactly three months of living with Erin, Beth, Tara and Alex to know that these weren't just her housemates. They were her sisters.

In 2.2 kilometres, turn left.

'All I'm saying is that some people struggle to let go of previous relationships,' Christine said. 'And not just romantic ones. Christ, dealing with this particular issue is probably ninety percent of my job.'

Becky nodded.

'And obviously it's a shame about your friend's husband. To be a widow at thirty-two must be quite daunting, especially when you're in the public eye. I mean, it's perfectly understandable not to want to go through the grief process alone, but I'm just not entirely sure that reviving dead friendships is the best way to deal with a dead husband.'

'Did you really just say that?'

Christine didn't respond. She just turned left and continued until Becky saw a glimpse of Loughview. It was at that moment that Becky regretted asking Christine to join her. Instead, Becky wanted to politely ask her girlfriend to get out of the car so she could run her over.

You have reached your destination.

CHAPTER 6

The departure lounge at the airport was heaving, not unusual for Dublin Airport, but Alex thought that just once she would like to sit and have a drink without having to share her table or become unreasonably annoyed at the blokes (because it was always the blokes) who'd slam their almost empty, dreg-splattered pint tumblers down in front of her and rush off to catch their flight.

She ordered a small glass of chardonnay and took it to a table near the window where a couple had just left, pushing their coffee cups to one side as she sat down. Hopefully no one would spot the empty chair beside her and she could sip her wine in peace.

Her feet were beginning to swell and throb a little. These sandals, beautiful as they were, perhaps were not meant for moving feet, only feet which rested on bar stools or dangled from the ends of elegantly crossed legs. Still, it was only half past one, she had an hour before boarding, plenty of time to let her feet deflate and watch the world go by.

'Hello, again.'

In the window she caught sight of a figure at her table. It

was the handsome man from the book section in WHSmith. *Oh good*, she thought, *he's come to return the dignity I dropped earlier. Brilliant.*

'Hi!' she responded, because that seemed far more rational than 'marry me.'

'I'm not following you, I swear!' He presented his beer bottle as corroboration that he too had a reason to be within fifty feet of her. 'It's kinda crowded so...'

She saw his eyes dart to the empty chair.

'I mean, I can sit on that guy's lap if he'll let me?'

Alex smiled as he gestured to a rather formidable-looking tattooed man in a polo shirt, sitting at the table to their left.

'It's fine,' she replied, 'Please, sit down. Those coffee cups were terrible at conversation anyway.'

'Very kind,' he said, sitting across from her. 'Hopefully I'll do a better job. I'm Aiden, by the way.'

'Alex,' she replied. 'Nice to meet you. You off anywhere nice?'

Jesus, Alex, you sound like a hairdresser.

'I'm not even sure,' he replied, 'I've never been to Kerry before. My girlfriend tells me it's beautiful though.'

Girlfriend. Of course, he has a girlfriend because there are no decent single men left. Not any that look like him, anyway. Well, Alex, it's just going to be you and Winston until you decided to bring a cat into the picture and—

'You alright?'

'Oh, yes! Sorry, where did you say you were going?'

'Kerry,' he repeated. 'You?'

'Same,' she replied. 'What a coincidence! Unless you *are* following me...'

'I'm absolutely not... not unless you're also going to meet my girlfriend's family for the first time?' He smiled sheepishly. 'Sorry, I'm a touch nervous.'

'Has she met yours?'

'No. We've actually only been dating a few months.'

Alex sipped her awfully dry chardonnay. 'Wow, that is a big deal, isn't it? Irish families are brutal. A few years ago, I took my boyfriend to meet my ma and they never found his body. I think she battered him to death with her slippers.'

He laughed. 'You're not helping.'

'I'm only messing. They got on really well. I think she liked him more than she liked me.'

'Your boyfriend obviously has skills,' he replied, taking a swig of his beer. 'I should ask him for notes. Or maybe some tips from your mother?'

'Ex-boyfriend,' she informed him, 'and my mother has passed since then, though I'm sure that wouldn't stop her having some thoughts on the subject.'

Aiden's eyes widened to the size of his beer bottle.

Overshare some more, why don't you, she thought. *Make the man uncomfortable.* God, she would have kicked herself if her feet weren't throbbing.

'So, do you live in Kerry or...?' he asked politely, because what the hell do you say after someone makes a joke about their dead mother.

'Weekend with some old friends,' she responded. 'Should be fun... God, I'm sorry, that mother thing was misjudged, my mouth just runs away with me sometimes.'

He shook his head. 'Please don't be. I've lost both of my parents. Sometimes humour is the only way to cope. Besides, I'll take misjudged over the usual humdrum small talk people swap at airports any day.'

———

Forty very enjoyable minutes later, Alex heard their flight being called over the tannoy.

'I'll walk with you if that's OK,' he said, picking up his back-pack. 'I think I've done enough following for one day.'

'Agreed,' she said. 'At least this way I'll know where you are.'

Thankfully for Alex's feet, the walk to their gate was short, but she still felt sad that their time together had come to an end. Meeting Aiden had been unexpected to say the least but the most fun she'd had in ages.

'Well, I have to make a quick phone call,' he said, 'but have a nice flight! It's been really great meeting you. Surprising.'

'You too,' she replied. Would it be weird to give him a hug? *Of course it would, you loser, he has a girlfriend, just say good-bye.* 'Hope everything goes well with the family!'

Alex got in line for boarding while Aiden walked to the side to make his phone call.

Surprising. She smiled. What an excellent way to describe it.

Once on board, Alex took her seat by the window and slid her shoes halfway off. Instant relief. All that feminine click-clacking was starting to take its toll but rather than unleash her trotters on unsuspecting passengers, half-off meant she was being socially responsible in keeping her sweaty feet to herself. People shared that kind of thing online. Viral photos of passengers with their feet on display being torn to shreds by a comments section baying for blood. The last thing she wanted was to be foot shamed and cancelled by the time they touched down in Kerry. She sat back in her seat and giggled to herself. *Foot shamed.* Becky wouldn't have cared about that. Becky and her need to be at one with the ground would have been nude-footed by now, her little blue anklet jingling as she pranced around.

As the rest of the passengers boarded, she lifted the inflight magazine from the seat pouch. *Maybe I should bring something for Erin*, she thought while flicking through. Some Ray-Bans or perhaps some all-purpose skin cream that was featured in *Vogue* because nothing said *sorry your husband died* quite like a tax-free overpriced moisturiser and—

'This is getting ridiculous.'

Alex turned to see Aiden, placing his bag in the overhead compartment, right next to hers.

'You're kidding?' she said, watching him reach to the back of the storage area while simultaneously making a bold effort not to stare at the flash of toned stomach which appeared every time he stretched. Didn't they have longer T-shirts across the pond? High-waisted jeans? Onesies?

'I swear, I'll show you my ticket,' he said, continuing to struggle with his carry-on bag. 'I'm just as surprised as you are.'

Finally, he closed the compartment and sat in the aisle seat, placing his water bottle in the seat pouch in front.

'Is it weird that I'm happy about this?' he asked. 'Like it's weird as hell but also strangely brilliant. I usually get stuck next to middle-aged men with perspiration problems. Gum?'

His hand reached across the empty middle seat, holding a packet of chewing gum. So far, no one had taken the seat between them. She hoped it wouldn't be the tattooed man from the bar.

'I'm good,' she replied. 'But thanks.'

'My ears pop, It's very annoying.'

'Yeah, it must be,' she replied, her eyes still scanning the magazine. Would Erin like a box of airplane Pringles? Everyone liked Pringles.

'Although, probably not as annoying as the American who keeps showing up and making silly conversation, right?'

American. Not Canadian. Noted.

Alex smirked. Normally he would be correct. Like most women, she hated it when men just inserted themselves into her space uninvited. The truth was in this case, she feared that if she looked directly at him for too long, she might drool.

'Sorry,' she replied, flipping over the magazine, 'I was just a little distracted, but please, continue with the silly conversation, I can't get enough of it.'

He glanced at the magazine. 'Ah yes. Duty-free: the attention killer. Anything good?'

She shook her head. 'Just wondering if bereavement warrants some new sunglasses or—'

The sudden, loud roar of the engine surprised Alex, cutting the rest of her mumbled sentence off. She hadn't even noticed they'd started moving.

'Any last words,' she said as the cabin began to shake. 'You know, just in case we explode mid-air?'

'Yeah,' he replied. 'I really like your shoes.'

I knew it, she thought as the plane took off. *See! These shoes are fucking magical.*

CHAPTER 7

Erin quickly checked her face in the hall mirror as she heard the first car pull up at the front of the house, swiping away a large mascara fleck from under her eye, which then smudged down her cheek. *For feck's sake*, she thought, using the sleeve of her cardigan to clean it up. *Twenty-six euros for Yves Saint Laurent mascara and I look like a bleedin' panda.*

She was surprised at how nervous she felt. In her line of work, nerves were nothing new and something she generally controlled quite successfully, but this felt different. This wasn't remembering lines in front of an audience or hitting her mark on time, this was unscripted. Unplanned. She wanted so badly for this to go well.

What if we have nothing in common now? People change. Jesus, sure you bumped into that shagger Frazer O'Leary from high school last year and he was a bloody born-again Jehovah's Witness!

She straightened her sleeve, took a breath and threw open the front door to see a tall, blonde-haired woman exiting the passenger side of a white Kia.

The woman who scurried towards Erin was understandably less baby-faced than the last time she had seen her. Her once wild, wavy hair was straight and tidy and she wore trousers instead of the flowing maxi skirts that Erin used to admire so much. But her huge, bright smile remained unchanged.

'Becky!' Erin bellowed, her arms outstretched. 'Agh! It's so good to see you!'

'Oh my God!' Becky responded, flinging herself at Erin. 'You look amazing! How are you?'

'Oh, you know; same old,' Erin replied, which she immediately thought was an odd thing to say, but it was better than *a bit shit to be honest. Husband's dead. Don't leave the house much.* Thankfully, Becky didn't respond, instead going in for a second hug.

'I can't believe you're selling this place. I'd forgotten how beautiful that view was,' Becky remarked. 'If I had a spare million, I'd buy it from you. Hey, do you remember that time—'

'Rebecca, can you give me a hand please?'

'Oh jeez, sorry, yes, of course!'

Becky darted back across the gravel towards the woman standing at the open boot of the car. Erin hadn't even noticed her get out. She waved over to the woman who stood with one hand on her hip and the other on the lid of the boot, looking like a slightly irritated mum. Older than Becky definitely, much shorter and, although pretty, Erin thought she currently had a face like a skelped arse.

They each took a bag, their feet crunching across the driveway.

'Erin, this my girlfriend, Christine.'

'Partner,' Christine quickly corrected, firmly shaking Erin's hand. 'Thanks for inviting us.'

'Pleasure,' Erin replied, her eyes darting towards Becky, who apparently now dated rather lugubrious women, unlike the giggling hipsters she used to go out with at university.

'Won't you come in? You're the first to arrive. Dump your bags in your room and we'll have a drink, yeah?'

She led them upstairs to the first bedroom and left them to unpack while she fixed the drinks: margaritas. They had made and consumed hundreds during their house share and Erin thought it would be a nice homage to their university years, hopefully minus the outrageous hangovers. She giggled to herself as she remembered a particularly boisterous party, at the end of their third year.

'Christ on a bike, Erin, did you just pour a whole bottle of booze in there?' Alex had asked. 'I can't feel my legs.'

The 'end of third-year exams' party was a rather raucous one. Countless people crammed into their small house, with the rest spilling out into the even smaller garden outside. Thankfully most of the neighbours were students too, so noise complaints were non-existent.

'No, just the normal amount,' Erin had replied, peering into the bowl. 'Though maybe I did add a little extra... who can say? But it's not that strong, no one else is complaining!'

Tara laughed. 'She has a point, to be fair. I'm frightened to light my ciggy in case I'm eighty percent proof and combust. Beth, I think your boyfriend just threw up in the sink.'

Beth leapt off the edge of the couch, yelling for him to get his disgusting puke hole away from her dishes.

'I don't see any of you lot offering to bartend,' Erin replied indignantly, squeezing the life out of another lime. 'When did you all become such lightweights? Besides, it's fruit based. It's good for you.'

Becky dipped her cup into the large punch bowl. 'Unless we all have scurvy, I'm not sure that's true. Has anyone seen Luna?'

'She was in the garden, talking to that weird guy from next door,' Tara replied. 'I swear, Becks, if you ever date someone who doesn't sound like a character from a gothic novel, I'll drop down dead.'

'She's very bubbly,' Erin remarked with a sly grin. 'Better than the last one, what was her name? Raven or Crow something?'

'Wren,' Becky reminded her. 'And she was perfectly nice... well, apart from that whole cheating on me fiasco.'

'You only dreamt that,' Tara said. 'Pretty sure she didn't actually do it.'

'Only because I broke up with her first... Jesus, Erin, this does taste like rocket fuel!' Becky exclaimed. 'Dilute this before someone dies or worse.'

Still laughing at the memory, Erin began rubbing the glasses with lime before edging them in salt. Then she squeezed more limes to add to the tequila and triple sec. Reaching into the cupboard for the cocktail shaker, she smiled as she noticed the one Scott had bought her for Christmas a few years back. It was shaped like a pineapple and played a jingly jangly version of 'Tequila' by the Champs when picked up. It had once made them both laugh, but soon the song began to grate on her nerves and she banished it to the back of the cupboard to be forgotten. As she lifted it out and the familiar song played, she felt a hot, fresh wave of sadness wash over her. God, she missed him. Everything still felt so raw.

'I'm afraid the damage from the crash was catastrophic. We did everything we could, but your husband died a few minutes ago. I'm very sorry. Is there anyone we can call for you?'

Catastrophic. Erin always thought that word was perfect. Not only to describe her husband's injuries but to define the impact it had on everyone who loved him.

She placed the musical cocktail shaker back in the cupboard, instead choosing a plain silver one to work with instead. As much as she loved this house, everything in it reminded her of Scott. Everything he touched, everywhere he sat and every word they said to each other, it was all deeply ingrained in the walls. As much as she found comfort in this, it was a constant reminder that he was never coming back.

One more weekend and then it would officially be on the market and she could attempt to start over.

CHAPTER 8

'You're kidding?'

Alex liked the way Aiden's head cocked to the side like a puzzled puppy. When Pete was confused, he used to retract his neck like a turtle, but this was far more endearing.

'Nope,' she replied. 'It was my book. I just get a bit embarrassed around readers. Normally I like to write the thing then hurl it into the void and get on with the next one.'

Ten minutes into the flight, Alex had confessed her connection to *Midnight* in a feeble attempt to explain why she'd acted like an absolute eejit at the bookshop. She could have told the truth and informed him that she was simply thrown by his handsomeness, but that would have meant spending the rest of the flight having him think that she was an absolute danger.

'I'm not sure I believe you,' he stated. 'That's just too uncanny.'

'It's true,' she insisted. 'If you google my name, you'll see my picture pop up.'

'Oh really?'

'However, please don't do that as the photos are all hideous. I've seen blobfish that are more photogenic.'

Showing her face, whether in a photo or a promotional video, was the one part of the job Alex hated.

'A.S. Moran – what does the S stand for?'

'Siobhan. It's my middle name. After my ma. I don't really use it, but I like the use of the initials. Alexandra was after my granny on my dad's side. I never met her, but she was Greek, fierce and apparently I have her hair. Not her actual hair, that would be unsettling. Just her type of hair… you know. Curly.'

What in God's name are you talking about? she thought, her soul slowly leaving her body. *Either get a grip or get the cabin crew to duct tape your trap shut for the next hour. I've heard they can do that now.*

Aiden grinned. 'I've never met an author before. I'd love to be able to write, but it might get in the way of my reading time.'

'You read a lot then?'

He turned in his face towards her. 'Always have. My mom and dad were big readers, I guess it rubbed off. I think I read every book that they owned.'

Alex felt a warm, cosy feeling wash over her. She imagined that must have been a nice home to grow up in. 'Do you have a favourite genre?' she asked.

'Not particularly,' he replied. 'I'll read anything. Growing up, Mom was big into King, Koontz, Herbert, Shirley Jackson. Dad, big Grisham fan but also had quite the passion for romcoms. Interesting choice for a six-foot-two truck driver, but he loved those stories. Mom said it reminded him that the world didn't have to be such a grim place.'

'They sound like nice people,' Alex responded. His voice was soothing. She could listen to him talk about books and his family for hours.

'Great people,' he affirmed, softly. 'But yeah… actually being the one to write those stories… it's very impressive.'

'You think?' Alex asked. 'I can think of a million more impressive jobs. Running a homeless shelter, being a doctor, human rights lawyer – you know, that kind of thing. All I do is type words.'

'Well, I'm a vet and to me it's—'

'A vet?' Alex asked. 'Wait, like a *n animal* vet, or a you-used-to-be-in-the-army-type vet?'

He laughed. 'A veterinarian. I have a clinic in Cedar Park– well, had a clinic, until I moved to London.'

Oh, feck off, Alex thought. *He saves animals for a living? There must be something wrong with him. No one is this perfect.*

'Sorry?'

She froze. Had she just said that out loud?

'Nothing. I have a dog. He hates everyone.'

'Tea? Coffee?' At that moment Alex was grateful to the flight attendant for giving her brain an opportunity to remember that it was capable of rational thought and conversation and not whatever she'd been doing up until now. She ordered a coffee and a small box of sour cream Pringles while Aiden ordered a coffee and a couple of KitKats.

'So, your name, Aiden. That's more Irish than mine.'

'We're Irish American on my great-great-great-grandfather's side or something. There's probably a distant cousin or two kicking around somewhere. My mom just liked the name. I hear she also liked *Tige*, spelled T-A-D-H-G, so I think I dodged a bullet there. My last name is Smith, however... really can't get anything more generic than that.'

He broke a KitKat in two and offered her one piece, which she accepted without hesitation.

'And your girlfriend is Irish? Does she live in Kerry?'

He shook his head but remained silent.

'Sorry, that's none of my business.'

He sighed. 'I was working in Dublin, helping set up a new clinic. She's back in London, on a later flight. She's really excited about this trip.'

'And you're not?'

'Well... I guess I just didn't think we were at the 'meeting family' stage in our relationship. It's always been really casual, you know? The whole thing makes me a little nervous, but she seemed adamant that I come along.'

Alex grimaced. His honestly was unexpected. 'I see. Hmm... tricky.'

He sighed. 'Tricky indeed. And I probably shouldn't be talking about this, but who better to discuss my love life with than a stranger from the airport? Completely normal behaviour.'

'It's not that peculiar,' Alex replied. 'I mean, therapists are strangers. You just have to pay them money. I, on the other hand, accept KitKats.'

He laughed. 'Seems like a fair deal.'

'Though I'm probably the last person to ask for relationship advice. I ended things with my ex and he still lives next door. We co-parent the anti-social dog.'

'That's incredibly civilised. Not many people stay friends with their ex.'

'I know. To be honest, I don't think he was that bothered when we split. I had a whole big speech and he was all, "OK. Makes sense."'

He took a sip of his coffee. 'You're very easy to talk to, you know.'

'I am,' she replied, resisting the urge to beam like a great bloody idiot who'd never had a compliment before. 'But I am also not free. Pay up.' She held out her hand for more KitKat.

'Ladies and gentlemen, we'll shortly be arriving at Kerry, where the weather is a beautiful twenty-four degrees and sunny.'

'Can I ask you something?' Aiden requested. 'Though it may sound somewhat odd.'

'Sure.'

'Do you believe in fate?'

Alex looked puzzled. 'Fate?'

'Yeah,' he replied. 'Because I think this is fate. You know, this. Us meeting.'

Alex felt her face flush in delight. 'Um, that's not fate, it's Ryanair.'

Aiden chuckled as they pushed back their trays and buckled their seatbelts for landing.

'I mean, think about it. Complete strangers until one minute we're talking about books, then we're having a drink, now we're seated together—'

'Well—'

'And you just happen to be the author of the book I was recommending! There's definitely something otherworldly at play here.'

Alex snorted. 'You should meet my friend Becky. She talks to the moon; you would love her.'

Aiden did not push the matter any further, but regardless the conversation continued to flow, even as they disembarked and headed towards the baggage area. Before long she spotted her green case making its way around the carousel.

'So, this is me,' she informed Aiden, grabbing her case. She swung it onto a trolley with a grunt.

'I get to hang around here for a while,' he said, 'Have some more terrible coffee while I wait.'

'Lucky you,' she replied. 'And enjoy your weekend. I'm sure everything will be grand.'

Aiden extended his hand towards her and as Alex slipped her hand into his, she felt every nerve in her body react. They paused, neither of them letting go right away.

'I guess this is goodbye,' he said. 'It's been—'

'You should take my number,' Alex blurted out. 'You know, for pet emergencies or advice, whatever.'

His gaze dipped momentarily. 'Pet emergencies,' he repeated, considering this.

Alex knew this was not her finest hour. Offering up her

number to someone else's boyfriend was icky at best, but in that moment, she knew she'd regret it if she just walked away.

'I can do that. Sure.'

'Great,' she replied, feeling like her heart might just beat out of her chest cartoon style and give her away completely. Still holding hands, he reached into his pocket and handed Alex his phone.

CHAPTER 9

'You know, I'm certain this is the room I stayed in last time I was here,' Becky noted, flopping herself down on the bed. 'I remember that little alcove by the window... but the walls... ugh, they were this disgusting mustard colour and I think the bed was on that—'

'This wardrobe looks vintage,' Christine said, paying no attention to anything Becky was saying; these days, she rarely ever did. Becky would often realise mid-sentence that Christine hadn't heard a word, or worse, Christine would interrupt her to start a different conversation entirely. Becky wondered if she acted like this at work. For someone whose job it was to listen, sometimes Christine sucked at it.

'Probably,' Becky replied. 'I expect Erin would have kept some of her grandparents' things. I think her nana had good taste... her gramps not so much. This bed is new though... want to break it in?'

Christine chuckled as Becky bounced on the bed. She didn't chuckle that often, but when she did, Becky loved the way her nose wrinkled. 'Is that all you think about? Maybe later, I want to get my clothes out of the case before they crease.'

She watched Christine carefully unpack, shake and hang her clothes for the next three days. All designer and all still immaculately pressed, while Becky predicted that her clothes were already like a jumble sale in her suitcase. Christine's meticulousness, in all aspects of her life, was something that Becky admired, envied even, and she had hoped in the two years they'd been together that somehow all of that fastidiousness might have rubbed off on her, given her focus when she tended to daydream and set goals that weren't just 'be kind' – to be anything really, other than her unconventional self.

Early on in their relationship, Christine had made her feelings on Becky's fashion sense quite clear. She remembered the day when everything really started to change.

'Ta-da!'

Becky twirled around in her half-price, deep red, Monsoon maxi skirt that she'd grabbed as soon as the January sales hit.

'What do you think?' she asked Christine. 'It's super festive, right? I mean, I know Christmas is over, but I absolutely adore it.'

'Very nice,' Christine replied as she watched her girlfriend gush over a piece of fabric. 'The colour reminds me of mulled wine. It suits you.'

'Thank you! I'm thinking I'll wear this and that little black vest for your work party next week. Dress it up with some jewellery. Maybe a little shawl...'

'Oh,' Christine replied, her eyes scanning the skirt again. 'Hmm... you sure?'

Becky stopped admiring herself in the bedroom mirror. 'Yeah... unless you don't think it's suitable?'

Five months into their relationship, this would be their first major outing together as a couple. Dinner and drinks at some exclusive club in Knightsbridge that Becky had never heard of. Knightsbridge wasn't an area that Becky frequented often, she preferred the laid-back vibe of Shoreditch or Peckham, but, still, she was looking forward to it.

'I think it's amazing, darling,' Christine said. 'Though you'd look amazing in a potato sack. It's just...'

'What?'

'I'm not sure it's entirely appropriate for the venue.'

Becky took another look in the mirror. 'Seriously? It's a skirt, not a pair of cowboy chaps. What's wrong with it?'

'It's perhaps a smidge too bohemian,' Christine suggested. 'You know that the circles I move in are less avant-garde than you're used to. I'd just hate for you to feel self-conscious.'

Becky rarely felt self-conscious, but she was now.

'So, what should I wear?'

Christine thought for a moment, her eyes still fixed on Becky. 'You know how much I love you in a trouser suit, with your hair back. You remind me of Cate Blanchett. You just look like you mean business.'

'Business? But I thought this was a party?'

'It is a party... a work party. *My* work. Again, it's completely up to you what you wear, I'd just hate for you to stick out like a sore thumb.'

Becky felt herself shrink as she realised this wasn't about how she looked at all. It was about how she looked on Christine's arm.

She felt the annoyance creep in. From the moment they met she had been toning down the way she looked. No gothic jewellery, no crystals, no pigtails, nothing that would stop Christine from taking her seriously. Becky might have gotten away with that free spirit look in her twenties, but she was in her thirties now. Time to grow up. However, this was an expensive skirt, not some floor-length tie-dye effort from the local hemp shop. Yet it still wasn't good enough.

'Are... are you embarrassed to be seen with me, Christine?'

'Heavens no,' she exclaimed. 'Why on earth would you think that?'

'Just a feeling I get,' Becky replied. 'Sometimes it's like I'm just on the edge of being good enough but I never quite get there. I know you like trousers over skirts and suits over casual, but I just don't feel they're quite me. My style is more... girly.'

'Feminine,' Christine corrected. 'And I really think you're overreacting.' She sighed and sat on the edge of the bed. 'I knew you might take this badly. I was reluctant to say anything at all. Your defensiveness might become a problem if you're not careful.'

'I'm not being defensive!'

Which is exactly what a defensive person would say. Well played, nitwit.

'It's perfectly normal for couples to give opinions in relationships, Rebecca. To guide each other. I don't want anything to detract from your full potential. You deserve to have every pair of eyes in the room on you next week... but for the right reasons. Yes, this is a lovely skirt, but I think you can do better. Is that really so bad?'

Becky took one last look in the mirror and sighed. The old Becky would have worn the skirt regardless, but the old Becky was dumped for being ridiculous. She could do better, she could *be* better. Christine was right.

'What trouser suit did you have in mind then?'

Becky finished unpacking in the other side of the wardrobe, thinking that side by side, their clothes looked like a before and after in one of those makeover shows: *From Basic Witch to Boss Bitch* or *Queer Eye for the Bohemian Bi.*

'I'm sure Erin has an iron you could borrow,' Christine remarked dryly.

Becky quietly sighed. She'd really tried to make an effort to smarten up. To become more polished. To leave behind her more unconventional fashion and join Christine in a world of trendy labels, delicate jewellery, and unpatterned tights, but given the creased garments in front of her, it obviously hadn't worked as well as she'd hoped.

'Shall we go back downstairs?' she asked, and Christine nodded, her eyes still on Becky's clothes.

She'll loosen up after a couple of drinks, Becky thought. *She might even be fun. She used to be fun.*

CHAPTER 10

'Stop fussing, love. I'm fine. Honestly, just grab the bags.'

Beth's left leg exited the car with ease, followed by her right which had to be physically lifted with both hands in order to join its partner. Paul meant well, as always, but her stubbornness to be as self-sufficient as possible was powerful. Besides, Beth knew that someone would be watching from that big, tinted living-room window and she didn't want them to see her struggle. She grabbed her walking stick from the back seat and plastered on a smile.

Since she'd experienced her first symptom at university in 2011, it had taken ten years for her to need a walking stick. Back then, well before the diagnosis two years ago, her leg had decided to play silly buggers every year or so, becoming numb and dragging with no warning at all before returning to normal like nothing ever happened. *Trapped nerve*, they'd said. *Bit of physio and you'll be fine.* But then she'd woken up one day with double vision and sometimes her bowels had decided they'd rather not wait for a bathroom. *IBS*, they'd said. *FODMAP your way into a healthy digestive system, while you wear a weird prism on your glasses for that weak eye muscle. It happens. Sometimes, it just happens.*

She saw Erin open the door, waving profusely. She looked almost exactly as Beth remembered.

But when the eye gets better and the bowels get worse and then the leg starts shaking and won't lift more than two inches off the ground and you get so tired you cannot function, an MRI reveals that your brain and spine have significant lesions and there's no way to undo the damage.

'Erin!' she yelled, 'Oh my God, you look amazing!'

Beth approached the door as fast as her one good leg would carry her, with Paul rolling the cases behind.

'Erin Carmichael, I can't believe it!' She placed her cane against the wall and hugged her hard.

'I know,' Erin replied. 'Way too long. I'm so happy to see you!'

Paul reached the door, where he rather awkwardly received his hug.

'You both exactly the same,' Erin exclaimed. 'And I'm glad to see some things never change!' She motioned to Beth's leg brace and stick. 'What the hell have you done to yourself this time, clumsy?'

'Well, I'm never jet-skiing off my yacht again, I'll tell you that much,' Beth replied quickly, going in for another hug. She'd had that line prepared. It was funny enough to ensure that no one would think it was anything serious and would also make them more likely to believe her next lie. 'I just had a run-in with a bottle of wine and some particularly steep stairs.'

Paul laughed along with everyone else, but she knew he did not approve. He didn't understand why she couldn't just be honest about her illness.

'An entire weekend of everyone feeling sorry for me? Nope, no thank you.'

'But they're your friends...'

'Yes, and one of them lost her husband recently. I can easily pass this off as a sprain or something.'

'Come away in. Becky and her partner are already here! I was going to put you upstairs, but I'll swap you with Tara. She can have the upstairs beside Alex and Becky.'

Smiling, Beth shuffled her way through to the living room, while Erin helped Paul with the cases. *I can do this*, she thought. *Clumsy Beth will not be pitied or coddled and maybe, for a few days, everything won't be about this bloody illness.*

'I love what you've done with the place,' Beth remarked as Paul and Erin returned. 'It looks so modern! Paul, the last time I was here, I spent the weekend glued to an old-fashioned brown recliner which belonged to Erin's grandfather. In fact, the whole room was brown.'

'It's nice!' Paul agreed. 'But there's a lot to be said for old-fashioned recliners.'

Beth rolled her eyes. 'He has one in the work shed that he refuses to throw out, even though the neighbours' elderly cat pissed on it.'

'Unfair of you to assume it was the cat.' Paul smiled wryly.

Erin listened to them go back and forth. They were still as fun to be around as they were ten years ago. They also looked genuinely happy, unlike Becky and her girlfriend, which was a relief as the thought of a house full of miserable couples for the weekend was soul-destroying. However, the sight of them together stung, far more than she had anticipated. It only reminded her of everything she'd lost.

Beth took a seat near the window and rubbed her finger down the glass. 'You know, vinegar and newspaper will get those streaks right out.'

'Jesus, Beth, we've only been here five minutes!' Paul exclaimed. 'Sorry, Erin.'

'What? I'm just saying...'

Erin laughed loudly. She'd missed that bossy cow.

CHAPTER 11

Alex didn't remember the lough being so close to the house, but as she stepped out of the taxi, she was greeted by a long, wide stretch of pale blue water, just beyond the garden path which led to the beach.

The beach.

'Rebecca Murphy, I love you, but I swear if you start summoning demons or walking on water, I will leave.'

The memory escaped from her brain and settled in her throat, forming a lump. She hadn't thought about that in years: the affirmations they'd made for the life they hadn't lived yet.

Taking her case, she wheeled it to the front door and rang the bell. The house had been given a much-needed fresh coat of paint since last time, but it still looked as charming as ever, with quaint dormer bedroom windows at the top of the house and the large tinted living-room window which might just have the best view in the whole of Kerry.

Within seconds, the door flew open and a familiar face greeted her.

'Alexandra bloody Moran!' Erin squealed, flinging her arms around Alex. 'God, it's good to see you!'

'You too!' Alex replied, squeezing her back. 'It's been so long. You look great!'

Alex was surprised at just how well Erin looked. Not that she expected her to answer the door dressed head to toe in black, wailing and clutching her rosary, but she seemed cheerful. Happy.

'I'm so pleased you made it,' Erin gushed, grabbing at the handle of the suitcase. 'Come away in, Becky and Beth are already here. We've already had a wee cocktail, so you'll need to catch up.'

Alex stepped over the threshold and back into the house she'd last stayed in a decade ago. The fresh air followed her in and filled the hall, mixing with the musky smell from the hallway candle. Sandalwood perhaps? It smelled like the little spa in Portobella where she'd once had her eyebrows done and they'd coloured them in ten shades too dark.

'I hope there's a wee margarita with my name on it,' she said, glancing around the room. Beth, Becky, Paul and another woman she didn't recognise. The sound of her name being screeched was joyous. She couldn't remember the last time people had genuinely been this happy to see her.

'One margarita coming right up,' Erin said as Alex was surrounded by Beth and Becky. She breathed a huge sigh of relief. Everyone was just as wonderful as she remembered. Erin handed her the pre-made cocktail and took her coat.

'Paul, would you be a love and take Alex's case to her bedroom? Top of the stairs, door on the left.'

Paul obliged, likely happy to get a quick respite from all the hugging.

'Beth, are you alright?' Alex asked, noticing her leg brace. 'My first editor had one like that, but she's got foot drop from hip surgery.'

'Oh, it's nothing,' Beth replied. 'Parkour is trickier than it looks. I'm in physio, but it's getting better!'

'Great news! I'm sure Paul can carry you if you get too pissed.' Alex said, her lips tingling from the salt on the edge of the glass. 'Although if I don't get these shoes off, I might have to borrow that stick. Honestly, I love them dearly, but they're killing me.'

Everyone glanced down at her feet as she kicked off her shoes.

'Look at you, Miss Fancy Feet,' Beth remarked, happy to steer the conversation away from her. 'They're gorgeous.'

'Are those Louboutins?' Erin asked, snatching one up. 'I'm absolutely having a shot of those.'

'No Tara yet?' Alex asked, watching Erin slip off her ballet pumps. 'I thought she'd have been first here. She could always sense a cocktail from a hundred kilometres.'

'She's coming,' Erin replied, 'At least I hope so. Bringing a lad with her too.'

'Oooh,' Beth replied, 'How nice. Anyone with you, Alex?'

'Nope,' she replied. 'I'm free as a bird. Although, I did meet this absolute ride at the airport. We had a drink, we sat together on the plane. He gave me half of his KitKat and I gave him my number.'

'Seems like a fair exchange,' Erin replied.

As Paul returned to join Beth on the couch, Alex couldn't help but notice how he'd changed, probably more than anyone. The last time she saw him, he was skinny and clean-shaven with a small amount of acne which had followed him from his teenage years into his twenties. Now he had a proper salt-and-pepper beard, a thicker waist and a much less gangly look about him.

Erin brought through a massive jug full of margarita mix and plonked it down on the table. 'So, Christine, what do you do?'

'Psychologist,' she replied. 'Mainly clinical but I run a private practice twice a week from home.'

'Really?' Erin replied. 'That's fascinating!' As she topped up Beth's glass, she noticed that Christine had barely touched her cocktail.

'It can be,' she replied.

'Fascinating,' Erin repeated. 'Now, are you not a fan of the ole margarita? Can I get you something else. Wine? G&T? Coffee?'

'Water would be fine. I'm not much of an afternoon drinker. I'll have some wine with dinner.'

It's half five, that's practically night-time, Erin thought but headed to the kitchen anyway to grab her some water. *Let's hope she likes the chardonnay later.*

Beth sat quietly while Becky recounted the tale of how she met Christine at a wellness retreat and how her eyes had been opened to the real advantages of therapy. Beth wasn't so convinced. Since her diagnosis, she'd had three Zoom sessions with a therapist named Lucian who was getting on her last nerve with his incessant *hmm*ing and asking *how does that make you feel?* every three seconds. Fifty quid an hour to tell a bloke in a deep V-neck that feeling sad made her feel sad didn't help at all. She was also somewhat surprised at Becky's enthusiasm for conventional therapy, given that she'd once overheard her asking a cat for advice.

'And you, Becks, what are you up to now?' Beth asked, darting into an empty space in the conversation.

'Massage therapy,' she replied, 'I love it. You should give me a wee shot on your leg while we're here.'

'Maybe,' Beth replied, hesitantly. Having her leg massaged was the opposite of not drawing any attention to it. 'If we have time.'

'You could work on my shoulders,' Erin said, placing Christine's water on the table. 'I swear I have a knot there like a ball of yarn.'

'Stress will do that,' Becky replied without thinking. 'Grief is the worst...' She caught Beth's eye and stopped herself mid-sentence. 'Sure, I can,' she said softly. 'No problem at all...'

Erin smiled but swallowed hard. She'd misjudged things. Ten years ago, there would have been no elephant in the room, no awkwardness. Someone might even have made a rather inappropriate joke to break the ice around Scott but not now. Now the tiptoeing had begun and she didn't want to be the one to stomp all over everything with her big size-seven grief boots.

'Alex,' she began, changing the subject. 'How's the—'

'Have you bitches really not aged in ten years?'

Startled, everyone turned to see Tara standing there, e-cigarette in hand and a massive grin on her face. 'Sorry, we parked the rental round the back and the patio door was open.'

Erin was the first to give a little squeal before pouncing on Tara, wondering how it was possible that she looked the same yet entirely different. Her formerly short black hair was now long and red, her skin now way more sun-kissed and her boobs now noticeably three sizes bigger on her slim frame. But the glint in her eye and her slightly crooked smile was absolutely the Tara she'd always known.

'You came!' Erin exclaimed. 'I wasn't sure if you were flying or driving or...'

'We flew,' Tara replied, now being hugged by Beth as well. 'And of course I came! You think I'd miss this... wait, Beth... what happened?'

'Free-climbing on Everest,' Beth informed her. 'Trickier than it looks. You remember Paul, right?'

'Of course! How are ya, fella? Jesus, you two stayed the course, huh? Amazing.'

Paul joined the scrum of a hug, before Alex excitedly popped up in front of him. 'It's sooo good to see you! Your hair! Really suits you.'

'Thanks,' Tara chirped. 'Oh my God, this is so fucking surreal, right? All of us together.'

'Well, not quite all of us,' Erin replied, her eyes darting towards the back door. 'I feel we're missing someone, no? You mentioned a *we*?'

Tara smirked. 'Yes, he's just getting the bags. I brought far too many, as usual.'

'What's his name?' Beth asked. 'Your butler?'

'Aiden,' Tara replied, making a face at Beth. 'His name is Aiden and be nice.'

'Um, where should I put these?'

Alex barely had time to process anything before he was standing in front of her. It was Aiden. Airport Aiden. Her Aiden. Tara's Aiden.

She quickly sidestepped behind Paul, her stomach plummeting towards her feet. *Tara is his girlfriend? This cannot be happening.*

'Everyone, this is Aiden,' she heard Tara say. 'Aiden, these are my friends: Erin, Beth, Becky, Paul, squashed behind Paul is Alexandra... Alex, come say hi to Aiden!'

Jesus, can you stop saying Aiden!

Alex stepped out and smiled meekly. 'Hi. Nice to meet you.'

The look of confusion on Aiden's face only lasted for a moment before reality set in. 'Hi,' he blurted back, his gaze quickly leaving Alex and focusing on anything else.

'This is Christine,' Becky said to an increasingly pale-faced Aiden. Christine raised her hand to greet him.

'Lovely to meet all of you,' he said. 'I'm just going to grab the last bag from the car.'

'I'll give you a hand, mate.' Paul insisted. 'Give this lot a chance to squeal at each other properly.'

While everyone interrogated Tara on where she'd met such a fine specimen, Alex considered her options. She could tell everyone that it was Aiden she'd met at the airport, but then she'd have to explain why she gave him her phone number despite knowing he had a girlfriend and that would be almost as awkward as Aiden explaining why he'd taken her phone number in the first place. The second option was to mention none of this and continue acting like they'd never met. The third and final option was to flee, never to be heard from again.

'Dinner's in an hour if anyone needs to freshen up?' Erin asked. 'I'm so excited to see you all, you have no idea! I'm sure this'll be a weekend we'll never forget.'

Alex smiled and secretly agreed with every word Erin said, but for all the wrong reasons.

CHAPTER 12

With Aiden unpacking upstairs, Tara watched Erin bustle around the patio table, making sure every piece of cutlery was in the correct position, every napkin was folded and everything capable of being blown away by the breeze was secured in place. Tara had offered to help, they all had, but Erin had graciously refused, determined to be the perfect host.

Tara remembered the patio area as being a large, grey slabbed space with a couple of potted plants and a small table and chairs where she'd parked herself and smoked as many cigarettes as possible over graduation weekend. Now it looked like something from *Homes & Gardens*. It was covered in white tiles, with pale grey couches at either side of a fire pit to the left, and a dining area to the right with a long table which could easily seat ten. She could imagine Erin hosting dinners and entertaining guests, while she herself was barely able to work a microwave.

'So, what are you doing with yourself these days?' Erin asked. 'I think last I heard you were in America.'

'I was in New York. I worked in media sales. The bonuses

were ridiculous, I made a small fortune. I do think the accent gave me an edge, you know? They love a bit of Irish.'

Erin smiled. 'I'm sure. It sounds very exciting though, good for you. Are you still there?'

Tara scrunched her nose. 'Nah. It started to bore me, so I moved to London last year. Doing a bit of freelance at the mo.'

Tara thought about telling Erin the real reason she left. How her shitshow of a life had led to her wake up one morning, book a ticket to London and leave everything behind except her passport, laptop and mobile phone. Turned out that drugs and stress weren't exactly a winning combination. When she checked herself into rehab two days later, she didn't even have a toothbrush. But perhaps now was not a good time. She didn't know if there ever would be. As much as she felt like she had a handle on things now, the shame of it all was still very much present.

'I don't think I could live in New York,' Erin replied. 'It's a fun place, but I prefer the quiet. Kerry girl at heart, I suppose. I hate it when I have to go away on long shoots.'

'But you must get lonely out here,' Tara said, while Erin filled the breadbaskets. 'I mean, especially since your husband passed away.'

'Scott,' Erin informed her, somewhat relieved that he was being spoken about directly. She paused for a moment to consider Tara's question.

'I do' she answered. 'I guess that's part of the reason I'm selling up. It was a big house for two anyway, so sometimes I feel like I'm rattling around in here, but I have Jasper at least.' She glanced at her cat who was happily stretched out in the evening sun. 'I have a really great pet sitter who stays here if we're... if I'm working away. Not that I do much of that at the moment.'

'I've never had a pet,' Tara said, watching Jasper with amusement. 'Was never that into animals. But he's very cute.'

'Sure, he's cute until he brings home presents...'

Tara frowned. 'Ah, Jesus! What, like mice?'

'Mice, birds, the odd rat. Usually alive and very hard to catch. Scott was chief bird wrangler. Does Aiden like animals?'

'He's a vet, so I hope so,' Tara replied, grinning.

Erin stopped rearranging the condiments. 'You're dating a vet? I so never saw that coming. Honestly thought you would end up with a musician or some indie, activist movie director, you know, someone a bit less domesticated. I don't think I remember any of your old boyfriends even being housebroken.'

Tara laughed, but truthfully, she had expected to end up with someone a little rowdier too. It wasn't like she hadn't tried, but the reality of those musicians and indie artists wasn't as exciting as she thought it would be. They left her emptier than she'd been before she met them. But Aiden... Aiden was reliable. He was good-looking, kind and he just let her get on with things. No arguments, no jealousy, he was a good, stable, guy for a somewhat unstable girl.

'The heart wants what the heart wants, I guess,' she replied. 'And right now, my heart wants this beautiful view.'

She envied Erin's home, much more now than she had all those years ago. Back then she didn't yearn for sea-view patio areas or private parking, nor did she give seclusion a second thought because she was determined to live in the centre of everything. Be part of it all. Live life in an apartment with traffic on either side and a view over a multicultural city which would be humming with activity twenty-four hours a day, and where everything she would need would be within walking distance. But she'd had all that in New York and it was nothing like she hoped for. Now, seeing Erin potter about Loughview, she found herself longing for even just a smidge of what Erin had.

———

'And if you look to the left, you'll see a lough, the name of which, right now, completely escapes me...' Alex paused to watch Becky grab a cardigan from her room.

'Lough Currane,' Becky informed them, popping her head around the door. 'Gorgeous view from up here, isn't it, Aiden? I must show Christine, she loves a good sunset.'

'Great idea,' Alex agreed, watching Becky vanish back downstairs and into the living room.

'Well, this is insane,' she whispered. 'Completely insane.'

Aiden nodded, his eyes still fixed on the view that Alex was pretending to educate him on while everyone else got ready for dinner.

'She said it was a family gathering...' he mumbled. 'I thought grannies and cousins... not this. This is—'

'Insane,' Alex repeated. He nodded again.

They both stood silently for a moment, just staring out of the top-floor window. Alex hoped that if she stood there long enough, it might reverse time. The confusion was almost as strong as the guilt she felt for unknowingly flirting with her friend's boyfriend.

'What do we do?' she asked. 'We can't suddenly announce that we've actually already met. That would be too weird.'

'Yeah, I guess so,' he replied.

'OK then.'

Aiden edged a little closer, their arms briefly touching. For a second neither of them pulled away.

'Alex, I don't want you to think that—'

'Dinner's ready!'

'Be right there!'

'Fuck,' he mumbled to himself before heading downstairs while Alex followed behind.

CHAPTER 13

'Before we begin, I'd just like to say how thrilled I am that you all came. I also want to thank all of you for your kind words after Scott passed. It was rude of me not to respond to your cards and flowers; I just wasn't in a good place. Anyway, you're probably wondering why I asked you here. Why now?'

Erin had tried to prepare a speech in advance, something to welcome everyone without getting overly emotional. She knew in the first three seconds that she might fail spectacularly. Glass in hand, she continued.

'The last time we gathered here, we were all—'

'Hammered!'

She laughed and nodded at Tara. 'Indeed. There was that. But we were also so young and so eager to get on with living, that we quickly forgot about the life we had together in Dublin. God, the laughs we had, I'm not sure I've laughed so hard since... but as you know, I'm selling the house. So, this weekend, I just want to say goodbye to it in style. With my oldest mates. I've missed you all so much.'

'I've missed you all too,' Alex replied, raising her glass to a wobbly-lipped Erin. 'And I wouldn't have missed this for the world.' The others repeated the sentiment as they toasted the weekend.

Erin took a deep breath and composed herself. 'For dinner, we have spaghetti and meatballs for the meat-eaters and veggie spaghetti for the vegetarians, which I believe is also vegan although I might have used the butter spoon to give it a quick stir at some point. Help yourself to wine, there's plenty more in the kitchen.'

Erin took her seat at the head of the table. For the first time in a decade, they were finally all together and for the first time since Scott died, she didn't feel quite so alone. As she watched them pass the dishes around the table Erin felt a sense of relief that these women were still willing to make the journey, however far, to be together again.

'This really is the most gorgeous dining area,' Beth remarked. 'Absolutely beautiful. You'll love the beach, Paul, it's proper lush.'

Paul grunted in agreement through a mouthful of pasta, his eyes already focused on the bread basket.

'Are you teaching, Beth?' Erin asked. 'I remember you were quite the technical genius.'

Beth bobbed her head. 'Yeah, at Cardiff. Computer science, though some of the kids there are much smarter than I ever was at that age.'

'So, you're Welsh?' Aiden asked. 'Sorry, I'm still trying to get my head around UK accents.'

'I am,' Beth chirped in response. 'I'm a valley girl, Pontyberem originally. What about you? I'm guessing Texas?'

'Correct,' he replied, delighted she recognised his accent. 'Born and raised in Austin.'

'Amazing! Did work bring you over here?'

'Family,' he replied, twisting spaghetti around his fork. 'My brother married and moved to England in the nineties. When he got sick, I decided to be nearer to him.'

'Oh, I'm sorry. How old is he?'

'He's forty-five, so ten years older. He's alright at the moment,' Aiden replied. 'But thank you. I work as a vet so it wasn't too hard to find a vacancy at the time. Doesn't matter where you go in the world, people still love their pets.'

Alex found herself staring at her dinner plate as he spoke, hoping to avoid eye contact with Aiden, in case her face erupted into one great flaming ball of shame.

'How's your folks, Beth?' Alex enquired, trying to pull the focus away from Aiden and his stupidly charming voice. Coming from Wales, Beth's parents had visited her in Dublin as often as they could. Everyone loved them.

Beth beamed. 'They're fantastic. Mum and Dad are still in Glamorgan, though they downsized last year. Dad retired, but Mum's still working at the post office. I don't think she'll ever leave; she'd miss the gossip too much.'

'How about your brothers?'

'They're very well. They're all married now which I still find mindboggling. They obviously don't annoy their wives as much as they annoyed me growing up.'

'How many brothers do you have?' Aiden asked.

'Three older,' Beth replied. 'Leo and Richie are twins, they're thirty-nine and then there's Rhys who's just turned thirty-six. They all live abroad, but we FaceTime quite often. I have two nieces who are also twins.'

'That's lovely,' Becky said. 'You must miss them.'

Beth nodded. She missed them terribly. Leo had married a Korean woman and moved to Seoul. Richie had immigrated to Australia, and Rhys and his wife just floated around the globe like farts in the wind. Last she'd heard they were in Amsterdam. She was surprised at how badly they'd taken the news of her MS, Richie especially, but slowly, she'd managed to assure them that it really wasn't that bad at all. Only her parents knew the reality. That she'd had to reduce her working hours, that her mobility was bad, even on her good days, and that the unpredictable nature of it all was terrifying. Her parents seemed to be able to handle the news much better than her brothers could, maybe even better than she did.

'Beth's parents are so lovely,' Tara informed Aiden. 'In fact, I think she's the only one who had a semblance of a normal family life. I think we all wanted to be her at one point, especially when her dad brought her trays of his homemade lasagne. My mother probably couldn't even spell lasagne.'

'And what about your family, Alex?' Beth asked, determined not to get lost in her own secret self-pity. 'Everyone alright? God, remember when your baby sister came to visit? What a laugh.'

Fiona was two years younger than Alex and completely unplanned. Apparently, her mother, Siobhan, had been horrified to discover she'd fallen pregnant so soon after Alex while still being equally horrified that she'd even had one child to begin with. Siobhan Moran never hid the fact that she found children to be more of a hindrance than a blessing and, in time, her children felt the very same way about her.

Where Alex clearly inherited her genes from her father's Greek side of the family, Fi looked like her mother, petite with dark blonde hair and blue eyes. She was also more driven academically, more outgoing and voted *most likely to get a tattoo on her arse while holidaying in Ibiza* by her classmates. Alex tried to talk her out of it and failed.

'I do remember.' Alex winced. 'Three tequilas and that girl was unhinged. Fiona's doing alright though, she's a GP. Lives in Galway. Has two mad dogs and a blind fish.'

'And your mum?' Beth continued. 'She was a singer, right? I remember seeing her YouTube videos.'

'She was,' Alex confirmed. 'Never a famous one but she did reasonably well around the pubs and clubs.'

Siobhan Angelos. Even after the divorce, she had kept her husband's last name, as it sounded far more exotic than Siobhan Moran, especially while promoting her work.

If Tina Turner gets to keep her name, so can I.

Alex cringed at the memory of her mother's voice. That women frightened the life out of her and her sister. A voice that sang beautifully yet constantly boomed at two young children because their father George had decided that he'd rather live with a woman named Nina O'Driscoll in Crete than spend one more minute married to her. She immediately changed her children's names to her maiden name, just to spite him. Not that he knew or cared. They never heard from him again.

'And is she still performing?'

Alex shook her head. 'She had aggressive cervical cancer. She died five years ago.'

She heard everyone around the table gasp in pity.

'It's alright,' she reassured everyone. 'We really were not that close. Shit, I've just bummed everyone out, haven't I?'

'A little,' Tara replied, smirking. 'But we'll forgive you.' She passed Aiden the garlic bread.

'How did you two meet?' Beth asked. Tara locked eyes with Aiden and giggled.

'Funny story actually. My neighbour Lisa's dog was hit by a car—'

'How is that funny?'

'No, Becks, I wasn't implying that was the funny part, just hang on. So, Lisa's going mental and the dog's howling and she doesn't drive – Lisa, not the dog – so I loaded them both up in my Ford Escort to take them to the twenty-four-hour vet in Wanstead. Aiden was the vet on call. Trouble was, with Lisa in the throes of despair, I was left to carry the dog, who pissed all over me. Aiden kindly lent me his T-shirt.'

'Was the wee doggie OK?'

'The dog was fine,' Aiden reassured Becky. 'Fractured leg, she was lucky.'

'And I returned his T-shirt a couple of days later... now here we are.' Tara raised her glass to Aiden and Alex felt her stomach twist a little. *Of course he'd give Tara his T-shirt. I mean look at her. She's bloody gorgeous, even covered in dog piss.*

'And, Becky,' Tara continued, 'now you know that the dog survived, care to tell us how you and Christine met?'

'Wellness retreat,' Becky responded. 'We were both working there and—'

'God, it was awful, wasn't it?' Christine interjected. 'Like a giant Live Laugh Love convention. Rebecca was about the only other person in the entire building who didn't think that bloody chakras and reiki were the key to good mental health and wellbeing.'

Alex glanced at Becky who pursed her lips.

'Becky?' Tara said with a grin. 'Seriously? Woo-woo Becky? Becky-who-gets-overly-excited-at-a-full-moon, Becky? I thought she'd have been reading auras and starting a coven!'

'Sorry?' Christine looked confused while Becky glared at Tara, shaking her head as surreptitiously as possible. Her eyes pleaded for Tara to pack it in.

'Nothing,' Tara replied. 'I'm just messing. Because she hates all that stuff. Old joke between old friends, right, *Rebecca*?'

Becky laughed and nodded, knowing she'd have to explain herself later.

'What about you, Alex?' Paul asked. 'Are you seeing anyone?'

'Nah, not at the moment,' she replied, doing her best not to get ragu sauce on her white top. 'I broke up with someone last year. Pete. Really good guy, he lives in my granny flat still.'

'I hear your books are doing well.'

'Ah, they've done alright,' Alex replied modestly, when in

fact they'd actually done remarkably well. She'd sold over ten million copies, been translated into thirty languages, with one film made and she had a decent advance to write the next three. She considered it to be eighty-five percent timing, ten percent luck and five percent talent. She wasn't perhaps as well-known as other thriller writers, but she was known enough – enough to be financially comfortable, at any rate.

'Hang on, back up... you live with your ex?' Beth exclaimed. 'I could never!'

'You've never had an ex,' Paul reminded her.

'I'm not living *with* my ex... not exactly. He just rents the flat from me, it was there when I bought the property. It sounds weird but it—'

'But you're just friends?' Erin asked. 'Nothing more?'

She nodded, wondering why everyone found their relationship so hard to understand, when in practice it was simple. Not every couple had to hate each other when they broke up.

Tara grinned. 'But do you still... you know?'

Alex laughed. 'God, no. That ship has sailed.'

'And is he seeing anyone?'

All eyes were now on Christine, who lifted her wine glass, her own gaze fixed firmly on Alex. 'Is he in a relationship now?'

Why yes, he is, prying woman I've never met.

'Yeah,' Alex replied. 'Florence. The complete opposite of me, which is probably a good thing.'

'Can't imagine she's too thrilled with that arrangement,' Christine said, picking at her spaghetti. 'It's quite common for a rivalry of sorts to rear its head in these circumstances.'

Alex looked at Becky who was clearly uncomfortable with her girlfriend's line of questioning.

'Hmm,' Alex replied, rather agitated by Christine. 'I don't—'

'Alex met a man on the plane today and apparently, he's an absolute ride. She gave him her number.'

Beth laughed loudly at Erin's attempt to break whatever

tension was mounting, while Alex cringed so far back in her chair, she feared she might break it.

'Really?' Tara asked, tearing at her garlic bread. 'Good for you! What's his name?'

Aiden. He's sitting right beside you.

'Um... Daniel, and it's no biggie, I probably won't ever hear from him again. Ships passing in the night and all that.'

'Another ship analogy,' Christine mumbled. Alex was certain she saw Becky nudge her girlfriend under the table.

'Oh, course you will,' Tara insisted, before elbowing an awkward-looking Aiden. 'I mean, look at you! Aiden, look at her, will you? Can you imagine any man not calling that absolute goddess?'

Aiden, now forced to look, smiled weakly. 'No. Of course not.'

'See!' she exclaimed triumphantly. 'You were always too hard on yourself, Alexandra Moran, you need to nip that shite in the bud. If he has half a brain cell, I guarantee he'll be thinking about you as we speak.'

'Enough about me,' Alex insisted. 'I want to hear about Erin. We're all just casually ignoring the fact that we're sat here next to a genuine film star.'

The table whooped while Erin shuddered. 'Oh God, enough. Being in a couple of movies does not make me a movie star.'

'Well, two superhero movies, that's a huge deal,' Alex insisted.

'I barely had any lines! It was a minor role!'

'Superhero?' Aiden asked before it finally clicked. 'Oh shit, you were Mother Earth! I didn't recognise you, I'm so embarrassed.'

Erin laughed. 'Don't worry about it. The makeup department were amazing.'

'I didn't see those films,' Tara said to Aiden, lowering her voice. She speared a mushroom off Aiden's plate. 'Were they any good?'

'They were excellent,' he replied, whispering back. 'Idris Elba was the lead villain.'

'And you did that indie film with Jennifer Coolidge,' Becky said. 'God, she's a legend.'

'She's lovely,' Erin replied. 'We went drinking in Soho, she's hilarious.'

'What's Idris Elba like?' Tara asked. 'Can't believe you've been in the same breathing space as that hottie. It would be the first thing I told everyone. I'd be telling people who hadn't even asked.'

Everyone looked at Aiden who lifted his palms off the table. 'I mean, she's not wrong.'

'Super nice,' Erin replied. 'And yes, he's just as handsome in real life.'

'Have you done any stage work?' Christine asked. 'Any theatre?'

Erin nodded. 'Lots actually, mainly in my twenties. *The Mousetrap*, some Shakespeare, though it isn't my favourite thing. I did a *Rocky Horror* tour when I was twenty-six, playing Janet – that was probably the most fun. Funnily enough, that's when I first started dating Scott.'

'Was he in the show?' Becky asked.

'God no, he wasn't theatrically minded at all, he just catered for film and TV sets. I'd met him briefly on my first film, just before I went on the tour. Turns out he was friends with the actress who played Magenta,' she informed them, leaving out the small yet not insignificant detail that Scott and Magenta were actually engaged at the time. No point adding 'home-wrecker' to her CV, she thought. 'Anyway, we have the whole weekend to catch up. Please, eat, drink and leave some room for dessert!'

'How tall is he? He looks tall.'

'Who?'

'Idris!'

'Oh, dear God, he's about seventeen feet tall, Tara. I'll ask him to bound over a mountain for you later.'

Alex thought the rest of dinner was a delight, despite the fact she had nearly disappeared into a black hole of shame. For dessert they had the most divine strawberry pavlova, followed by cheese, biscuits and some coffee with Scottish tablet. And as much as she laughed and conversed with her friends, she struggled to keep her thoughts away from the man on the opposite side of the table who, as his eyes met hers and his face flushed, seemed to be struggling too.

CHAPTER 14

Dinner was a success, Erin thought, ushering everyone inside to relax in the living room. And for the first time in weeks, she felt happy. Positive. Having a home full of people for the first time since Scott's death wasn't nearly as stressful as she thought it would be.

'What can I get everyone?' she asked, turning on some music. 'Tea, more coffee? A cocktail perhaps?'

'A c-type charger if you have one?' Aiden said, looking at his phone. 'I can't find mine anywhere and I'm down to four percent.'

'There's one on my bedside table,' Beth said. 'Just take that, I have another in my case.'

'A Baileys coffee would be good,' Alex suggested. 'Been ages since I've made them. Do you have skooshy cream, Erin?'

'Affirmative,' she replied. 'Anyone else?'

'Ooh, yes please,' Beth answered while she swiped through Erin's Spotify. 'I swear, Erin, your musical tastes have gotten worse. How is that possible?'

Becky raised her hand in agreement.

'Nothing for me,' Christine responded. 'I'm rather tired. Aren't you, darling?'

Becky lowered her hand again. She wasn't tired, but it didn't feel right, leaving Christine to go to bed alone while she stayed up. Not when they were trying to work through things. 'Yes actually, maybe we should turn in. We've had a long journey.'

'It's only ten o'clock,' Tara remarked. She almost sounded offended. 'Alex's coffees are legendary, totally worth losing beauty sleep over. You can make up the extra hour in the morning.'

'We'll catch up properly tomorrow,' Becky insisted, putting an end to the debate. 'Night, everyone.'

Aiden returned, passing Becky and Christine on the way out. 'Thanks for the charger, Beth. You're a lifesaver.'

'No worries,' she replied. 'We're making Baileys coffee if you're interested.'

'Absolutely. Can I give anyone a hand?'

'Yeah, I'm sure Alex could use some help,' Beth replied. 'Mumford & Sons, Erin, really?'

Alex was already in the kitchen, filling the kettle. 'How do you not own a coffee machine?' she asked, 'I'm having to use the council coffee.'

'I do own a coffee machine,' Aiden replied, 'I just don't tend to travel with it.'

Alex spun around, soaking her hand under the tap. 'Oh! Sorry, thought you were Erin!'

He laughed. 'I gathered that. I've been sent to assist.'

'We need six mugs.' Alex informed him, plugging the kettle in. 'Fancy ones if she has them.'

Erin's kitchen wasn't overly large but had obviously been designed by someone who had an unhealthy penchant for storage space. There were so many little cupboard doors and hidden units it looked like a blueprint for an advent calendar.

Thinking logically, Aiden tried the cupboards above the kettle first.

'Can I just...' He brushed past Alex and opened the door above her head. Bingo. Mugs.

'First time lucky,' he remarked. 'Now, what do you consider fancy, because these all look a bit fancy, to be honest.'

'Hmm, glass ones to the left, I think.'

As he handed them down, she felt proud of herself. Actually, she felt proud of them both. *Just two adults behaving like grown-ups*, she thought. *People fancy each other all the time, it's normal. It's human. It's goddamn biology. It doesn't always have to mean something. This was just a blip on what will be a wonderful weekend.*

Coffee made, Alex added the Baileys and Aiden the whipped cream. 'Teamwork,' she said, as they admired their rather infantile-looking drinks.

'How are we getting on in there?' Erin yelled from the living room. 'We're all gasping.'

'Coming!' Alex shouted, lifting the first tray, while Aiden followed behind with the second. If they carried on like this, the weekend might not be so awkward after all.

Beth had decided on something a little less folk-rock for their soundtrack, instead choosing an upbeat 2000s playlist she'd found on Spotify. Erin had given up protesting by this point and found herself humming along to Lily Allen. Coffees sufficiently drowned in overly sweet whipped cream, the conversation continued.

'I honestly can't believe you're selling up,' Beth said. 'I think you're mad. This house is everything. I mean, we have a nice home, but to be honest, I'd set it on fire to live here.'

'Maybe she's ready to move on,' Tara said, giving Beth a deliberate glare.

'Oh. Of course. Sorry.'

'No, it's grand,' Erin replied. 'And you're both right actually.

I am mad to sell it, but it's time to go. It should be up on the agent's website next week.'

'It should sell quite quickly,' Paul remarked. 'Private beach and all.'

'Totally,' Beth agreed. 'And with all the work you've put into it. It's beautiful; your grandfather would be proud.'

Erin felt a lump appear in her throat. She hadn't even been thinking about her grandfather and now she felt guilty for selling off the home he'd shared with his wife. The only real home she'd ever known as a child.

'Oh shit, what have I said now?' Beth exclaimed as Erin's eyes filled up. 'I'm sorry! Look, I'll put Mumford & Sons back on. It'll be fine!'

Erin smiled, wiping her eyes. 'Don't be daft. I'm sorry, it's just an emotional time.'

Tara stood up and gave her a hug. 'We're here for you, you know that.'

Erin thanked her.

'Maybe sharing some more stories about Idris Elba will make you feel better.'

Erin laughed loudly as Alex's cushion hit Tara squarely in the face.

CHAPTER 15

'I guess I am a little exhausted,' Becky said as she took out her earrings. 'I think it's the fresh air... or maybe the wine.'

Her heart sank a little as she heard everyone laughing downstairs. They sounded like they were having a blast. Was that Lily Allen? She loved Lily Allen.

'Did you have a nice evening?'

'I did,' Christine replied. 'Your friends are an interesting bunch, aren't they? A *lot* going on there.'

Becky frowned. *Interesting.* There were a million other words that Christine could have used – nice, funny, amazing, welcoming – but no. She chose *interesting.* She only chose interesting when she was about to verbally dissect something or someone.

'They are,' she agreed, rummaging through her case for a vest top to wear to bed. 'Very interesting. And they are all just as wonderful as I remember.'

Christine slipped on a silk pyjama set and climbed into the right side of the bed. 'They're definitely not what I was expecting. They seem older than you in some ways – not physically. Mentally, perhaps.'

'What do you mean?'

She paused, taking off her watch. 'More grown-up, maybe. Oh, don't look at me like that, Rebecca, darling, it's really not that uncommon to still be finding your feet in your thirties.'

'Finding my feet? What exactly are you trying to say?'

'Just that perhaps they've been more selective with their career path. More driven.'

'I have a career!' Becky responded, pulling her vest over her head. 'Yes, I'm not a lecturer or an actress or an author, but massage therapy *is* a career. It's just not one you deem particularly worthy.'

Christine rolled her eyes. 'Not this again. We've been over it before. If you were really happy with your job, you wouldn't care what I thought either way, darling. Maybe it's you who doesn't deem it worthy.'

Becky's career had always been a touchy one. Christine couldn't understand why someone with a *perfectly good* degree in philosophy had chosen a job, which, in her words 'takes very little training or brainpower'. Becky found that rather rude, but Christine had never been one to mince her words. She used to find that refreshing, now it was just irritating.

Not only was her 'perfectly good' degree a first-class honours with distinction, she was paid well, very well in fact, with regular clients from all over London and a successful training academy under her belt. Regardless, it didn't sit well with Christine, whose ex-wife was a barrister and previous girlfriend before Becky, an architect.

Becky removed herself from the conversation and made her way to the bathroom, leaning against the sink. Her tiredness had now been replaced by frustration.

Stay calm, she told herself. *As much as you want to fly back in there and tell her to fuck off, you don't need anger issues being brought into question as well as your job and your friends.*

As she looked at herself in the mirror, she wondered how it

had come to this. how she would rather repress her feelings for fear of having them used against her. But deep down she couldn't help thinking that this was her fault. She hadn't exactly entered into this relationship being herself. She'd so desperately wanted to be taken seriously by someone that she'd stripped herself of everything she once held dear, to finally be in a proper grown-up relationship.

But she felt that Christine hadn't exactly been honest either because this version, the one sitting in bed belittling her, wasn't the one she fell in love with. She'd fallen in love with a woman who'd initially showered her with love and affection. A woman who couldn't bear to be apart from her. A woman who made her feel like she mattered.

Becky couldn't pinpoint exactly when that stopped; all she knew was she'd been chasing that feeling again, ever since. That, if they'd just work through things, they'd could get back to where there were in the beginning.

She turned off the bathroom light and got into bed. Christine was already asleep.

CHAPTER 16

'You shattered, love?'

Beth assumed that the fact she had fallen face first on to the bed might have been a small indication, but she groaned in agreement anyway.

'Want me to rub your leg?'

Beth groaned again and Paul lifted her skirt, rubbing from the thigh down, something he had gotten quite adept at over the past few years. Her thigh was almost completely numb on one side, but the cramps and the spasms still caused her enough pain to stop her in her tracks occasionally.

'Dinner was great,' he remarked. 'Do you think Erin cooked it herself or got a chef to rustle it up?'

Beth laughed, the sound muffled by her face planted into the pillow.

'I mean, it's very possible she's gotten better,' Paul continued, 'but do you remember that corned beef hash monstrosity she made that one weekend? My stomach still hasn't recovered.'

Beth, still chuckling, turned on to her back. 'I'm going to say she made it. Her husband was a chef, right? She must have learned something from him, surely.'

Beth had read about Scott Flynn's death in the newspaper. Car crash, dead at forty-three. He ran a successful film and TV catering business, but the only reason he made the paper was because of Erin.

'I should have tried harder to contact her when he died,' Beth said as Paul proceeded to work his way down to her calf. 'I mean, a card and flowers via her agent... She probably never received it. If I'd known she still lived here...'

'Don't beat yourself up,' he said, 'You've had a lot on your plate. You know better than anyone that shit things happen to good people. You're here now.'

'True. And I'm very glad. Glad to be with Erin again. And this place is beautiful.'

He agreed.

'Especially this bedroom. Are the floors heated or are my feet just hot from the nerve damage?'

Paul laughed. 'They're heated.'

'Oh, thank God. And also, wow!'

Paul leaned in and kissed his wife.

Although Beth hoped that losing someone so suddenly was a type of grief she'd never have to endure, she couldn't help but think about her own kind of grief. She was grieving the loss of herself.

2020

'Hi, Doctor O'Hara.'

The first thing that Beth noticed was that this consulting room was far less plush than the one she'd had her initial appointment in. Then again, this was the NHS and not some two-hundred-quid-an-hour private hospital.

'Hello, Beth. Take a seat.'

The second thing she noticed was his gaze fixed behind her on the closed door.

'Oh, you didn't bring anyone with you?'

'No, just me,' she replied, sitting down. 'Hubby's working.'

'Are you sure you don't want me to come with you?' Paul had asked. 'Bit of moral support?'

'No point in us both taking time off,' she'd replied. 'Besides, I think I'll be fine. I'll call you when I'm done.'

'Right, OK,' the doctor said before opening the file in front of him. 'Beth Cooper, 19th May, 1990? Thirty years old.'

'That's correct.'

'Great, just checking I have the right information in front of me. So, you came to see me two weeks ago at my private clinic regarding your leg weakness. You first noticed this in 2011 when you were twenty-one. Back surgery two years ago, L4/5 microdiscectomy.'

'Yes,' Beth replied. 'That's correct.'

'We decided on a brain and spine MRI, which you had two weeks ago.'

'Yep.'

'OK. So... I'm afraid it's not good news.'

'It's MS, isn't it?'

He looked a little taken aback. 'Well, yes.'

'I knew it!' she replied, almost triumphantly. 'I mean, I hoped it was just a trapped nerve, but I just had a feeling it was something more. It's not like I haven't googled, even though my husband told me not to, but the more I searched, the more it pointed towards this. Or...'

She watched as the consultant pulled his screen around to show her the white spots on her brain and spine. To show her where her own body had been slowly and silently destroying itself.

I have MS.

'We could also perform a lumbar puncture, but given the number of lesions I see here, along with your symptoms and history, I'm more than confident that we're dealing with multiple sclerosis. Do you have any questions?'

Yes. How in the flying fuck do I have MS?

'What happens now?'

'You'll be referred to our specialist team to discuss your options. They'll be able to answer any questions you have. You'll get an appointment letter in due course.'

'So, you won't be my consultant?'

'No,' he replied, 'I specialise in a different area of neurology.'

'Oh. So, with all due respect, if it's not your area of expertise, then you could be wrong?'

She saw his face soften. 'It's extremely unlikely. Do you take vitamin D?'

'No.'

'We advise everyone with MS to take a daily supplement. Levels tend to be lower in MS patients. We'll get your blood work checked so they have everything for your first appointment. The nurse outside will take you along.'

Beth nodded and stood up. She felt numb.

'I'm sorry it wasn't better news,' he said, shaking her hand.

'At least now I have answers, I suppose. Thanks very much for your time.'

The nurse outside led her along the corridor towards phlebotomy, but she didn't make it that far before reality began to sink in. She stopped, held on to the wall and sobbed harder than she ever had in her entire life.

2021

'Paul, come and look at this!'

Beth sat on the toilet, waiting for her husband to appear. Not an ideal position to be in but after nine years of marriage he'd undoubtedly seen worse.

Paul popped his head around the bathroom door and glowered. 'I don't like the fact you've asked me to look at something while you're on the pan,' he said. 'Please don't let it be gross.'

'No, it's nothing like that! Just look.'

Beth raised her left ankle onto her toes. 'See, normal.'

'OK.'

Then she lifted her right ankle into the same position. Her whole leg began shaking uncontrollably.

Paul frowned. 'How long has it been doing that?'

'I'm not sure,' Beth answered. 'I only noticed when I was trying to lift my leg to pull my knickers on. Oh, and I can't do that now either, you'll need to give me a hand.'

It had only been a year since Beth's diagnosis, but she'd already started to see new symptoms, including her fingertips becoming numb and no feeling at all on her abdomen.

'Shit,' he said, rubbing his forehead. 'What else did the great and powerful Google say? Will it go away?'

Beth smiled gently. 'Babc, none of this will go away. It's only going to get worse.'

Paul nodded and silently helped his wife pull her underwear on.

CHAPTER 17

2009

'So, does your hair always look like that?'

Alex peered up from her magazine to see Tara on the opposite bed, staring suspiciously at her. In nineteen years, Alex had never shared a bedroom, let alone one with a roommate who wouldn't look out of place in the copy of *Vogue* she was currently perusing.

'Look like what?' she asked Tara, her hand self-consciously reaching towards her head. 'God, has it gone all weird? I got caught in the rain earlier. It tends to go a bit all over the place at the mere hint of moisture. It once got so floofed up, my bobble hat pinged across the lecture theatre.'

Tara smiled. 'No, it's deadly! I love it. Massively curly, isn't it? I'd kill to have a mop like that.'

'Oh, thanks,' Alex replied, hoping the kill comment wasn't to be taken literally.

'What products do you use then? My hair's so bleedin' fine, I need some papier-mâché and an electrical socket to get any kind of volume. We've all got thin hair in my family. Thin everything really.'

We're the opposite, Alex thought to herself. *Thick everything. I could crack bloody walnuts with these thighs.*

'I use a few things,' Alex replied. 'Mousse, gel... maybe a bit of serum for the frizz if I'm going out.'

The smile remained on Tara's face, but she didn't reply, her gaze now fixed on Alex's toiletries basket.

This was Alex's second week in the house and the first week Alex and Tara had shared a room together. However, she'd been dreading this week. Tara was such a big presence in the house, she wasn't sure how they'd get on.

The bedrooms themselves were reasonably sized – two single beds in the shared rooms and a double in the biggest room which also had a small bathroom attached. Alex had not had the double room to herself yet, but she'd heard great things from the others.

Her first week in the house, she'd shared with Erin in the bedroom across the hall. It was identical to this one, apart from a huge crack in the ceiling which Beth was currently chasing the landlord to fix. Alex got the sense that Beth liked to take charge. To be invaluable. If she wasn't studying computer science, Alex thought she'd have made an excellent police officer.

Erin was fun to share with. She came across as quite delicate at first, sensitive. She read constantly, loved music and never once made Alex feel unwelcome.

However, out of everyone in the house, Tara was the most unpredictable. While she was funny and smart, she could also be incredibly snarky, to the point of offensive. Intimidating even. Not quite a mean girl, she'd never waste time saying something behind your back that she could say to your face. Tara was definitely blunt. So far, Alex had found they had absolutely nothing in common.

'Give as good as you get,' Erin had advised. 'She's really not as daunting as she seems. You'll get used to her. She loves a bit of banter, does Tara. Make her laugh and she's yours forever.'

Alex wasn't even sure whether she wanted Tara to be 'hers forever', but what she did want was a friend who wouldn't scalp her in her sleep.

'I hear we've got a new housemate coming next week,' Alex said, hoping that a change of conversation might encourage Tara to change her facial expression. 'That'll be fun, right?'

'Hmm,' Tara replied, her eyes still scanning Alex's side of the bedroom. 'Let's hope so. I met her briefly when she came to view with Erin. Rebecca something. Seemed nice enough. So, what size are you? I really like that top. It goes with that lipstick. What brand of—'

'Tara, do you want to have a rummage through my stuff or would you prefer to just keep questioning me on everything until we both eventually pass away?'

She grinned. 'Rummage. One hundred percent. Thought you'd never ask.'

Tara leapt off the bed and headed straight for Alex's wardrobe. Alex didn't mind. Not really. While she knew that nothing she owned would fit Tara's skinny arse, she was delighted that Tara seemed to admire her fashion sense. As she went back to her magazine, hearing Tara rake through her makeup basket somehow made Alex feel happy. Tara liked her. In this house, that was a big deal.

'So does your family live near?' Tara asked, inspecting a lipstick. 'Any handsome brothers I should know about?'

'Nah, just a sister,' Alex replied. 'Fiona. She's just been accepted to med school in Brighton. My dad lives somewhere in Crete and my ma's in Blanchardstown.'

'Ah, a broken home!' Tara remarked. 'Splendid. Is your mother a raging narcissist too?'

'Something like that.'

Tara held a large shirt up against her small frame. 'And your dad's off living his best life?'

Alex laughed. 'How did you know?'

'Lucky guess,' she answered, 'or maybe we all just have that look about us...'

As she gave a little wink, Alex smiled. It seemed they did have something in common after all.

CHAPTER 18

As she watched Aiden undress for bed, Tara felt glad that she'd brought him to meet her friends. Aiden was easy on the eye, funny and, so far, he'd been a hit with everyone. He was certainly far more personable than Christine, a woman she hadn't warmed to at all.

'So... verdict?' she asked, slipping out of her jeans. 'Everyone's so great, right?'

'Totally,' he replied. 'Very welcoming. Big fan of the coffee. Ten out of ten.'

She laughed. 'You were a good sport for coming. Not sure I would have agreed to a weekend away with a group of your mates.'

'Hmm, well, technically, I didn't agree to a weekend with your mates. You said it was a family gathering.'

'These people are my family! But yes, I can see the confusion. Regardless, I really wanted you here.'

While true, part of the reason Tara really wanted him there because she had expected everyone else to show up with husbands and partners, maybe even children or at least an endless camera roll with photos of them doing things only other parents would find adorable. She did not want to be the only singleton there, having to watch them all be annoyingly happy and content. She was far from content, but at least by having Aiden there, she could pretend to be. She'd never met anyone quite like him.

Tara had been upfront with Aiden about her rehab and follow-up therapy, fully expecting him to drive off into the sunset, never to be seen again. However, Aiden took the information in his stride. He was the most accepting man she'd ever met.

'I am good enough. I am smart enough. People like me, for me.'

Tara thought she'd throw herself under the nearest bus if she had to repeat that mantra one more bloody time, but she had to trust the process, despite feeling utterly foolish. Still, by the look on their faces, she guessed that at least seventy percent of the people here felt the same.

'Today we're going to talk about acts of kindness—'

'I helped save a dog recently!' she exclaimed.

'—towards ourselves.'

'Ah shite. I have nothing then.'

She sat back in her seat and let Jerry, the group director, continue. Her mind wasn't entirely focused on group anyway, not after the Facebook invite she'd received that morning.

A reunion, if you will. It's long overdue.

I've missed you all.

Erin x

Erin bloody Carmichael, though now she was Erin Flynn, up-and-coming actress who recently did that superhero thing with that actor whose name she was totally blanking on. Good-looking big fella. Played that detective on telly.

She'd replied yes, of course, thrilled at the prospect of getting together with her oldest friends, some who had become incredibly successful. Unlike her.

Hi everyone. I had a nervous breakdown, fled my life in New York and went into rehab. Kicked the powder and now currently taking group therapy on how to deal with processing the shame that is my life. How have you all been? Normal? That's nice.

She felt her stomach knot. Though they had kept in touch sporadically after university, it had been ten years since they'd all sat down together. Was she really going to show up and tell tales about her crappy life?

She nodded along in group when the others did, pretending to listen.

You could bring Aiden, she thought to herself. *Handsome man on your arm, bit of moral support... but would he even want to come? Four days with people he doesn't know, Christ, he hardly knows you.*

'Tara? Are you with us?'

She snapped back to reality, greeted by a room full of faces all staring in her direction.

'Yes. Sorry. Totally here.'

'I was asking if you could tell us a way in which you exhibit self-love?'

She smirked. 'Self-love? Fella, I'm not sure I want to be telling you all about—'

'No. Nonono. I mean how are you personally *kind* to your-self?' Jerry asked, clearly a little irritated by the giggling from certain members of the group.

After a pause, Tara finally said, 'I'm reconnecting with old friends... but I'm pretty certain the dog thing still counts.'

Group over, Tara left the building, quickly spotting Aiden's car in the car park. It looked rather out of place sitting between the Mercs and the Teslas.

'Thanks for picking me up,' she said, climbing in. 'Very sweet of you.'

'It's no trouble,' he replied. 'I have the day off. Can I ask how it went?'

'Hmm, not bad, I guess,' she replied. 'Lots of talking and feelings, which is fine if you like that sort of thing.'

She buckled her seatbelt before waving to a mousy-looking woman called Jessica that she had grown quite fond of over the past few weeks. Despite her timid appearance, Jessica, a former criminal lawyer, was an absolute riot.

'Idris bleedin' Elba!'

'Sorry?'

She laughed. 'Nothing, I was just trying to remember his name earlier.'

'So, what's actually involved here?' Aiden asked. 'In your group. Do you have steps to work through or...'

'Nah, it's not like AA or those kind of support groups, I'd imagine. This is like a weekly meet-up for people who have self-esteem issues. They call it an empowerment group, which to be fair is a shite name, but it costs a bloody bomb and has a waiting list as long as your arm. You'd be surprised at the types of people who don't like themselves very much. I can't name names obviously, but there's quite a few famous people.'

'You're very brave' he said, starting the car. 'Not sure I could handle something like that. *Empowerment group!* It all sounds very American, doesn't it?'

'You're American.'

'I know. I'm sorry.'

Tara laughed. 'It would be pointless for you anyway, because you like yourself,' Tara replied. 'And you should, you're deadly.'

Tara had only been dating Aiden for twelve weeks, but he'd

been entirely chill with her current situation. She'd already completed rehab but still felt she had a long way to go. She wasn't completely sure why he hadn't run for the hills, given the absolute state of her, but perhaps, Tara thought, this was another reason she was wise to keep attending the group.

'So how was work?' she asked. 'Save any animals?'

'Well,' he replied, 'someone did hand in a five-foot python they found in their garden.'

'I dated a guy who owned a python once,' Tara replied. 'It didn't do much, but then again, neither did he. They made a good pair.'

Aiden smiled. 'Yeah, they're pretty docile. She was microchipped though, so we found the owner quickly, which was good.'

Tara liked listening to him talk, even though she found his job to be somewhat boring. Unlike previous boyfriends, he wasn't flashy or arrogant or vain (even though he had every right to be), he was just a sweet guy who made her laugh and, right now, that was all she needed.

'You ever been to Ireland?'

'No,' he replied. 'You?'

She laughed loudly. 'Not for a while. I thought I might take a trip, in a couple of weeks. See some family. You up for it?'

'Sounds nice,' he replied. 'Yeah, I'm definitely up for that, I just need to check with work.'

'Excellent,' she responded, kissing him on the cheek. 'We'll have a great time, I promise.'

CHAPTER 19

Beth awakened early on Friday morning to a quiet house. As she hobbled her way to the bathroom, she passed by Jasper the cat who sat perfectly still at the bottom of the stairs, seemingly unfazed by the influx new visitors in his home. He observed as she held the walls, hobbling into the loo, her leg unsteady, almost floppy without the weight of the brace.

The main bathroom was large and bright, with pale yellow walls and a white tiled floor. The clawfoot bath looked incredibly inviting, however Beth knew that she'd never be able to get in or out safely on her own. There was a shower over the bath, but again, she would have to hike that bad leg over the side and hope she stayed upright. Not a challenge she was willing to accept.

No, you are not waking Paul, she thought to herself. *He does enough for you – let the man sleep!*

Asking for help was tough at times, even from her husband. It was hard not to feel like a burden, but she was stubborn, sometimes to her own detriment. While keeping this a secret from the girls was tricky and exhausting, it was still better than having them pity her.

———

Upstairs, Alex was also wide awake with only one thing on her mind. Aiden. Bloody Aiden. Walking around with his stupid *howdy, ma'am* voice and his stupid excellent face. *Dammit*, she thought, *pulling a pillow over her head, this is ridiculous. He's Tara's partner! Remember Tara, your old bestie who would absolutely never steal your boyfriend? Well, there was that incident in second year at uni, but he technically wasn't your boyfriend so that doesn't count.*

She screamed into the pillow before throwing it on to the floor. It was only Friday. They didn't leave until Monday afternoon, which meant another three days of smiling and ignoring her libido which was determined to make itself known.

She looked at her phone. Half past seven. Not quite the long lie-in she had planned, but she could make some tea and bring it back to bed. Maybe snag some of those biscuits left over from last night.

Throwing on her dressing gown, she tiptoed her way downstairs and into the kitchen. Hungrier than she thought, she wondered if there might be any of that nice bread left and—

'Morning.'

Alex jumped at least two feet in the air. 'Christ on a bike, you scared me!'

Aiden smiled from behind the fridge door before returning inside to rummage. 'Sorry,' he whispered. 'I was starving. Do you know if there is any of that crusty bread left?'

'Try the breadbin,' she replied, quickly flattening her hair, though his bed head was almost worse than hers.

She filled the kettle and stood awkwardly while it boiled, watching Aiden, in his boxers and T-shirt, carve into a tiger bloomer.

'Do you always wander around someone else's house half-naked?' she asked.

He turned and smiled. 'I'm hardly half-naked, though you don't appear to be wearing much under that bathrobe yourself.'

As they locked eyes for a moment, Alex felt her pulse rate soar. The sound of footsteps coming down the hall snapped them both out of it.

'Oh good,' Beth said as she limped into the kitchen, 'I could murder a cuppa. Morning, Alex... Aiden. Oh, Paul has those boxers. I think. Hugo Boss? Anyone know where the mugs are?'

One by one, everyone in the house began to rise and before long the living room was full again.

'Sleep well?' Erin asked, yawning. Alex thought she looked as if she hadn't slept a wink. Underneath her eyes, her face looked almost hollow.

'If you're still tired, go back to bed,' she suggested. 'I'm sure we can all amuse ourselves for a few hours.'

'But breakfast...'

'We can manage,' Becky said. 'Besides, I intend to do nothing this afternoon except take advantage of those sun loungers. It's supposed to be scorching. Go and rest for a bit.'

Erin conceded and headed back to her bedroom, where Jasper had taken up residence at the foot of the bed. She was tired, but this was nothing new. She'd often sleep in the day because night-time was the worst. Night was when she missed Scott most intensely. She'd dream about him constantly, always happy dreams. Dreams where everything was the way it had been. The way it still should be. It wasn't lack of sleep that left her fatigued, it was the dreams; the sheer force of missing him was exhausting.

'How can it be this hot?' Becky asked, fanning herself with a magazine. 'It's Ireland. We have two seasons and both of them involve rain.'

As there were only three sun loungers, the rest of the group made do with beach towels on the grass. Beth and her leg brace were assigned one of the loungers, with Becky and Tara taking the remaining two.

'So, you left university, only to go back to university?' Tara asked Beth. 'Weren't you sick of it?'

Beth shrugged. 'It's different when you're on the other side of the lecture hall. I love my job.'

Tara thought that she'd rather clean toilets with her own toothbrush than go back into education. 'And what else do you get up to when you're not teaching?'

'Sorry?'

'Fun, Beth. What do you do for fun?'

I try not to fall over, Tara. It's quite the rush.

'Usual stuff,' she replied. 'Movies, gigs, Saturday markets in the park and I...'

'What?'

'Nah, you'll laugh!'

'Possibly,' Tara responded, 'but don't let that stop you."

'I have an allotment.'

The smile flew across Tara's face quicker than expected. 'An allotment?'

'Yes.'

'Like a patch of grass you grow vegetables in? Ha, I never took you for a farmer, Beth.'

'See, I knew you'd make fun of me!' Beth exclaimed. 'And no, I'm not a bloody farmer. Gah, you're still so annoying.'

'Sorry,' Tara replied, laughing. 'Do you bring your own hoe or is there like a communal one?'

'Forget it.'

Beth was reluctant to carry on the conversation. She'd had the allotment for years. Their garden at home was completely paved over and too small to transform into anything worthwhile. All they had was a wooden shed, left by the previous owners which Paul had immediately commandeered.

'I'm just messing,' Tara assured her. 'Tell me.'

'It's actually quite a young crowd that have patches there,' she said defensively. 'Not everyone is retired. And I enjoy it. I grow veg, plants, flowers and it calms me. In the summer it's a glorious place to be. It might not be London or New York, but it makes me happy.'

'It sounds like hard work,' Tara replied. 'Fair play to you, I wouldn't have a clue where to begin. Besides, I'm not the biggest fan of nature.'

She swatted at a wasp which seemed to take offence at her last statement.

'I swear, if this wasp doesn't piss off, I'm going to flatten it,' Tara said, flapping her hands around her face. 'It's basically goading me at this point, it's like Conor McGregor at weigh-in.'

Alex squirmed. 'That's what you get for eating fruit outdoors,' she said, keeping one eye on the wasp in case it decided to have a go at her next. 'You're practically inviting it to dinner. Jeez, you're waving at it as well; did they teach you nothing at primary school?'

'Becky, help me out, will ya?'

Becky raised her sunglasses and looked over. 'Me? What can I do?'

Tara was now standing. 'Anything! Come on, you're the bee whisperer. Tell it to bugger off.'

'Bees and wasps are very different,' she replied, lowering her glasses. 'Wasps are much harder to reason with. Just stay still, it'll move on.'

'You can talk to insects?' Christine enquired from the shaded patio.

Becky gave a little laugh. 'God no, that would be ridiculous. They're just joshing because I've never been stung. Like I must have some affinity with bees or something.'

Christine went back to reading.

By now, Tara had returned to the patio area and the wasp had moved on. Paul quickly moved onto her lounger.

'Whatcha reading there, Christine?' Tara asked. 'Any good?'

'*The Guest List*,' she replied. 'Lucy Foley. I borrowed it from Erin's shelf. I'd usually choose non-fiction over fiction, but it's not bad, I suppose. From what I have read so far, it features a group of people staying together in a large house, all keeping secrets from each other.' Her eyes darted among the group, looking for a reaction. 'These types of scenarios never go well, do they?'

'Not for the one who inevitably gets murdered,' Tara mumbled.

'I thought it was excellent,' Alex interjected. 'She's brilliant.'

Christine sniffed. 'I mean, I've never heard of her, but there are so many writers just lobbing out books these days, aren't there? Hard to keep up.'

'She's actually a *New York Times* bestseller,' Alex replied, feeling herself getting defensive over an author she'd never met. 'I love her writing.' Comments like that annoyed her. One does not just lob a novel out.

'I might head to the beach,' Beth suggested. 'Sprawl out on a beach towel if anyone wants to come with?'

'Sure,' Alex replied, grateful for the excuse to get away. 'I could use the sea breeze. Have a paddle with my pals.'

'Maybe later,' Tara said, 'I'm not in the mood to get sandy feet.'

'No, thanks.' Christine said. 'I prefer the shade.'

'Becky?'

She glanced at Christine before shaking her head. 'I'm good here.'

'I have a ball in the boot of my car if you want to have a kick around?' Paul said to Aiden.

'Absolutely,' he replied. 'I haven't had my ass kicked at soccer for a while. Bring it on.'

Aiden followed Paul to his car while Alex helped Beth walk down to the beach.

'I can't believe she's leaving all this,' Alex said, looking out on to the lough. It was clear, calm and the sky bright blue. 'It's like her own little paradise. Who the hell sells their own beach?'

'I genuinely thought she'd pass this down to her kids,' Beth replied. 'You know, keep it in the family. But I guess the memories here are just too painful. Shame though. She'd be a great mum. I hope she gets the chance one day.'

They found a spot and placed their towels on the sand. Beth awkwardly manoeuvred down, her legs stretched out in front.

'I can run back and get you a chair,' Alex offered. 'Kick Tara off the sun lounger?'

Beth snickered. 'No, this is fine. I need to stretch anyway.'

'Nice kick!' she heard Aiden say as a ball flew over their heads. She wondered if she'd ever not find his voice appealing.

'Could you live in the same house still if anything happened to Paul?' she asked, watching the guys run around the beach.

'I'm not sure,' Beth replied. 'I mean, there would certainly be more space.'

Alex giggled. 'True.'

'Actually, I don't know,' she said, staring at her feet. She tried to will her right ankle to bend, but it stayed motionless. 'Hard to know what you'd do, unless you're in that situation.'

'Yeah.'

'Not the same, I know, but you're living with the memories of your ex. Isn't that tough?'

'Hardly memories,' Alex said, 'Pete's still around. He's like a living ghost who stomps around in his work boots.'

'So, what happened with him? How long were you together?'

'Five years,' she replied. 'We've been apart for one.'

'Why did you break up?'

Alex sighed. 'Honestly?'

'No,' Beth replied. 'Lie to me.'

She smiled. 'Well, I woke up one morning, looked over at him and realised that I wasn't in love with him anymore. That I could absolutely picture my life without him in it, romantically.'

'Oh dear. Was he devastated?'

'Not at all,' Alex replied. 'In fact, I think he was grateful I said something first. I'm not sure we ever fell in love to be honest. We were young. I think we just fell into a relationship. One minute he was good company, the next he was moving into my new house with me.'

'And no one since him?'

Alex felt her eyes drift towards Aiden.

Oh God, he has his top off! The boxers were bad enough, now I'm forced to see his torso? Is this a Texan thing?

'Alex?'

'Sorry. No, not really. All the good ones are taken ... God, this is depressing. You want to paddle?'

'Definitely,' Beth replied. 'I'm roasting.'

Alex helped her up and they walked over to the shoreline and stepped in.

'Christ, that's colder than I expected!' Beth squealed. 'I remember now why we didn't go swimming and, oh my word, Aiden appears to be shirtless.'

'Really?' Alex replied. 'I hadn't noticed.'

'How is it?' Paul yelled, pulling their focus away from Aiden's flesh.

'Baltic,' Alex responded. 'Enter with caution!'

Alex barely got the words out before Beth's leg went out from under her. She shrieked as her knees hit the water. Paul immediately sprinted over.

'Fuck, are you OK?'

'I'm fine, I'm fine' Beth reassured everyone. 'Just lost my footing. God, my arse is soaking.'

As Paul leaned in and helped her up, he noticed blood running down her knee. 'You're bleeding! You should have had your stick.'

'Don't fuss,' she said. 'I'm fine, just a scratch. Help me back to the house, will you?'

Alex and Aiden stood back, watching Paul help his wife hobble home. 'Well, the beach trip was fun while it lasted,' Alex remarked.

Aiden shrugged. 'Doesn't have to be over just yet. We could do a little wading.'

'Paddling,' she corrected with a grin. 'You're not in Texas anymore.'

'Fine... paddling. We should paddle.'

Alex instinctively looked towards Tara's direction. 'I'm not sure.'

'We're just talking,' Aiden said. 'People do that, you know. I've heard it's quite popular. We did enough of it on the plane.'

'I know! But see, the problem is that now I know who you are, I'm finding it hard to know what to say! Or what to do... or even where to look, for feck's sake, can you just put your shirt back on.'

He glanced down at his bare chest. 'It's summer, Alex.'

'It's obscene is what it is.'

'Are you a prude?' he questioned, still not putting his damn shirt back on. 'I don't understand.'

'A prude? Jesus, Aiden, do I have to spell it out? In order for me to make it through the rest of this weekend, I need you to not look like that.'

'Oh. Right, gotcha,' he said. 'I'm not trying to make this difficult, you know. But know that the more time I spend with you, the harder this becomes.'

'What becomes?' Before she could even engage her brain, her eyes wandered down to his crotch.

'I meant the situation, Alex.'

Her face flushed with mortification and she picked up her shoes. 'So, I'm just going to throw myself in the lough now.'

Aiden's laughter echoed across the beach as she scurried away.

CHAPTER 20

2011

'Who has the room next week?' Beth yelled from the kitchen.

'My turn,' Alex shouted in reply. 'And it cannot come quickly enough. I swear I'm going to murder Becky if she doesn't stop sleep-talking.'

'I can't help it,' Beth heard Becky respond. 'I just happen to have a lot of conversational dreams.'

As roommates went, Beth enjoyed sharing with Erin the most. She was the calmest of the group, unlikely to sweat the small stuff and most importantly she didn't snore. Tara on the other hand sounded like she was sawing wood, especially after a few beers. She was also the most likely to wind Beth up. She'd *open her mouth and let her belly rumble* as her mum would say, often bluntly speaking before she'd had time to think. Person-ally, she hadn't heard Becky's sleep-talking, but Alex was known to giggle at nothing in the dead of night.

'Would you mind swapping with me?' Beth asked. 'Pretty please?'

'Why?' Alex enquired. 'Did you not just hear my I'm going to murder Becky story?'

Beth took a deep breath. 'I'd quite like Paul to stay over next week and I know that we all agreed—'

'NO SLEEPOVERS!' was the loud response in unison from the living room. She sighed. She knew they would say this. They had four house rules that they swore to stick by:

1. If you mess it up, tidy it.
2. If you finish it, replace it.
3. Ask before you borrow it.
4. No sleepovers.

Originally there had only been three but then Becky bumped into one of Tara's naked acquaintances in the hallway at am and almost had a heart attack.

This is our home, our safe space! None of us need to be seeing random hairy arses and dangly bits in the dead of night!'

Tara initially protested until she realised the following day that the random dangly man had stolen her bank card and new electric toothbrush. The new rule was quickly added to the list on the fridge in block capitals.

'Oh, come on, it's Paul!' Beth insisted, stomping through from the kitchen. 'You've met Paul. He's harmless and very respectful. You won't even know he's here!'

'Unless you've both taken a vow of chastity, I think we will,' Erin remarked. 'But why does he need to stay here? He has his own flat share – in a much nicer part of town, might I add.'

Beth shoved Tara's legs off the arm of the couch and sat down. 'Two reasons. Number one: it's my birthday and Paul wants to cook me dinner. Our kitchen is far better equipped that his one dirty microwave and a hot-plate setup. And number two: his place is a smelly nightmare. It's just *eau de testosterone* the moment you step inside. It's so hard to get any real privacy and God, the toilet in the morning – it's unbearable. Pube soap in the shower, questionably damp loo roll – it's like a festival Portaloo covered in tiny beard shavings. Boys are so gross.'

'And yet you want to let one of them loose in here?' Alex questioned. 'I don't think so. Also, bars of soap are still a thing? What is this, 1950?'

'It's actually better for the environment,' Becky added. 'No plastic waste.'

Alex shrugged. 'I'll let the planet burn before I touch boy soap.'

'Can we get back to my request please?' Beth exclaimed, in an attempt to get the conversation back on track. 'If we can't stay here, I'm not sure what we'll do.'

'See, that's why God invented hotels,' Tara said. She paused. 'Although it didn't work out too well for Mary, Joseph and the wee fella, but you get my point. This is the only other option. No exceptions. Just get a room and go out to eat. I have student vouchers for Pizza Hut!'

Beth threw her head back in frustration. 'Have you seen how much a hotel in Dublin costs these days!'

'Yes. Four million euros.'

'Oh, ha-ha, very funny, but it might as well be,' Beth replied, glaring at the incessantly sarcastic Tara. 'It's more than we can afford to spend anyway, vouchers or not. Please, just one night! I'll take over the chores for a week. I'll even wash all of the bedding, not just my own.'

Becky's ears pricked up. 'Oh really?'

Beth smiled, moving closer to Becky. 'Uh-huh. I'll even use some of that spring breeze fabric softener that you like so much... *like the outdoors, indoors...*'

'They also have a new lavender one,' Becky informed her, now totally invested. 'It's really sooth—'

'Stand down Becky,' Erin laughed. 'We know you're partial to a freshly changed bed – we all are, but rules are rules.'

'Oh, fuck's sake,' Beth mumbled. 'Fine. I hope you all get bedbugs.'

'I think we need to have a house meeting about this,' Alex decided, rather forcefully. 'Beth, if you'd like to wait upstairs, we'll call you down when we've made the decision.'

They watched Beth close the living room door and heard her trundle upstairs. The subsequent door slam let them know she was in her room.

'So, we'll just let her sit for a bit?' Tara asked, hanging her legs back over the side of the couch.

'Yep,' Erin replied, 'It'll make it look like we're actually giving it some thought.'

'Did Paul say what time he wants us to scarper on Tuesday? I have those student vouchers for Pizza Hut, remember.'

'Can't believe he's asking her to marry him,' Becky said in her best 'I'm trying very hard to keep my voice down' voice. 'She's totally going to cry.'

Erin laughed. 'I think *you're* going to cry.'

'I so am. Think she'll say yes?'

'Absolutely,' Tara insisted. 'As ridiculous as I find the whole concept, those two are going to be married forever.'

Everyone nodded in agreement.

'Ready?' Alex asked, getting up to open the living room door. They all tried to look as innocent as possible.

'BETH! One night! Only because it's your birthday.'

There was a muffled scream of delight from behind the door.

CHAPTER 21

'Maybe you should be using that walker more?' Paul said as he hunted in the medicine cabinet for a plaster. 'I think you need a bit more stability on your feet.'

Beth sighed like a petulant child. 'I hate that bloody thing. I feel like one of those old ladies you see at the shops. It's so... uncool. I'm only thirty-two.'

'So I'll get you a funky one,' Paul replied. 'They have some more modern ones online, I've seen them. Sequins and all sorts. They even have ones which turn into a wheelchair for when—'

'I don't need a wheelchair.'

He saw the look of disdain in her eyes. 'I know... but it's only for when you get tired. You know how tired you get.'

Beth felt her eyes welling up. 'I don't want this,' she said. 'I don't want any of this.'

Paul finished tending to her knee before sitting next to her on the bed. He placed his arm around her as she wept.

'I know it's tough,' he said softly. 'And I don't want to upset you. I just want you to live your life as normally as possible. I want you to be safe.'

He swallowed as he remembered an article he'd read about

a man with MS who'd fallen into a glass table and died from the lacerations to his arms. His mobility issues prevented him from getting help. Paul never told Beth about the article though.

'I miss my life,' she said. 'I miss being who I was. Inside I'm still the same and that's the part that hurts more than the nerve pain or the accidents.'

Paul hugged her tightly.

'I still feel the same as I always did. I still want the same things. This breaks my heart.'

'Do you want to go home? We can make an excuse.'

Beth shook her head. 'No. I came here to forget about all of this for a while, not wallow in it. I'm going to wash my face and enjoy the rest of my weekend. It's not going to take that away from me too.'

———

Aiden and Alex could hear everyone laughing as they walked up the garden path. Beth, her knee now sporting a rather fetching plaster, had an announcement to make. 'Oh good, you're here! Sooo, I was thinking. Tonight. Who fancies some karaoke?'

There was a united groan from Aiden and Paul.

'Oh, fun!' Tara replied. 'I haven't done karaoke for ages. Ha, remember when we used to go to the student union. Cheap beer and bad singing, it was a gas!'

Even though none of them could sing a note, Friday nights were always reserved for karaoke. There were two rooms in the union, the smaller one jammed packed on a Friday with drunken academics, all grabbing for the song books.

'What was the name of the wee fella who ran the karaoke night? Dead smooth, could have sold sour milk to the cows.'

Alex laughed. 'Davey Dawson. God, I haven't thought about him in years.'

'I bet he's thought about you though, eh, Moran?'

Alex scowled at Paul. 'I'm sure I have no idea what you're talking about, *Cooper*.'

She absolutely did. Davey Dawson, all five-foot-two of him, had taken a shine to Alex and wasn't shy about letting her know. He was harmless but made no secret of the fact that he thought Alex was the most beautiful woman in Dublin.

'He was loaded,' Tara stated. 'You could have done a lot worse.'

'She did,' Beth replied, smirking. 'Two words: Aaron. Keating.'

Everyone began to roar with laughter, except Alex, Aiden and Christine. In fact, Christine hadn't look up from her 'it's not bad, I suppose' book for the entire conversation.

'Care to explain?' Aiden asked, over the top of the laughter.

'Not really.'

'Oh, go on,' Becky encouraged.

Alex threw her head back and quietly screamed. 'Fine. I just happened to date... I mean, I wouldn't even call it dating, it was more of a short-lived—'

'Sexual catastrophe?'

As her hands covered her face, Alex made a noise like a dying animal. 'I hate you all.'

'I'm completely invested now,' Aiden said, laughing. 'What happened?'

'I can't,' Alex mumbled from behind her hands. 'Just kill me and get it over with.'

Tara immediately started the story. 'So, Aaron was the year below us,' she told Aiden. 'First year in agricultural science or something farmer-y, I can't remember. You'd have liked him. Anyway, he was fresh off the tractor... just eighteen. Big lad, y'know... sturdy and also, like Davey, thought Alex was the cat's ankles.'

'This makes me sound like I was a much sought-after

woman,' Alex interjects. 'And I really wasn't.' In fact, she remembered the struggle she'd had getting ready.

'I can't go out like this!' she'd yelped, fussing over her dress in front of the mirror. 'I'm practically falling out of it. It'll give him entirely the wrong idea.'

'Oh I think it'll give him entirely the right idea,' Tara replied, helping Alex scoop her chest properly into her low-cut red dress. 'Though, I'd maybe give dancing a miss. One misplaced jiggle and it's game over.'

'See!' Alex cried. 'That's it, I'm wearing the black one.'

By now, Erin and Becky had joined them to see what all the fuss was about. 'You look lovely,' Becky insisted. 'No offence but the black one makes you look like you're going to a funeral.'

'I'd rather be going to a feckin' funeral,' Alex mumbled. 'That's way less depressing than a first date.'

'Come on now,' Beth said. 'Alan seems lovely and it's been ages since you've had a date.'

'His name's Aaron.'

'Whatever. It's all just rehearsal for the main event. You're not going to marry this boy, you're just going to practise on him. Just have a good time.'

'I guess...'

Despite her concerns, Alex had found herself enjoying her first date with Aaron. Although rather shy, he was fun to be around. She also enjoyed her second date and by the third they both knew that things were going to go further.

Observing house rules, Alex found herself in Aaron's room in student halls, which looked exactly like she imagined it would. Film posters on the walls, bed in disarray and clothes scattered on the floor.

'Sorry about the mess,' he said, trying to kick a pathway through his room.

'It's fine,' she replied, 'My room isn't much better.'

She could almost hear Beth cackle at this outright lie. While

Alex didn't have her own room, any room she did sleep in was spotless but giving an eighteen-year-old boy advice on cleanliness might have killed the mood.

They kissed. They had kissed before, but this time it was with purpose. This time it had intention and would lead to more than a 'thanks for a lovely evening,' or 'I'll call you'.

Clothes off rather hurriedly on Aaron's part who appeared to be down to his boxers before Alex had even unzipped her dress. He turned her around and began kissing her neck.

'Bend over,' he whispered, which surprised Alex, given that he was the least assertive guy she'd ever met. She was pretty sure if she'd said no, he'd have agreed that it was a terrible idea and begged for forgiveness.

As she assumed the position, she felt his entire weight on her back followed by his arms wrapped around her. Sweet Jesus, he's literally mounting me, she thought to herself.

'Um, I'm not sure that this will—'

'Just give me a second,' he mumbled. 'Nearly in.'

'I don't think you're anywhere... WOOAHHH!'

She heard a crash as he fell sideways onto the floor. She wanted to laugh, so badly, but didn't have the heart to humiliate him further.

'How about we just do it normally?' she suggested. 'You know, facing each other?'

He agreed, apologised profusely and six minutes later they were done.

'That was amazing,' he declared. 'I mean, I knew it would be, but woo-hoo!'

Oh God, I'm his first, Alex thought. In fairness he was only her third, but still, she was well past the woo-hooing stage.

'Was it alright for you?' he asked. 'Was I—'

'Perfect!' she replied quickly. 'Couldn't be happier. If I didn't have an early exam, I'd be climbing back on.'

She leapt from his bed and gathered her clothes.

'I can drive you home,' he insisted, pulling on his boxers. 'Kev has a car. KEV, CAN I BORROW THE CAR?'

'Aye,' a voice through the wall replied. 'It'll need some petrol though.' Oh dear God, Kev must have heard everything.

'Honestly, it's fine, I can—'

'I think I love you.'

Aware that Aaron was behind her again, she spun around quickly. One surprise mounting was enough for the evening.

'Oh no,' she said, smiling. 'You don't.'

'But I do. Come here.'

Three seconds into the world's most awkward hug, Aaron stepped forward and Alex felt a searing pain shoot through her foot.

'My toes!' she yelped as Aaron removed his nineteen-stone body weight off them. 'I think you've broken my toes!'

Alex pulled herself back to the present, on the patio, where Aiden was laughing just as hard as everyone else. Christine – still nothing. The woman was clearly dead inside.

'In two places,' Alex continued. 'My middle toe is now forever wonky. Horrible experience altogether but thanks for bringing it up, everyone! I mean it's not like anyone else has any embarrassing stories from university, and definitely not any involving chewing gum...'

It was Alex's turn to laugh with the group as Tara let out a little shriek.

'I had forgotten about that!' she exclaimed. 'Bloody Keith! Oh, the horror. I mean, who the hell goes down south on their unshaven girlfriend with chewing gum in their mouth?'

CHAPTER 22

2014

'You busy?'

Erin turned to see a stern, tall, stocky man standing on the steps of the catering truck, his dark blonde hair, unruly from the cooking heat.

'Me? Um, no, I'm not busy... I'm just—'

He moved towards her. 'Good, taste this.'

Erin leaned in and sampled the red sauce on the end of the spoon.

'Delicious!' she enthused. 'It's just the right balance of sweet and sour.'

'Oh great,' he replied. 'Exactly what I was going for... except it's supposed to be spicy. Definitely needs more chilli.'

Erin didn't think that her last day on the set of her very first film would be spent hanging around the catering truck. Her minor role did not afford her a trailer so she was left to her own devices.

'Well, your food is excellent,' she informed him. 'I had the chicken at lunch. Really delicious.'

He frowned. 'That was lamb.'

'It was? God, I'm sorry, maybe I'm not the best person to—'

'I'm joking! It was chicken and thank you. Chef's gone home but I'll let her know.'

Erin peered into the trailer. 'What, so you're just here, messing up her nice kitchen?'

'It's *my* nice kitchen, actually, I own the business. But you're right about the mess part.' He glanced down at his striped apron, splattered with the same red sauce she'd just sampled. 'I should clean up.'

Erin glanced at the side of the truck. 'So, you're not a chef, *Scott Flynn Catering?*'

'I am,' he replied, smiling. 'More planning than cooking these days, unfortunately.'

That smile. Erin felt her knees go weak and her brain completely evacuate all rational thought, leaving an awkward silence hanging in the air.

'You alright?' he asked, his eyes meeting hers.

'Uh-huh,' she replied, wondering if it was too soon to propose. Usually, Erin was a normal human being around men. They rarely made an impression, if at all, but this was completely unexpected. A few seconds later she realised that neither of them had broken eye contact. He blushed as he realised this too.

'Um, don't you have lines to be going over or something?' he asked, swiftly moving back inside the truck. From the door she watched him shake something red and powdery into the pot. 'I mean, I am assuming you have a part in this film. Either that or you just really like wearing Victorian corsets.'

'Both actually,' she replied, finally finding her voice. 'And I have a whole three lines, two of them have already been shot. This is my final one, my *piece de resistance.*'

'Let's hear it then.'

'What, now?'

'Sure, why not?'

She liked his accent. West Country, she guessed, Devon perhaps.

She cleared her throat dramatically. 'The horses are ready, ma'am. Be safe. We'll await your return.'

He laughed and applauded. 'Bravo. I completely believed you were...'

'Mary Ronan. Second Housekeeper.'

'Of course!' he replied, stirring his sauce once more before turning off the heat. 'So, this is your last day? Got anything else lined up after this?'

'I do actually,' she replied. God, his eyes were so green. Like little emeralds—

'And...'

'Oh, sorry. *Rocky Horror* tour. I'm really excited.'

'More corsets,' he said. 'Interesting.'

'Mary Ronan, you're up.'

Erin waved towards the assistant. 'Shit, OK, I'd better run. Really nice to meet you!'

'It was really nice to meet you too, Mary Ronan.'

'Erin,' she replied, grinning. 'My name's Erin.'

———

Erin awoke to the sound of her friends laughing in the garden. Five-thirty in the afternoon; she'd been asleep for nine hours. She sprang out of bed, chastising herself for being a terrible host.

That's right, just you sleep the entire weekend away and leave your guests to starve.

Pulling on a cardigan, she scurried down the hall to the kitchen where she was reminded that her guests were grown adults, capable of finding food in a fully stocked fridge. Panic over, she poured herself a drink and stepped out on to the patio.

'I'm so sorry,' she said, pulling up a chair. 'You must think me so rude.'

The weather was still unreasonably warm for half past five. The cardigan was immediately removed.

'No, we think you so tired,' Alex replied with a smile. 'Please don't worry about us, we've been catching up on old times... some of them less worth remembering than others, I might add.'

'Really? Anything interesting?'

'Aaron Keating,' Becky mouthed behind Alex's back.

Erin snorted. 'Aaron Keating? I ran into him a few years back.'

Alex spun around to throw daggers at Becky.

'I was doing some god-awful play in Mayo or Galway; I can't remember but he was there with his wife! I seem to remember he was quite high up in soil science or something.'

'Did he ask after Alex?' Paul enquired. 'Maybe a longing look off into the distance at the mention of her name. A small tear of nostalgia shed? Anything?'

Alex snorted. 'Did his wife at least have both of her feet intact?'

By now Erin was laughing too hard to reply, all she could do was shake her head. Eventually, she calmed down enough to ask about dinner.

'I was going to do salmon,' she suggested, 'with a spicy veggie stir fry for Christine, Becky and Aiden? I should still have some bread for—'

'No bread.' Tara interjected. 'We got peckish. And you might be out of hummus too.'

'And soft cheese,' Paul confessed.

'Oh no worries, I get an extra delivery in the morning anyway.'

'Salmon sounds delicious,' Aiden remarked. 'I'm pescetarian so fish is fine with me too. Don't go to too much trouble.'

'It's no trouble at all,' Erin replied. 'We can eat in an hour, oh and feel free to use the shower in my bedroom, I've popped some extra towels in there.'

Beth breathed a small sigh of relief. She might just be able to manage that by herself. 'Can I give you a hand with dinner?' she asked. 'You're actually in luck, as I'm an absolute whizz at nothing at all – *except* stir-fry.'

'Nonsense,' Paul replied. 'She's also excellent at boiled eggs.'

'That'd be nice,' Erin replied. 'Thanks, Beth.'

'No problem. I'll jump in for a quick shower first.'

Erin's bedroom was nestled away at the back of the house. Beth had seen it in its previous incarnation – huge but very beige, with heavy dark wooden furniture which undoubtedly had a past. Ten years later and it was a completely different room. Soft lemon walls, white furniture and peach accessories scattered throughout. She wondered whether it looked like this while Scott was alive or if she'd redecorated to try and minimise some of the memories she held there.

The bathroom was also updated. A wet room with nothing to step up to or fall over. As she undressed and walked in, she realised that this was the first time she hadn't struggled to shower in over a year. For a moment, she felt like her old self.

———

'Kerry is quite a beautiful county, it seems,' Christine noted as they got ready for dinner. 'Bigger than I thought.'

'It is,' Becky replied, watching Christine sweep blusher over her cheeks. 'I haven't seen as much of it as I'd like to. Maybe after we leave on Monday, we could do a little exploring for a couple of days? Find a guesthouse or a B&B?'

'No, I have clients booked in when we return.' Christine didn't look at Becky, preferring to move on to her eyebrows.

'Me too, but I'm sure I could rearrange my appointments.'

'People rely on me, darling. I can't be that cavalier, it's unprofessional. But maybe another time.'

Becky fastened her trousers with such force she feared she'd broken the zip.

'You know, Christine, sometimes I hate the way you speak to me.'

The corners of Christine's mouth twitched downwards, an expression she sometimes gave when she heard something unfavourable but was still, on the whole, unbothered. 'Really? And how would you like me to speak to you?'

'Like a normal person!' Becky exclaimed. 'Like someone who's actually conversed with another human being before! Like a girlfriend who—'

'Partner, Rebecca, we're not teenagers.'

Becky felt the vein in her forehead throbbing. Christine was remarkable at staying completely cool, unmoved by any kind of confrontation. Becky had never even heard her raise her voice. Once a quality she admired, now she found it rather perturbing. Her girlfriend was like a robot.

'I'm sorry you're upset,' Christine said. 'How would you feel if I said that perhaps it wasn't the way I speak to you that upsets you, but the way you choose to hear my words?'

How would I feel? Becky thought to herself, unable to even look Christine in the face. *I would feel like losing it. I would feel violently pushing you out of that second-floor window and then I would feel sad that I'd ruined Erin's lovely driveway.*

'I would feel like you're just saying shit to get out of having a real discussion about this,' she finally replied. 'To avoid taking some responsibility.'

'Interesting.'

Becky pulled her shirt over her head, mouthing expletives.

'I'm starting to wonder whether coming here wasn't quite as wonderful as you'd hoped,' Christine continued. 'A lot of big personalities here, not many boundaries. I'm struggling to see where you fit in, if I'm honest.'

'Look, I know you're miserable here, I get it. My friends just aren't your bag and that's fine. But we will be out if here soon enough and then you can continue to rip them to shreds at a more suitable time. All I'm asking is that you just make the best of it while we're here. Maybe even try and have a little fun, God knows you need it.'

'I'm sorry you're under the impression that I dislike your friends,' Christine began. 'I really have no feelings towards them one way or—'

'See you downstairs,' Becky said as she firmly closed the door behind her.

———

Erin's karaoke machine was at least two hundred years old and had Beth known this she would have brought her own or at least a better microphone.

'This machine takes CDs, Erin!' she declared. 'Do you even have the CDs?'

'Hmm, probably not,' Erin replied. 'I think we donated them all to charity a few years ago.'

'Testing... testing...' A loud feedback whine was quickly followed by complaints from the room and a pillow tossed her way from Tara.

'We can't use this either,' she grumbled. 'Not if you want the volume above two.'

'We don't even need a mic,' Erin declared. 'And I guarantee every song ever written is on YouTube as a karaoke version.'

Beth frowned. 'But without the mic, it's just someone standing in front of the telly singing. My four-year-old niece does that.'

'We'll use it as a prop then,' Alex suggested. 'Like a hairbrush when you were a kid.'

'God, have a mojito,' Erin insisted. 'A couple of those and you won't care.'

Cocktails and karaoke were soon underway at Loughview House, blank cards for writing song requests were making the rounds. The more ridiculous the song, the better.

'By the way, Erin, I'm vetoing Whitney Houston right now. No offence but "I Will Always Love You" is an absolute mood killer.'

'Fine,' she replied. 'As long as you're not singing Snoop Dogg.'

Beth's love for old school nineties rap had been legendary while at university, a genre Erin couldn't stand.

'It's rapping, not singing, Grandma,' she mumbled.

'Oh, I would very much like to hear that,' Aiden said, grinning, much to Beth's delight. She immediately started writing on her card.

With the first few requests in, Tara was up first, excitedly belting out the first few bars of 'Red Alert' by Basement Jaxx.

'This song suits her perfectly,' Becky said to Christine. 'I mean not her voice but her energy, you know? It should be her theme song.'

'Yes,' Christine replied, watching Tara flounce around. 'There's a certain mayhem to it. And her. I think you've hit the nail on the head.'

'Mayhem? No, I just meant—'

'Maybe I should sing something...'

The thought of Christine getting involved made Becky perk up. She'd never seen Christine let loose in a setting like this. Or any setting really. They didn't do karaoke or pubbing or clubbing or anything Becky once considered the most fun on earth. Christine was almost forty and thought it was uncouth to be doing any of that past thirty. Her friends held small dinner parties, or dined in restaurants, occasionally moving on to a wine bar if they felt somewhat frisky. Although Becky had never said anything, she found Christine's friends (all older academics) to be incredibly dull. So many thoughts in so many heads and not one of them witty. Becky tried hard to fit in, to take her place at the grown-up table, but really, she'd rather have been anywhere else.

'I hear your family were travellers, Rebecca. How interesting.'

They had been, about five generations ago on her mother's side. She'd made the mistake of casually mentioning this to Christine, as well as the fact that her devout family now lived in Valencia. Christine of course took this disclosure as a sign of unprocessed trauma when Becky really couldn't have given two shits either way.

Still, to Christine's friends this traveller news was like having their very own caravan-owning, bare-knuckle brawler at the dinner table. Quite the curiosity. Sometimes she felt like she'd been brought along for novelty value.

'You should absolutely sing,' she said, handing Christine a piece of card. 'Did you have anything in mind?'

'Oh, maybe something a little more lyrically driven,' she replied.

'Like Adele? Taylor Swift?'

Christine looked offended. 'God, no, nothing quite so basic...'

On the other side of the living room, Alex tentatively took the only free seat next to Aiden, who seemed entirely riveted by Tara, dancing wildly in her short black dress. To be fair, those boobs of hers were enough to rivet anyone, but she still felt a little sad that his eyes weren't on her. *Grow up*, she told herself. *Tara's his girlfriend, and who wouldn't want to look at her? She's beautiful! Stop being ridiculous.*

'Are you singing?' Alex asked him, now feeling altogether frumpy in her jeans and off-the-shoulder T-shirt.

'I probably should, shouldn't I?' he replied. 'I don't embarrass easily, but this is always kinda mortifying.'

'It's only us!' she answered, playfully nudging him. 'We encourage everyone to be their worst. What would you sing?'

'Something silly, probably'

She grinned. 'What, like 'Barbie Girl?'

'Not quite... you know Eddie Murphy?'

'The actor? Yeah. He doesn't sing though. Does he?'

She watched as he scribbled on his card and handed it to Beth. Before he could answer, Tara finished her song.

'That was fun!' she chirped. 'One down, fifty to go... Paul, I think you're up next.'

While Paul, in his red checked shirt, was enthralling everyone with his version of 'I Wanna Be Your Slave' by Måneskin, Christine handed her card to Beth who, like Becky, was also surprised by her participation.

'Oh. Wow, interesting choice. OK, you can go after Paul.'

Unlike Aiden, Christine was completely unfazed by all of this. She pulled her shawl around her arms and when her turn came, casually took the microphone from Paul, everyone intrigued to see what song she planned to sing.

'La Vie En Rose' by Edith Piaf.

OK, Alex thought, *maybe she doesn't quite get the vibe of the evening but it's fine. At least she's joining in.*

No one expected Christine to be good and she wasn't; she was magnificent. Pitch perfect and every word sang like she meant it, even if half the room didn't understand French. Becky melted as Christine, occasionally catching her eye, crooned one of the most romantic songs ever written. Becky knew it was for her.

'Bravo!' Alex yelled as she finished. 'What a voice!'

Christine half smiled and put down the microphone. 'Thank you. It's a timeless song.'

She sat down beside Becky who threw her arms around her. 'That was incredible!'

'Do you speak French, Christine, or just those lyrics?' Tara asked. 'I know all the words to "Sonne" by Rammstein, but I can't speak a word of German.'

'Je parle français,' Christine replied. 'I lived in Paris for eighteen months in my twenties and was madly in love with a textile artist there. The song always reminds me of her.'

Becky's arms slithered back off Christine. She hadn't been serenading her. She had been serenading a memory.

Beth lifted the next card. 'Aiden!' she announced, handing him the mic. 'And another unusual song choice!'

'Woo!' Tara yelled in anticipation. 'Go, Aiden!'

Sheepishly, he put down his drink and walked over to the television. 'I apologise in advance.'

The entire room broke out into a cheer as Aiden launched into 'Party All the Time' by Eddie Murphy, while Alex remained puzzled. How could she be the only one who'd never heard this song before?

As the song continued, she realised she did know it, at least the chorus. Alex knew it quite well – she just had no idea Eddie Murphy sang it.

Surprisingly, despite his forewarning, Aiden wasn't terrible. He wasn't West End stage level like Christine, but he could absolutely hold a note. His greatest skill however was getting the entire room up to dance.

'Oh my God, Alex!' Beth exclaimed at end of the song. 'You used to sing this whenever one of us suggested going out for the night!'

Becky laughed. 'Yes! And she'd change *my girl* to the name of whoever it was. I'll never forget that!'

Alex laughed, pretending that this wasn't yet another

fucking weird-as-shit thing to happen this weekend. He could have chosen any song, yet he chose the obscure one she was remembered for. Aiden didn't say anything but as he handed the mic to Becky, his eyes darting towards her, she could tell he was just as mystified as she was.

CHAPTER 23

At 6.30am, Alex sat up in bed, wide awake. This was unheard of. At home she'd very rarely surface before nine and, even then, she'd try and squeeze in a few more minutes before zombie walking herself to the kettle. Working from home meant she kept her own hours, sometimes writing at 10am and finishing by 1pm, sometimes starting at 10pm and writing into early morning. Back when they were together, Pete always scolded her for not having a set routine, for wasting so much time which could otherwise be filled with productive endeavours. Trying to explain to someone who enjoyed rules and schedules that writing doesn't always work that way was pointless. Still, this morning he'd be proud that she was alert and ready to go so early. Alex felt like texting him, just to hear the distance thud of him keeling over in shock.

She kicked off her covers and walked over to the window. *I should go to the beach*, she thought. Become one of those pensive, serious writers who gets inspired by being near a vast body of water. She'd seen authors like that on Twitter, posting photos of their reclusive writing retreats where all they had was a MacBook, thirty-six woolly jumpers and a view of the sea.

Tumbling into a pair of leggings and an oversized cardigan, she crept downstairs, past the sound of loud, rhythmic snoring which echoed throughout the house. Grabbing an apple, she quietly opened the back door and headed down to the beach.

Although bright, it was still a tad chilly, with the sounds of seagulls piercing the quiet air. She pulled her cardigan around her as she bit into her apple. She hadn't had fruit for breakfast, well, ever. Maybe this reunion was making her a better person already.

'Couldn't sleep either, huh?'

Alex spun around to see Aiden coming down the side of the embankment and on to the beach. She immediately pawed at her wild morning hair. She hadn't even run a brush through it.

'No,' she replied. 'Thought I'd take a little walk.'

Aiden lifted the bottom of his T-shirt to wipe the sweat from his face.

'I googled you, by the way. Definitely nothing like a blobfish.'

It took her a second before she remembered their conversation on the plane.

'That's good to know,' Alex replied, trying not to blush, though maybe some colour in her cheeks might be an improvement. 'Don't let me keep you from your run.'

'I'm done. I was just making my way to the house.'

'OK.'

'Mind if I walk with you?'

Alex considered all the reasons why this was a terrible idea. *You fancy him. He's Tara's boyfriend. You fancy Tara's boyfriend.*

'I'd feel better if you let me,' he continued. 'It's really deserted at this time of the morning, and worse than any villainous humans out there are many, many psychotic seagulls.'

Alex grinned. 'Oh really?'

He nodded. 'I mean, look at that a massive bastard over

there. I don't trust him. He's got apple snatcher written all over his face.'

'Fine,' she replied, 'The safety of my apple is now in your hands.'

'Excellent. Let's walk and talk. Is it weird that I've been wanting to talk to you?'

Alex brushed her hair from her face and took another bite. 'Everything about this whole situation is weird. I mean, what's even left to say?'

He shrugged. 'I'm just curious. Normal stuff. Like, what's your favourite movie?'

'Anything with Eddie Murphy.'

She heard him snigger. 'But seriously. These are innocent requests.'

'So, are we doing twenty questions?'

'We can start with one.'

She pondered this. 'Impossible to choose just one. Like trying to choose your favourite child.'

'Every parent has a favourite child.'

'True.'

'OK, but what if you *had* to because, well, it's my game and you have to...'

Alex smirked. 'Fine... *Sense and Sensibility.*'

'Is that Brontë?'

'Austen,' she replied. 'Emma Thompson kills me every time.'

'Not a bad choice,' he said. 'Though period dramas are not—'

'Wait... maybe *Never Been Kissed*,' Alex interjected. 'I love Drew Barrymore.'

'Right, OK—'

'Actually, scrap that, I'm going with *Oldboy*. I've watched that film a million times. Have you seen it? Utterly brilliant.'

'*Oldboy*?' he repeated. 'Are you serious?'

'Yes. It's genius.'

He began to chuckle.

'What's so funny? I'm a big fan of Asian cinema.'

He paused and lifted some pebbles from the embankment. 'It's nothing. I just love that movie too.'

'And what would your number one be?'

He shook his head. 'Impossible to choose just one. Like trying to choose your favourite child.'

Alex laughed loudly.

Skimming the pebbles into the lough, he considered this. 'I'd probably have to say... *True Romance*.'

'Good choice,' she replied. 'You like a little violence with your love life, eh?'

He smiled. 'Maybe. I think it's just like the idea of two people just being so hopelessly right for each other.'

'And here's me choosing a film about unspeakable revenge.'

'I know, right?' he replied. 'God, Alex, you're so edgy. Who's your favourite band? Napalm Death?'

Despite having never heard of them, she snorted at the name alone. 'No,' she responded. 'Though they sound super fun. Any more questions?'

'Yeah, one actually,' he admitted. 'What exactly is a lough? Is it just a lake?'

She giggled. 'That's technically two questions but fine. Yeah, it's just a lake. A sea inlet. Irish call them loughs, Scots call them lochs.'

'Easier just to say lake, huh?' he replied, grinning. 'And easier to spell.'

She playfully rolled her eyes. 'Sure, but where would you be without us Celts making the world a little more colourful?'

Bzz. Bzz.

Aiden pulled his phone from his pocket.

'It's Tara,' he said, briefly flashing the message. 'I should probably head back.'

'You should,' Alex replied. 'I think I'll hang out here a little longer, look at the *lake*.'

Hands in his pockets, Aiden gave a little chuckle, turned and made his way back to the house, soon becoming a speck in the distance. She couldn't help but smile. In fact, she was beaming from ear to ear like an utter fool. *Calm yourself, Moran,* she thought, *you are thirty-two, not thirteen.* In fairness though, she had not been quite so giddy over a boy since Jack McCarthy in the year above her at school in 2006. He had a provisional licence and facial hair; it was an exciting time to be alive but not a patch on this moment. Alex would never get to be with Aiden, but for now, for this moment, it was enough.

———

Half an hour later, Alex wandered back to the house, greeted by the smell of coffee and bacon. She followed the scent as if being pulled in by a delicious tractor beam. Tara, Beth, Erin and Paul were already seated. No sign of Aiden. Maybe a gull got him after all.

Beth looked predictably well put together: green dress, white shawl and a perfectly straight middle parting in her perfectly straight brown hair.

'Morning!' Alex said. 'Erin, this looks amazing. I think you've missed your calling running a bed and breakfast.'

'Oh, Lord, no,' she replied, cutting into a bread roll. 'I hate making beds. And making breakfast. And making small talk. Marian, who runs the hotel in Waterville, dropped this lot off earlier. Her catering is excellent.'

Beth and Paul side-eyed each other, knowingly. *Catering.*

'No Becky and Christine?'

'No sign of them yet,' Tara replied. 'Christine's probably bored them both into a coma.'

'Tara!' Beth scolded. 'Be nice...'

'Ah, come on,' she replied. 'She's not exactly a barrel of laughs, now is she... can you pass the butter please?'

Beth obliged. 'Aiden still in bed?'

'That fella was out for a run at stupid o'clock,' she replied. 'He was in the shower when I came down, he shouldn't be long.'

Alex bit into her toast, giving nothing away.

'Bit of a fitness freak, is he?' Paul asked, working on his second bacon roll. 'I went to the gym once. Awful experience. Zero out of ten.'

'Not a fitness freak as such,' Tara replied, 'We both like to run, he probably went earlier because it's cooler. I like to eat first and then burn it off... oh, here he is now.'

'Morning, everyone.'

Alex briefly looked up to acknowledge Aiden who took the chair beside her. God, this whole thing was clandestine as hell.

'Nice T-shirt,' Paul complimented. 'Is that a film? Don't think I've seen that one.'

As Alex's eyes scanned down from his face to his clothing, she nearly choked on her breakfast.

'Thanks,' Aiden replied. 'Yeah, *Oldboy* is one of my favourite movies. You should give it a watch.'

Oh, for God's sake, Alex thought, starting to giggle, *he kept that quiet on purpose to see my reaction.*

'Something funny, Alex?' Beth asked.

'Oh nothing,' she replied, sipping some water. *No problem here Beth, just having an existential crisis along with my bacon roll. No big deal.*

Moments later, Becky and Christine appeared. Becky bright and breezy as always, followed by Christine who did her best to appear happy to still be there. She wasn't.

'I was going to suggest that we all go for a walk along the beach after lunch,' Erin said, blowing on her coffee. 'There are stables nearby and they bring their horses to the beach at the weekend. However, since Johnny Knoxville over there has hurt herself, we might have to come up with something else.'

'I want to see the horses!' Beth protested, like a toddler. 'I can still walk, you know, albeit slower and not very far. It's fine, though; Paul can mosey along with me and carry me back if my leg falls off.'

She wanted to say that she had a rollator in the car – a very handy device, like a Zimmer frame on wheels with a seat in the middle, but that would be harder to explain. Those were for people with more serious mobility problems, not people who hurt their leg fake-jet-skiing.

'I might go for a run,' Tara said, completely missing the point of group activities. 'I'm not much of a horse person. Anyone want to join me?'

'I'm good,' Aiden replied. 'Once a day is enough for me.'

'I will,' Christine replied. 'Work off some of that food from last night.'

While Becky was somewhat narked that Christine would not be joining them, she was happy that she wouldn't have to spend the entire time making sure that her girlfriend was having fun. It was exhausting.

'OK, so just the rest of us then,' Erin said. 'I'll leave the keys under the doormat in case you get back before we do.'

CHAPTER 24

2012

'Alex, you're not seeing Niall Doyle, are you?'

Seeing Tara upright on a Sunday morning after a heavy night out was almost unheard of. She'd gone out with some friends from her business course and crashed through the front door around 5am. Seeing that she still had her makeup on and that, given the visible smudge level, the rest of it was presumably on her pillow, Alex immediately felt glad that she'd chosen to have a quiet night in.

'Seeing him? What, right now?' Alex asked, looking around the living room. 'Nope, he's definitely not here.'

She heard Erin chuckle from behind her book, another housemate who had chosen to spend Saturday night at home.

Tara smirked. 'Very funny, no I meant like dating him. I know you shifted the face off him in that club, and you had drinks the other week, but I just wondered if it was anything a little more serious.'

Niall Doyle was a six-foot-two, blonde-haired, third-year physiotherapy student that Alex had found herself locking lips with at Lillie's Bordello one Friday night. This had led to an afternoon bar crawl around Temple Bar where he'd spent the entire time staring at her boobs. Still, Alex quite liked him and had arranged another date for the following week. She was looking forward to it. It wasn't often that men who looked like Niall showed any interest in her. Personality wise, he maybe wasn't exactly her type, but physically, well, she'd never dated someone with visible bicep muscles before.

'Serious? Well, no,' she replied, 'It's a bit early for that, we haven't even done the deed yet.'

'Oh good! I didn't think it was. Just a wee casual thing then. Grand.'

'Why?'

Tara smiled sweetly. 'Nothing, just wondering.'

Tara never smiled sweetly. Alex heard Erin snap her book closed. She turned to see her glowering in Tara's direction.

'Tara...'

Tara didn't reply, her face beginning to scrunch awkwardly as she deliberately avoided Erin's gaze.

'Oh, you didn't!' Erin exclaimed. 'Please tell me you didn't.'

Alex watched as Tara pulled her polo neck over her face. 'Maybe,' came the muffled reply. 'Not on purpose.'

The penny finally dropped. Alex sat bolt upright on the couch. 'Wait... Tara, did you shag Niall?'

She peeled back her polo neck as Alex felt the colour drain from her face.

'Look, I'm sorry, I didn't *mean* to!'

'You didn't mean to?' Alex replied, 'What, was it an accident? Did he just trip and fall into your feckin' gee?'

'You know how I get on whiskey; I was absolutely rat-arsed! I don't care what it says on the label, I swear that stuff is like ninety percent horsepower. And the club was dark so I didn't even realise it was him until we got to his place, which by the way, smelled weirdly like mustard.'

'Did you realise it was him before or after you didn't mean to sleep with him?'

As she glanced at Erin, the look on Tara's face said it all. She threw her head back and huffed in annoyance.

'Look, under normal circumstances I wouldn't have ridden him if he had wheels,' she stated. 'He's not my type, *and* he kept his socks on throughout. I did you a favour, really, saving you from a very underwhelming sexual encounter.'

Tara found herself ducking at the plastic coaster Alex fired in her direction. 'Maybe I'd like to have found out for myself, you absolute arse. You're so bloody selfish sometimes, Tara, always taking whatever you want and to hell with the rest of us!'

'I do not just take whatever I want,' Tara protested. 'Wait, are you still mad that I ate your Pringles?'

'It's not about the Pringles!' Alex exclaimed (absolutely still mad about the vanishing Pringles). 'It's not just food: it's clothes, makeup and now apparently men.'

'For God's sake, I don't take stuff, I *borrow* it and I certainly didn't *take* Niall Doyle,' Tara insisted. 'You said it yourself, you two weren't serious.'

'That's not the point—'

'And, no offence, if he was serious about you, he wouldn't have bought me four of those dirty, vile drinks.'

Erin gave Alex a little heartening smile as Tara looked like she was going to vomit. 'She has a point, Alex. I mean, I'm not excusing her drunken need to shag the entire city of Dublin—'

'Hey!'

'—but regardless, he obviously wasn't madly in love with you and is therefore a feckin' eejit by anyone's standards because you're extremely loveable.'

'I am,' Alex responded quietly, giving a little sniff. 'But I'm still mad at Tara.'

Tara slunk down on the sofa beside her. 'I am really sorry,' Tara whispered, giving her a nudge. 'My bad.'

Alex rolled her eyes but felt herself soften.

'And she's right. You are too good for him and I think I should vet all potential suitors from now on.'

'Don't push it,' Alex replied with a smirk.

As Tara went back to bed and Erin returned to her book, Alex found herself in the kitchen making tea she didn't want, just to get some alone time. God, Tara was infuriating and as much as she liked her, Alex had come to recognise just how impulsive she was, reckless even, occasionally to the detriment of others but mostly to herself. She was a force of nature, but sometime nature could be the most damaging force of all.

CHAPTER 25

Tara had once thought that when two people who knew each other decided to go for a run together that they would run together. Side by side. A camaraderie of sorts, each driving the other on, perhaps chatting to pass the time. And if they didn't know each other particularly well, this might just be the opportune moment to remedy that. But as she watched Christine speed off into the distance, she realised that she was mistaken.

Well, fuck you too, she thought to herself. *I hope you get lost.*

AirPods in, she started off at a mild pace, following the GPS route she'd planned for this afternoon. She'd never run the roads around Erin's house before and she found the beach, while beautiful, to be a more demanding terrain to run on. Sometimes she'd lose her balance running on sand and feel like an idiot.

She cherished her new peach HOKA trainers, a massive step up from her old, worn-out Nikes which had torn up her feet and facilitated too many sprained ankles. Aiden had suggested she get them. He'd been running far longer than she had and he knew his stuff, in fact, it was Aiden who'd introduced her to running. She'd been resistant at first.

'It releases endorphins. Makes you feel good.'

'*That's nice. Do you know what else makes me feel good? Sitting down. Netflix. Being indoors where—*'

'*Tara. Just try it. Your K-dramas aren't going anywhere.*'

The first time she ran, she threw up. The second time, she threw up again but not quite so much. Four months later and there wasn't even a hint of nausea, well, except for that time she ran through a massive dogshit and nearly had to set fire to her shoes there and then. But Aiden was right – about the running at least. Netflix removed three of her shows before she could finish them.

Tara usually had a running playlist, something upbeat and bass-driven to keep pushing her on. Today however, she was running along country roads and had to keep her wits about her. She didn't want to end up face-first in a ditch or under a car. So far it had been spectacularly quiet. Peaceful. She'd known that Erin's house was remote, but this really gave her a sense of just how isolated it was. Just fields and trees and the odd sheep that had wandered too far. As she came around a bend, she passed a group of birds feasting on some roadkill. Charming. Maybe she didn't like the countryside as much as she thought.

Two miles in and she was hitting her stride. It gave her time to be alone with her thoughts, which for the most part involved her beating herself up or over analysing everything until nothing made sense.

She sighed. If empowerment group had taught her anything, it was that she really didn't know herself at all. She wasn't sure if she ever did. She had struggled her entire life with her identity, fighting against her mother's perception of what she should be. Eventually, she had no idea which version of *screw you* aimed at her mother, was actually her.

She hid it well though. To her friends she'd appear impulsive and confident, a free spirit. In reality, she was horribly insecure, surrounded by people who annoyingly seemed to have it all figured out: Erin, with her composed drive and focus; Beth, taking charge of everything around her; Becky, happily floating on a cloud above the rest of them; and Alex, a kind and beautiful soul, no matter what life threw at her.

And then there was Aiden. The first real connection she'd made after rehab.

Aiden's really great. An absolute treasure.

Not everyone you date has to like everything you do, Tara. So, what if he doesn't enjoy techno music, it's no biggie. Or clubbing... or the dance tent at that festival you went to (the only reason you went) and instead watched bloody men in beards play guitars and sound like every other male beardy guitar group.

And sure, maybe he's not the type to get tattoos on a whim, or be an absolute freak in bed, but that's the reason you chose him. Because he wasn't any of that. Stable, remember? Aiden is your rock. Your confidant. He's your pal.

However, as she ran, the thoughts did not dissipate. That something was missing. *Don't you screw this up like you've screwed up everything else. The grass isn't always greener, Tara, sometimes it's just more grass.*

CHAPTER 26

Beth was grateful they didn't have to walk too far before the horses came into sight. They were magnificent, two brown and one larger white one. If she knew anything about horses, she'd have been able to refer to them as something more technical than *beautiful*.

'Any idea what breeds they are?' she asked Aiden, who was trailing behind the others.

'I'm not an equine vet, unfortunately,' he replied. 'But I do know that the ones who wear the Ugg boots are Clydesdale horses.'

Beth chuckled, leaning up against Paul to watch them trot around at the shore. She was already tired. Getting here had been manageable but she hadn't given any thought to how she'd go back. Maybe they'd let her borrow a horse.

'You know, my brother, Eli. He has multiple sclerosis.'

Beth felt her stomach flip. She glanced at Paul who widened his eyes a little in surprise. 'Really sorry to hear that,' she replied. 'How's he doing?'

'It affects mainly his right side and his leg brace isn't as fancy as yours, but he's doing well. It's more common than people think, you know.'

'Really?' Beth replied, trying her best to sound naïve on the whole subject matter. 'You don't hear about it that much.'

Aiden sniffed. 'It took him a while to tell everyone too. I understand how hard it is.'

Beth gripped Paul's hand. 'I'm not sure—'

'He took Fingolimod too. You left them on your nightstand.'

The urge to ask what the hell he was doing in her bedroom was curbed when she remembered that he'd nipped in to borrow her phone charger.

'Look, it's none of my business,' Aiden added. 'Just wanted to let you know that someone else with MS is doing really well. It can be a lonely disease, huh?'

Beth nodded, her eyes brimming with tears. Before she could object, the teardrops began to fall.

'I... I won't mention it to anyone,' Aiden stammered, horrified that he'd turned the normally upbeat Beth into a blubbering wreck. 'God, I'm sorry.'

Paul wrapped his arm around his wife. 'It's been a tough few months,' he admitted. 'When was your brother diagnosed?'

'Fifteen years ago,' Aiden replied. 'He's now secondary progressive, but he's stable. They switched him to the infusions a while back. No new lesions in three years.'

'That's really good to hear,' Beth said, between sniffs. 'I'm sorry, it's just a little overwhelming at times and you're right. It is lonely.'

'All the more reason to tell your friends, then,' Aiden replied. 'When you're ready, of course. I'll give you guys some space.'

Aiden caught up to Becky, Erin and Alex, hoping that he hadn't just completely overstepped the mark and ruined Beth's day.

'Why is it so hard to believe that I've never been on a horse?'

Alex asked, now acutely aware that Aiden had joined them. 'I didn't even have a pet until I was twenty-five.'

'My mam made me ride ponies when we'd have trips to the seaside,' Erin said. 'I was never that bothered, but I think she thought it made us look quite prestigious. Like it was one step away from owning a bleedin' herd of horses and some stables.'

'What about you, Aiden?' Alex asked, 'Are you much of a horse fan?'

He smiled. 'I'm a fan of all animals.'

'You can't like them all?' Alex insisted. 'That's like a doctor saying he's a fan of all people. It's statistically impossible.'

'Fine,' he replied. 'I'm not crazy about Chihuahuas. There, I said it.'

Alex laughed. 'What's wrong with Chihuahuas? They're cute!'

'Uh-uh,' Aiden replied, scrunching his face. 'They are ugly, noisy and can be quite unpredictable if they're not well trained. See this...' He held out his hand. 'That scar above my thumb, courtesy of Princess the Chihuahua.'

Alex took his hand in hers to inspect it. She rubbed her thumb over the scar. Big mistake. This was a manly hand. Strong. Not too rough but not too soft either. And he had two of them. Two big manly hands. She swiftly let go.

'There's hardly anything there,' she replied, her voice strangely higher than usual. 'Very glad you survived.'

Erin and Becky had a much less carnal experience while examining Aiden's hand, but as they peered closely at it, he locked eyes with Alex, just for a moment, and it was enough to make her realise that she might be in serious trouble.

'I might head back,' Alex announced. 'Grab a shower before the joggers return and use all the hot water.'

'I'll walk back with you,' Aiden said. 'I need to make a quick call and my phone is out of battery. Again.'

'Keys under the mat,' Erin replied. 'See you back there.'

Alex counted thirty steps before she was certain that everyone was out of sight.

'What are you doing?' she asked.

'I'm going to charge my—'

'No, not that. With the hand touching and the eyes and the smouldering looks, what are you playing at?'

'Me? You touched my hand! I was just showing my battle wounds!'

'You know what I'm talking about. And in the kitchen yesterday.' She found herself stomping now which was rather difficult to do in the sand. 'Standing there in your T-shirt and your boxers with your hair. Ridiculous.'

He started to laugh. 'You're acting like this is all me. You were also in the kitchen yesterday. I might have been looking at you, but you sure as hell were looking right back at me.'

'I know. Shut up.'

They reached the house and held back a little before going inside.

'We're adults,' Alex insisted. 'We should behave as such.'

'I completely agree... but can I ask you something?' Aiden said. 'It's been bugging me since I got here.'

'Sure.'

'What exactly is *an absolute ride*?'

'Oh my God,' she mumbled, her face turning a delightful shade of beetroot as she rushed inside, almost tripping over the chairs on the patio.

Once in her room, Alex closed the door, grabbed a pillow from the bed and screamed into it. This was awful. If she'd known this was how the weekend would go, she'd have made some excuse and stayed home with Winston.

———

Everyone was exhausted when they returned from the beach, Erin especially who proclaimed that she could not be arsed cooking and did everyone want a takeaway? There was a general rumble of agreement.

'I could fair go a Chinese takeaway,' Tara said. 'Been ages since I had one.'

Becky could practically feel Christine die inside from disgust. She didn't do well with junk food and unless they had takeaway avocado and quinoa, she just might starve.

'What are the options?' she asked, hoping that at least somewhere would grill some tofu. 'Not sure I could handle anything too greasy.' This of course was a lie. She was ravenous. She would eat a deep-fried shoe if someone offered it.

'There's the usual Chinese, pizza, fish and chips but I was thinking lobster,' Erin replied. 'There's a grand wee restaurant on the seafront that does takeaway.'

Christine's ears pricked up. 'Lobster? Do they do also do oysters?'

'They do,' Erin confirmed. 'But I thought you were vegetarian?'

'I make an exception for oysters.'

'Right, well, they do most seafood. I'll pull up the menu online. They don't deliver, but I can go and pick it up.'

After much deliberation, Erin phoned in an order for two lobsters, a dozen oysters on ice, two fish and chips, scallops, a scampi, and a vegetable risotto for Becky.

'This is an outrageously expensive takeaway,' Beth declared. 'You're certainly not paying for it. Let me transfer you some cash.'

'God, yes,' Aiden agreed. 'It's very extravagant.'

'Totally,' Becky joined in, reaching for her phone.

'Please don't,' Erin pleaded. 'It's my pleasure.'

Beth reluctantly conceded. People splurging made her feel

uncomfortable, especially when she was the recipient of such a grand gesture. She knew she'd never make as much money as Erin or Alex, but she didn't want to take advantage of that either.

'Well, at least let me set the table outside while you're gone,' she offered, feeling like Annie in the Warbucks mansion.

'I'll help,' Tara said. She could sense Beth's uneasiness. 'Can't have you tumbling over with a dish in your hand.'

'I'll come and give you a hand with the food,' Paul said. 'That's a lot to carry for one person.'

'Great,' Erin replied. 'There are lobster crackers in the kitchen somewhere, you might need to rummage a bit. Shouldn't be too long!'

Trying to set a table for eight with a leg brace and a stick was much harder than Beth anticipated, still she powered through as best she could. She found that sitting and organising one side at a time seemed to work best.

'I've never known anyone who actually owns lobster crackers,' Tara mentioned, passing them to Beth. 'I mean, how often does a person actually eat lobster?'

'She does live by the sea,' Beth remarked, placing them in the middle of the patio table.

'And I live near a duck pond, doesn't mean I eat foie gras every week.'

'Not sure that's quite the same but I see your point.'

'I felt bad back there,' Tara said, helping Beth with the plates. 'You, Aiden and Becky all offering to pitch in, while the rest of us didn't even bat an eyelid.'

'That's because you all have money,' Beth replied.

'True, though I certainly don't have nearly as much as the others. I guess when you're around money all the time, you just don't think about it. It's kind of gross, actually.'

'Perhaps. I just didn't want Erin to think I was taking the piss. I'd have been happy with a kebab!'

Tara sat down beside Beth. 'You always were a good person. Bossy but really kind and thoughtful. I'm glad to see that hasn't changed.'

Beth felt caught off guard by Tara's heartfelt remarks and began to well up. Finally, someone who noticed that she was still the same person inside. This was what she needed to hear.

Tara noticed Beth's eyes glistening.

'Jesus, don't cry. I take it back, you're not bossy.'

'I am,' Beth replied. 'But thank you. I think I needed to hear that.'

———

'Tara's made Beth cry,' Alex announced as she peered through the kitchen window at the patio area. 'Oh, never mind, now they're hugging. Panic over.'

'She can be brutal,' Aiden said, appearing at the kitchen door. 'Need a hand with anything? Becky and Christine have gone upstairs.'

'Not really,' she replied. 'To be honest, I'm not really doing anything. I'm just trying to look busy. Is it working?'

He grinned. 'Absolutely. I was convinced there was work being done in here.'

'Excellent.'

'Should we talk about earlier?'

'Oh, God no,' she insisted, picking up a stray spoon, 'I think the best thing is to keep at least seven feet apart and get through this weekend.'

'Why are you waving a spoon?'

'No idea.'

'*Food's here!*'

Alex put down the spoon. 'Let's not make this any more difficult than it needs to be,' she whispered. 'Can't we just enjoy each other's company?'

'We can,' he mumbled. 'I'll just try not to look at you.'

Before Alex could reply, Erin and Paul appeared, laden with bags and boxes. 'Let's eat, people,' Erin yelled. 'This lobster isn't going to crack itself.'

CHAPTER 27

'We could have showered together, you know! Saved a bit of time.'

Becky finished tying up her hair as she waited for Christine to finish which wouldn't be long as, unlike Becky, Christine didn't take forever and try to become one with the shower.

'I'm done anyway,' Christine replied. 'Can you hand me that towel?' Becky obliged. 'It's all yours,' Christine added, covering herself before carefully stepping out. 'I'll just do my teeth before we have dinner.'

Becky took off her robe and stepped into the still running shower. It stung her shoulders initially, first sign of sunburn. *Must remember to cream up tomorrow*, she thought. The sound of Christine's toothbrush began whirring.

'How was your run with Tara?' Becky yelled over the noise. She watched the water run over her feet, removing the remnants of the beach she'd brought home between her toes. Although barefoot in the sand was her happy place, she hoped it wouldn't clog Erin's drain.

'We didn't run together,' she heard Christine say from the other side of the curtain.

'No? Why not?'

'I wasn't really in the mood to chat and Tara can be rather boorish, don't you agree?'

Becky didn't often get angry, but this absolutely rattled her cage. Jaw clenched, Becky turned and let the water run over her face. She was tired of biting her tongue, tired of clearly being the only one trying to work on this relationship. This new version of herself wasn't a patch on the old version because the old Becky would never have allowed anyone to disparage her friends.

Moments later, she turned off the shower and stepped out.

'It's always about you, isn't it?'

Christine stopped mid-floss. 'Excuse me?'

Becky grabbed her towel and wrapped it around her. 'It would have taken just a little effort... in fact, a tiny, minuscule amount of effort for you to get to know my friend a bit better but no. You didn't feel like talking.'

'Well, no. That's right. I didn't.'

'Do you even hear yourself?' Becky asked. 'Everyone here has welcomed you with open arms, but you have done absolutely feck all in return. What you have done is judge and sneer and generally make this weekend quite unpleasant.'

Christine bobbed her head. 'You're obviously angry that I haven't ingratiated myself into the group as you perhaps hoped I would.'

'I'm angry that you haven't even tried!' Becky exclaimed. 'And Lord knows, I try for you. All those evenings with your friends, all those boring bloody dinners—'

'The ones you said you enjoyed?'

'Of course I said that, because, unlike you, my main ethos in life isn't "fuck everyone else and their feelings".'

'Your take on this is quite interesting,' Christine replied. 'You're chastising me for being truthful while at the same time martyring yourself for lying.'

Becky sighed. 'It always amazes me how you do that.'

'Do what?'

'Hear everything someone says without really listening.'

'*Food's here!*'

Tara's voice yanked Becky's rage down a notch or two.

'I'm telling you right now that if you don't show my friends, not even me but my friends, some consideration, we are finished. Now go downstairs and enjoy your fucking oysters. I'll be there when I'm ready.'

As Becky left the bathroom, she realised that was the first time Christine hadn't had the perfect rebuttal. In fact, she'd said nothing at all.

CHAPTER 28

Alex peered apprehensively at the lobster on her plate like it had just crawled on there unexpectedly. It sat next to a dish of melted butter, a lemon wedge and a portion of seasoned fries.

'You alright there, Alex?' Erin asked. 'You did order the lobster, right?'

Alex nodded, her eyes still fixed on its bright red shell. 'I did,' she replied. 'I just assumed someone might have broken into it for me first. Aw, man, it still has its face on.'

Everyone started to laugh, watching as she tapped on the shell. 'Does it come with a power drill or what?'

'Is this your first-time having lobster?' Beth asked. She had decided to go with the scampi, which Alex thought looked far easier to navigate.

'No,' Alex replied, 'I've had lobster before, it's just never actually looked like one.'

'Some people call them cockroaches of the sea, if that helps?' Aiden remarked.

'Not really.'

Tara laughed. 'Want me to do it for you?'

Alex briefly considered this before refusing. 'No. No, I feel like this is a rite of passage. Car, house, lobster cracking, retirement, death.'

'Good for you,' Paul encouraged, tucking into his fish and chips. 'First time I did it, I nearly lost a finger.'

'Are you kidding me?'

'Don't listen to him,' Tara said, grinning. 'Just do what I do. It's not that hard, no pun intended. Grab a pair of those little pincer things and a seafood fork... yep, the long thin one.'

Alex followed her instructions, aware that everyone else now appeared to be very invested. 'God, please eat your food, people. I'm starting to feel like a sideshow here.'

'Please, if anyone would like an oyster, help yourself.'

Becky almost fell off her chair. Was that the sound of Christine making an effort?

'Ooh, maybe,' Beth replied. 'I've never tried them.'

'Excellent!' Erin exclaimed, 'We have another seafood virgin, ladies and gentlemen.'

'Do it,' Alex encouraged, dipping her lobster into butter. 'It's the worst experience you'll ever have, but it's character building.'

'Aren't they an aphrodisiac?' Paul asked. 'If they are, I am also in favour of Beth trying one. Or five.'

Everyone gave a small chuckle.

'They are indeed,' Christine replied, with just a hint of a smile on her face. 'And yes, they're an acquired taste, but I adore them.'

'Do you just swallow them down?' Beth asked. Their slimy appearance wasn't exactly inviting. Kinda like a little shell full of snot.

'You can,' Christine replied. 'You get the most flavour by chewing them however.'

As Becky listened to her girlfriend, she was dumbfounded. She was being helpful. Charming almost. Maybe Becky's ultimatum had actually worked. She placed a hand gently on Christine's knee.

Beth watched as Christine prised open an oyster before loosening it from the shell. She squeezed on some lemon juice and a little Tabasco before slurping it into her mouth. A little chew and she swallowed it down. 'See. Delicious.'

'I'll do one with you,' Aiden said. 'I've had fried oysters but never raw.'

Beth smiled at him gratefully. 'Deal.'

Christine loaded up both oysters and passed them across. 'Bon appétit!'

Beth gave the oyster a little sniff. Then a second sniff. She raised it towards Aiden. 'Bottoms up.'

They both knocked the oysters back, before chewing and swallowing.

A quiet fell over the table as they waited for the verdict.

'Oh, fuck me,' Beth exclaimed. 'That's bloody awful. That tasted as bad as it looked.'

'Is it too late to tell you that raw oysters are alive?'

She looked at her husband and gagged. 'I hate you.'

'Honestly,' Aiden said, 'the hot sauce masked the flavour a lot. The texture is a bit like... you know when you have phlegm at the back of your throat...'

Beth gagged again.

'I'm teasing,' he stated, over the sound of everyone laughing, 'It really wasn't that bad.'

Beth grabbed a handful of fries and stuffed them into her mouth. 'Never again,' she said. 'I'd rather starve.'

———

Dinner led to drinks in the garden, where Erin lit the firepit as the sun went down.

'Can I get anyone anything?' she asked, before spying Jasper at the side of the garden wall.

'Jasper... stop that,' she yelled. Everyone turned to see Jasper down low, his butt wiggling furiously towards something unseen.

'What on earth is he doing?' Beth asked.

'Hunting,' Erin informed her. 'If he drops a mouse on your foot, it means he likes you.'

Beth shuddered. 'If a mouse comes anywhere near me, I will pass away.'

She sunk back in her chair, keeping one eye on Jasper. She was exhausted and it was only 8pm. The evening hadn't even begun and she was ready to say goodnight. Beth closed her eyes for a moment, hoping the fatigue would wash over her and away, instead of wrapping around her, refusing to let go.

'Jeez, Beth,' Tara said, filling up the tank of her vape kit. 'How much did you drink? Get some coffee down you, before you keel over.'

'She's just tired,' Paul interjected. 'She'll be fine.'

'You always were a bit of a lightweight, eh?' Tara said, a huge cloud of vapour escaping from her mouth. 'Always the first to bail on a night out.'

'Maybe coffee is a good idea,' Erin suggested, seeing Beth's face scowl. 'I'll just—'

'You don't know anything about me!' Beth exclaimed. 'As usual you just love the sound of your own voice.'

Tara laughed in surprise. 'Relax, *Bethany*. Who pished on your chips?'

Beth could feel Paul's eyes burning into the side of her head, probably begging her to let it go. But she was rattled now.

'I really don't know how you can inhale those disgusting things,' she said haughtily. 'I see my students puffing away on them, really smart kids, and it just makes me sad. All these healthy bodies, just voluntarily damaging themselves. Morons.'

'Are you calling me a moron?' Tara asked through a cloud of smoke.

'I believe I called my students morons, but if the shoe fits...'

'Wow, Beth. Glad to see you're still as judgemental as ever,' Tara remarked. 'Thank God I'm not still smoking cigarettes; you might pull out a fecking PowerPoint and bore us all with a TED Talk.'

'I am not judgemental!' Beth replied, 'I'm just stating facts. I mean, I'm sure it's terrible to be addicted to something, but these kids—'

'But what, Beth? They should just have more willpower? Or maybe get a time machine and not even start in the first place? And they're not kids! They are young adults at university and they should be afforded the same rights to fuck up as we were.'

Beth sat upright in her chair. 'Really don't know why you're getting so upset but then again, you always were temperamental.'

'Ladies, maybe you should just calm down,' Erin suggested.

'I am calm,' Beth replied. 'I just don't think that inhaling chemicals or whatever should be so openly encouraged. It's like people don't care about harming the only body they'll ever have.'

'God, you're so feckin' pompous,' Tara said, laughing in disbelief. 'Just let folk live their lives. God, I bet you vote Tory now, don't you?'

'What does that have to do with anything, you libertarian tw—'

'Enough!' Erin yelped, before the political insults came out in full force. 'Christ, you two haven't changed at all, have you? I have enough going on without hearing you two sniping at each other.'

Beth pursed her lips and sat back. Sometimes she forgot that she wasn't the only person going through hard times.

Erin grabbed her hair and angrily twisted into a loose bun. 'If you're going to argue, can you do it somewhere else, please. The rest of us are trying to have a nice night!'

Beth cringed. 'Yes, sorry. You're right. I really am just worn out.'

'Yeah, apologies,' Tara responded, giving the group a remorseful smile. 'The heat must be getting to me.'

Erin rubbed her forehead. 'Sorry, guys. Just been a stressful few days.'

'No problem,' Tara replied. 'We're the dicks here, not you.' She smiled meekly, realising how trivial the argument had been.

'Well, that was intense,' Alex commented, trying to lighten the mood. 'They've even put Jasper right off his murder spree.'

All eyes fixed on Jasper who was now rolling around, belly up on the path. Even as Tara left the group and headed towards the kitchen, the air of tension remained.

———

It was close to midnight when everyone began saying goodnight. Alex was the first to go, but she was almost glad to. Apart from the bickering between Tara and Beth, she'd been sitting across from Aiden all evening. Not close enough for accidental physical contact but plenty of opportunity to catch his eye, sometimes the gaze lasting longer than it should have. It was completely inappropriate but utterly thrilling, a fact she wasn't proud of. Tara would be gutted if she caught wind of this and rightfully so.

After shooing a moth out of her window, Alex closed the curtains and began pacing the room. This was all getting too much. She needed advice.

Alex opened her phone and scrolled through her contacts. She needed to talk to someone, someone who wouldn't immediately judge her.

'Fi! You there?'

'Hello.'

'It's me.'

'I know it's you, your name comes up on the screen.'

Alex rolled her eyes. 'Fine, smartarse. Just thought I'd give you a wee bell. See how you are.'

'It's almost midnight, Alex, why are you calling... shite, hang on a second... *Romeo, if you do not stop barking, I will let Mercutio play with your favourite tennis ball...* Sorry, sis, I'm here. I swear that dog thinks the phone's for him when it rings.'

Alex sniggered, picturing him waiting by the phone. Romeo was the sweetest, daftest dog she'd ever met.

'Anyway, everything OK?' Fiona asked. 'What's the craic?'

'Everything's grand,' Alex replied, double checking her bedroom door was closed. 'Everything's going really well.'

'Why are you whispering? Oh, you're at your reunion, right?'

Alex perched herself on the edge of the bed, kicking her shoes off. 'Yes, and I just wanted your advice on something. It's a bit personal.'

'Did that fungal rash come back again? I told you; dandruff shampoo works a treat, but you really need to be consistent—'

'What? No, it's nothing to do with that,' she replied instinctively looking at the offending armpit area. 'I just have a small, non-medical related dilemma.'

'Oh right, shoot.'

Alex lay back on her cool bedsheets, scrunching her face apprehensively. 'So, I met someone—'

'You met someone!' she heard Fiona screech. 'Are you serious? That's amazing!'

'Yes, but... Fi... *Fiona*, can you stop...'

Alex pulled the phone away from her ear until her sister stopped squealing. And now Romeo was barking again. This reaction was louder than anticipated.

'Are you finished?' Alex whispered as she heard the chaos began to subside. 'Just shush for a sec and let me finish.'

'Sorry, I'm just thrilled at the news. I thought we were going to declare you a spinster, tie you to a lamppost and cover you in cinnamon, like they do in Denmark. Where did you meet him?'

'On the plane. Well, we met at the airport initially and then we had a drink... wait, why cinnamon?'

'No idea, I just read it somewhere. So, is he hot?'

Alex felt a grin take over her face. 'Hot doesn't even begin to describe him. And by some weird coincidence, we ended up sat next to each other on the plane ride to Kerry.'

'And does he have a name?'

'Aiden. We talked for ages, we laughed and when it was time to go, he took my number. Honestly, Fiona, I've never met anyone like him.'

'Well, that's great!' she replied. 'So, what's the problem?'

Alex paused, sat up and took a deep breath. 'He's with someone.'

'With someone?' Fiona questioned. 'Oh God, is he married?'

'No, he not married.'

'Engaged? Living together?'

'No.'

'Well, then I feel sorry for his girlfriend, but I'm sure she'll find someone else. There you go, problem solved.'

'Problem not solved,' Alex responded. 'Because his girl-friend is Tara.' Alex sat up in bed and sighed. Saying that out loud made her want to punch her own face in.

'Tara who?'

Alex said nothing.

'*Oh shite, Tara?* Your friend Tara?'

'Yep. She turned up with him to the reunion. Neither of us knew who each other really was. And now we're just pretending like it never happened.'

She heard Fiona start to laugh. 'I bet that's awkward as fuck. Oh, to be a fly on the wall!'

'You're really not helping. We've tried to ignore it but... there's definitely something happening here between us. I don't know what to do!'

'Maybe show him your fungal rash, that'll put him off.'

'Again, not helpful...'

'I'm sorry,' she said, still chuckling. 'So, there are two ways to look at this, right. Firstly, he's an absolute scumbag for taking your phone number when he's not single.'

'Or?'

'Or he's just a guy who was dating the wrong woman when he happened to meet the right one.'

'But?'

'But either way, you cannot do anything about it until he breaks it off with her, because then that would definitely make *both* of you scumbags.'

'You're right.'

'I know. Listen, I need to go, this dog is driving me nuts, but let me know what happens.'

'I will. Speak soon.' Alex hung up and flopped back on to the bed, her sister's words going round in her head.

You cannot do anything about it until he breaks it off.

Her heart sank. Even if Aiden did break it off with Tara, there was no way she'd just let Alex have him. There was more chance of Romeo willingly handing his tennis ball over to Mercutio. She realised that there was no world in which dating Aiden would ever be acceptable.

CHAPTER 29

'So, what was all that about?' Aiden asked. 'Last night, with Beth? I thought you were going to start throwing hands!'

'Ah, she's just so bloody judgemental sometimes,' Tara replied, rubbing the sleep out of her eyes. 'Even at uni, it was like living with a small Welsh mother, who would disapprove every chance she got. Like smoking within five hundred feet of her, or when you'd accidentally switch off the microwave and she'd have to reset the clock. Nightmare.'

'Sounds like you two didn't get along very well,' Aiden remarked. 'I guess that happens sometimes.'

Tara looked at him like he was daft. 'Nonsense!' she exclaimed. 'Why ever would you think that? We got along swimmingly, she's an absolute star.'

'But you just said—'

Tara sat up in bed, plumping her pillows behind her. 'Look, if you expect perfection from friends, you're going to have a very lonely life,' she told him. 'None of us are perfect but I don't think I'd change a single thing about any of them. Hmm, maybe Becky's new look come to think of it; I never thought I miss seeing someone's feet so much.'

'So, if they're all so perfect, why didn't you all stay in touch?' Aiden asked.

Tara paused to consider this question, like she had many times before. 'Initially we did,' she replied. 'For the few months after graduation, we'd text and chat loads. Then the messages became fewer, less frequent. Everyone got busier... got older. People moved, stopped updating their social media... Some of us just wanted to become someone else.'

'Have you told any of them about rehab?'

Tara kicked the covers off and walked over to the bedroom window. The morning sun was already warming the room. 'Nope. I mean, you heard the way Beth droned on about feckin' vaping, can you imagine if she knew that I sniffed half of Colombia up my nose?'

'That's true,' Aiden agreed. 'But she's only one person.'

She pushed open the dormer windows and took a moment to admire the view. In the morning light, the lough had never looked prettier.

'As soon as they know this about me, everything changes. I'm no longer just Tara. I'm Tara the druggy. Tara the trainwreck.'

'You know, someone once said that "If you expect perfection from friends, you're going to have a very lonely life."'

She glanced over at Aiden and smiled. 'I guess it's easier said than done.'

———

Having weather warm enough to sunbathe at 9am was a rare and unusual occurrence in Ireland but one that Becky was planning to immediately take advantage of. Her tanning level was slightly-done-toast, a sandy beige colour which never quite blossomed into a full brown. She did, however, enjoy the freckles which dotted her face during summer.

'Can you put suncream on my back?' she asked Christine who, still half asleep, sat on the edge of the bed. 'I'll do yours too if you like? Little Sunday morning tanning sesh?'

Becky was happy she'd cleared the air with Christine. Even after last night's argument in the garden, Christine has remained quiet and judgement free. Of course, she hadn't apologised for her behaviour, but it was a start.

'No, I think I'll just go for a run,' she replied. 'I'm too pale to sit directly in the sun for long periods.'

Becky had never seen Christine with a tan, but it was understandable. She had extremely pale, porcelain skin which looked like it might char like cigarette paper if left anywhere near a high heat. As much as Becky loved the sun, a beach holiday was not Christine's idea of a fun break. They had been on holiday together twice, once to Norway, which was beautiful but very mild weather, and once to Madeira which she loved but it rained for the whole week. She had seen the Northern Lights in Norway so it wasn't exactly a hardship, but just once she'd like to lie in the sun by a pool with her girlfriend.

Christine applied the cream to Becky's back before applying some to her own arms and face. She then threw on her running leggings, T-shirt and white cap. Even her running clothes were smart.

'Are you having breakfast first?' Becky asked, fixing her hair bun. 'I'm starving.'

'No, I think I'll run fasted. I'll grab something later.' She leaned over to kiss Becky, pausing close to her face. 'You look nice,' she said. 'Rested.'

'Thank you!' Becky replied. 'You too.'

As Christine gazed at her girlfriend's face, Becky smiled. She didn't often feel seen. These moments were so rare.

'You have a lot of broken veins around your nose, you know.'

Her words almost made Becky flinch. 'Sorry, what?'

'Broken veins,' Christine repeated. 'Little red ones.'

'I know,' she replied, her hand reaching to cover her nostrils. 'They've been there for years.'

'Hmm. Odd. Are you not a bit young to have them?'

Becky turned her face away. 'I really don't think my age has anything to do with it. And broken veins are—'

'You really don't need to get defensive. It wasn't a criticism, just an observation. I'll see you later.'

Wasn't a criticism? Becky watched Christine leave before flopping down on the bed, feeling more than a tad crushed. *Why tell me I look nice then follow it up with a flaw? What is the point?* Determined to brush it off, she headed downstairs for breakfast.

'Morning,' she said as chirpily as she could muster. 'I'm ravenous.'

'Morning, lovely,' Beth replied. 'There are pastries and fruit here, Erin's just taken a delivery if you want to wait for toast.'

Becky smiled, making a beeline for the pastries. Pain au chocolat was the ideal mood cleanser.

'Save some of those for your girlfriend,' Alex remarked, smiling.

'Christine's away for a run,' Becky replied, chomping into one. 'She can sort herself out when she gets back.'

Taking her pastries and tea to the sun lounger beside Tara and Aiden, Becky plonked herself down. She wouldn't let Christine ruin this beautiful day. Although Tara had positioned herself away from Beth, the atmosphere didn't feel strained now. Becky hoped that it had just been blip on their so far enjoyable weekend.

'Gah, we're missing a few things from the delivery,' Erin announced as she joined everyone on the patio. As no one had prepared for this heatwave, she was amused to see the other women wearing her beachwear, though a smidgen annoyed that Tara looked far more incredible in her bikini top than she ever did.

'I'll put away what has been delivered and then pop out to the store and pick up what we need. The main thing is the fruit juice for tonight. Hard to make cocktails without it!'

'Hey, Tom Cruise, I think you'll find you're booked in for a massage with me this morning,' Becky yelled from the garden, determined to soak up every ray of sunshine available. 'Can't someone else go?'

'Count me out,' Beth said, motioning to her leg. 'And I'm not entirely sure I'd trust Paul to drive this morning after the skinful he had last night... in fact I'm not even sure he's alive, I haven't properly checked.'

Paul and his white, hairy legs lay motionless on a beach towel.

'I can go,' Alex chimed in. 'Just make a list.'

'You don't have a car,' Erin replied. 'It's at least a good couple of miles on foot, maybe more.'

'I'll take yours,' she replied, 'My insurance covers me to drive any car, it's no problem. Fancy joining me, Tara? A girls' two-mile road trip?'

Tara pushed her sunglasses down the bridge of her nose. 'As tempting as that is, it's far too glorious out here. Aiden will help though, won't you, Aiden?'

Alex felt her chest tighten. 'Oh, it's fine,' she insisted. 'I'm sure I can manage!'

'Don't be silly, he can put those big arms to good use.'

Alex wondered how it was possible to feel like throwing yourself into the sea and also completely delighted at the same time, but regardless it was happening.

'I... um, sure.' Aiden replied, glancing at Alex. 'Happy to help.'

'Brilliant,' Erin replied. 'I'll make a quick list.'

Aiden followed Alex out to Erin's white Range Rover. *Be cool*, she thought to herself as she threw her bag into the back-seat. Act normal. Pretend he's just some guy that you're not ridiculously enamoured with after an absurdly short period of time.

'You didn't have to come, you know,' Alex said, fastening her seatbelt. 'I could have managed alone.'

'I know,' he replied. 'To be honest, I couldn't think of a reason not to help. I was caught off guard.'

Alex smiled. She admired his honesty.

'Damn, this is a nice car,' he exclaimed, feeling the material on the dashboard. 'My Yaris is like a toy car compared to this.'

'Don't feel bad, I don't drive anything particularly fancy either – I've had my little Fiat for years now. I guess you'd need something big like this for the winter out here. This is like a bloody tank compared to mine.'

'I had a Fiat Punto years ago; I don't even think they make that model anymore. What do you have?'

'Fiat 500,' she replied, peering suspiciously at the dashboard. 'It's an old model, but I love it. Parking's dead easy, which is handy in the city centre. Why is there no ignition in this car? Where is the gearstick?'

He started to snicker. She liked the way his shoulders shook when he laughed, even if it appeared to be at her expense.

'What's so funny?'

'How old exactly is your car? Just put your foot on the brake and push the button.'

'Old enough to remember what keys are for,' she replied. 'This is far too confusing.'

Successfully starting the car, she took a moment to look over the controls. 'Is all of this shit really necessary?'

With prompting from Aiden, Alex put the car into drive and tentatively pulled away.

'I may have finally found your flaw. You're a Fiat 500 girl.'

'Oh God, not you too,' she replied 'Why are men like this? My ex takes the piss out of me for this too! It is a perfectly good car!'

While Pete did make fun of her for driving a Fiat 500, it was more (of course) about the safety aspect.

'*It's an old car, Alex. Minimal safety equipment, average safety rating and well, up against a lorry on the M50, you wouldn't stand a chance.*'

'*So, that's reassuring. Anything else?*'

'*Aye, it looks shite.*'

'*Good talk, Pete.*'

'I'm just surprised someone like you drives one, that's all,' Aiden continued. 'I heard they were driven by twenty-somethings with too much fake tan, who watch *Love Island* and have a Starbucks addiction.'

'Where did you hear that?'

'Twitter.'

'Ah, Twitter. A credible source... and what exactly do you mean someone like me?' she questioned. 'You mean a thirty-something with no fake tan and an arse that takes up both front seats?'

'Well, no...'

'And what did you imagine I drove?' she asked, fiddling with the aircon. 'Some old lady car?'

'No, just something bigger than a matchbox, and—'

'You drive a Yaris! That's a teeny wee car!'

'—and, for the record, by someone *like you*, I meant someone cool.'

'Oh. Right.'

'Obviously I'm taking that compliment back now... My Yaris is not teeny. It can comfortably seat four and a half people.'

Alex laughed. 'Sorry. I stand corrected.'

Leaving the winding backroads from Erin's house, they reached the Ring of Kerry. In summer it was particularly beautiful with lush green trees, mountain views, interspersed by glimpses of the sea. However, given the narrow, snaking road, potholes, wildlife darting across and carefree hikers, their journey was a slow one. Alex didn't mind; driving Erin's car was proving more challenging than she had anticipated.

'It's like a bleedin' rocket when you accelerate,' she exclaimed. 'I'm hardly touching the pedal.'

Ten minutes from Erin's secluded house was Waterville, a small seaside village nestled between Lough Currane and the Atlantic Ocean, overlooking Ballinskeligs Bay. Living in Ireland all her life, Alex had seen many of these villages but as they drove through, Aiden seemed enthralled.

'I've been living in cities way too long,' he insisted. 'This is charming.'

'It's quite normal for Ireland,' Alex replied. 'Lots of coastline. Ha, I sound like the tourist board. Come to Ireland. It's quite island-ish.'

She found his enthusiasm for the scenery rather adorable. Had this man never seen a coastline before?

'Wait... was that a Charlie Chaplin statue?'

Alex slowed, almost to a stop, to see a green statute complete with cane and bowler hate to her left. 'Oh yeah,' she replied, squinting at the information plaque. 'I think he stayed here on holiday. It's a bit random.'

Aiden laughed. 'It says there's even a film festival in his honour every year. I love this place.'

Alex steered the tank off the main stretch of road and into the car park at the side of a small supermarket.

'Have you got the list?' Alex asked, taking a trolley. Aiden nodded, rummaging in his pocket. The shopping list was small and concise; two different types of bread, some soft cheese and six cartons of cranberry juice.

'Sex on the beach,' she concluded.

'Sorry?'

'The cranberry juice. She's either making sex on the beach cocktails or she has terrible cystitis.'

It didn't take them long to find what they were looking for, yet they strolled slowly up and down each aisle, like an old married couple.

'Are there any foods you miss from home?' Alex asked as they sauntered past the condiments, 'Anything you can't get over here?'

'Oatmeal crème pies, definitely,' he replied swiftly, obviously something he'd thought about previously. 'Oh, and honey buns... apple jelly... and root beer.'

'I've heard of honey buns,' Alex replied, picking up some hot sauce. 'But it's generally been from prison movies, you know where they trade them for cigarettes and shanks and the like.'

Aiden beamed. 'I'm sure they're a valuable commodity in prison.'

'Oatmeal crème pies sound vile though,' she said, making a face. 'It sounds like a dare.'

'Hush your mouth! They are delicious. Little Debbie is the queen of cakes. Next, you'll be telling me you don't like Oreos.'

Alex scrunched up her face. 'I mean, they're alright... a bit bland. Not exactly my go-to biscuit.'

'*Cookie*,' he reminded her. 'And what would be your go-to biscuit?'

'KitKats are good,' she replied. 'I'm also a big fan of the ol' shortbread, but I think chocolate digestives are my downfall. I didn't get this arse from playing nicely with a packet of chocolate digestives.'

'I feel like I should thank them,' he mumbled quietly.

Reaching the checkout, Alex placed her items on the conveyor belt. Everything on the list along with some lemonade ice lollies for the sunbathers back home.

'This wasn't on the list, was it?' Aiden asked, picking up the Tabasco sauce.

'No,' she replied. 'It's for me. I noticed Erin ran out last night. Thought we might make Bloody Marys. I've thrown in some tomato juice too.'

'Tomato juice is the worst,' he replied. 'First the car and the cookies and now this,' Aiden said, bagging the items. 'I think I've gone off you.'

Alex laughed. 'Yeah, well, you eat porridge pies! That's enough to make any women question her choices.'

'That'll be fourteen forty, love.'

'You do know they're not actually porridge pies...'

'Whatever,' Alex replied, tapping her card against the machine. 'Right now I'm just looking for any excuse not to be as attracted to you as I currently am.'

Alex pursed her lips, realising that saying that out loud was a huge mistake. Aiden laughed while the woman on the checkout quietly sniggered. Taking two bags each, they made their way back to Erin's car.

'Maybe we could take a walk,' Aiden suggested as they loaded up the boot. 'Just along the seafront...'

'These ice lollies will melt,' Alex replied. 'Besides, Erin's expecting us back soon. They'll be wanting this bread.'

Aiden slammed the boot closed and sighed. 'I don't want to go back. Not yet.'

'I know. Neither do I but—'

'The guilt I feel...' he said, his voice trailing off. 'God, I feel like a huge piece of shit.'

'Me too,' Alex agreed. 'And the more I get to know you, the more conflicted I become.'

'I need to tell Tara we're finished,' Aiden said, resting against the car. 'She deserves better. How can I keep pretending that everything is fine when... I should never have come on this trip; I should have told her when she first suggested it.'

'Don't do that because of me,' she pleaded. 'It would just be a waste.'

They climbed back into the car, neither ready to leave yet.

'A waste how?' he asked. 'After I tell her, then we're free to—'

'What, Aiden? What do you think will happen? We'll suddenly embark on some great romance? That all roads are now clear for us?'

Aiden looked confused. 'Well, why not?'

'You don't get it, do you?' Alex sighed. 'After you guys split up, you will be my friend's ex-boyfriend and that's all you can ever be!'

Aiden sank back into his seat. He looked wounded.

'Do you know what's been the hardest part in all of this?' he said. 'Getting to know you. Not just the physical attraction, but genuinely getting to know you. Discovering all the parts of you that make you amazing, everything I'd look for in a woman, and knowing that I can't do a thing about it.'

'We have to be realistic,' she said. 'I cannot start seeing you, Aiden... or worse, what if I *do* start seeing you and I have to lie about it to everyone? What if one day we fell in love and—'

'What if that day is already here?'

Alex shook her head. 'You can't possibly mean that.'

He turned to face her, resting his head against the seat. 'I have never, ever felt this way about anyone,' he insisted. 'And, yes, I am aware how ridiculous that sounds given that we only met three days ago.'

'Exactly!'

'Then tell me that you don't feel the same because I see the way you look at me.'

Alex flushed. She wanted to tell him that this was nothing more than a fleeting attraction, that this string of coincidences meant nothing. People met all the time; it didn't have to lead to anything. But what was the use of another lie?

'I do feel the same, Aiden, you know I do!' she exclaimed. 'But it doesn't matter how I feel!' She pushed her hair behind her ears and sighed. 'This is too hard. We should go.'

As she shifted the car into reverse, Alex felt Aiden place his hand over hers.

'It matters to me.'

She upturned her hand and interlocked her fingers with his, neither saying a word as she rested her head on his shoulder. Alex wasn't sure how long they sat in reverse in the supermarket car park, but it was long enough to realise that she just might love him too.

CHAPTER 30

'Oh my God,' Erin said, admittedly louder than she had intended. 'That feels incredible.'

Becky smiled as her hands pushed up and over Erin's back, kneading into her shoulders and neck. 'It's supposed to,' she replied, 'although I am going easy on you. I'd really like to go at you with my massage gun. Your hair looks really pretty by the way, they painted that balayage on with precision, eh? I once got one and it looked like someone had just tripped and fell into my hair with a tinting brush.'

Erin wondered if Becky spoke to all her clients like this, or just the ones she massaged for free on a patchwork couch.

'It makes sense that you'd end up doing something like this,' Erin remarked, allowing herself to melt into the sofa. 'I remember those head massages you used to give after a heavy night out – magical fingers. You always made me feel brand new. Pretty sure Tara cried during one, she was so relaxed.'

Becky laughed. Tara crying was almost unheard of.

'Well, back in those days it was all about releasing negative energy. I used to drag those demons out. It was all a bit amateur, but now I mostly relieve *muscular pain and specific concerns all in accordance with the ITEC.'*

Erin giggled at her professional tenor.

'But yeah, I enjoy it. Honestly cannot think of anything else I'd rather be doing.'

'Quite the team, you and Christine, aren't you?' Erin remarked, her face squished against a cushion. 'Like healers united.'

'Hmm,' Becky responded, 'I've never thought about it like that. I'm not sure she'd agree. Massage isn't on quite the same level as psychotherapy.'

'Rubbish. I've had my fair share of counselling and, what you're doing right now, it's just as therapeutic.'

Becky poured some more oil onto her hands. She'd normally use a wheatgerm and soya bean blend, but today she was using stupidly expensive extra virgin olive oil, courtesy of Erin's kitchen.

'It's certainly more relaxing,' Erin continued. 'Therapy stresses me out.'

'Really? Why?'

Erin repositioned her head on the pillow. 'Just the whole setup. You go in there and bare all. Open yourself up completely. But there is no instant healing. When your time is done, you leave with an open wound. Some people quite like having a big cry during their sessions but I hated it. Driving home with a soggy face and those hiccupy sobs that just won't fuck off. No thanks.'

'When did you have therapy? After Scott passed?'

'Yeah, for about three months. My agent recommended someone. Bereavement counsellor. Iris. Really lovely, patient woman. Her office smelled like coconut...'

Becky continued to work down her shoulder. 'I'm guessing there's a *but* coming.'

She felt Erin sigh. 'I think I went because everyone else

wanted me to. It's hard to explain. Don't get me wrong, it was helpful to talk about it... about him. I just feel sometimes that grief is a very personal thing, you know? No one's grief is the same. So, without actually knowing the person... it all feels a bit clinical... empty.'

Becky paused her hands on Erin's shoulders. 'Do you feel empty?'

Those words made Erin want to scream. Empty didn't begin to cover it. The void that Scott left, it was like a black hole that continually gnawed away at her. She felt hollow.

'Don't,' Erin began. 'I'll cry.' She reached up and touched Becky's hand.

Erin knew if she began to cry, she might never stop. The whole weekend wailing like a banshee while everyone else sat awkwardly on patio chairs eating all the bread.

'It all just feels a bit hopeless,' she said quietly. 'What if I move and the sadness just follows me there?'

'You'll be sad for as long as you're sad, I guess,' Becky replied softly. 'I don't think location will change that. Just know that when you're ready to talk, we're all here for you.'

'That's not what I wanted this weekend to be about,' Erin replied. 'But thank you.'

Becky understood. She imagined that everyone had something they didn't want spilling over into the weekend and ruining it. But every inch of Erin's body held on tight to her pain and so, for the first time in ten years, she placed her hands on Erin's head and without saying a word, began dragging out the demons.

CHAPTER 31

'Was it busy?' Erin asked as Alex dropped the shopping bags on the table. She had already started prepping for the evening meal. 'You guys were gone for ages! I was about to send out a search party.'

'It was mobbed,' Alex lied, feeling uneasy that they'd drawn attention to their time away together. 'Place was jam-packed. Busy morning in Waterville.'

'My bad,' Aiden interjected. 'I made Alex stop so I could look at the Chaplin statue.'

'Ah sure, I forgot he was there,' Erin replied. 'Maybe we should all have taken a drive, it's a lovely wee place. We could have had afternoon tea there.'

'Sorry if I held you up,' Aiden apologised. 'Typical tourist. But I'm at your disposal now if I can help out?'

'It's no problem at all,' Erin replied, 'and I'm grand! Becky gave me the world's greatest massage so I'm relaxed as hell with everything under control. I think Tara was looking for you anyway. Give her one of those ice lollies to appease her.'

Alex started to unpack the shopping, handing Aiden an ice lolly which was now ninety percent melted. He retreated towards the patio. She could still feel the warmth of his hand on hers and the way he looked at her still lingered—

'So, I was thinking that since it's our last evening, we'd have a picnic on the beach tonight,' Erin announced while Alex began unpacking the shopping. 'What do you think? Food, a little music, too much booze. Sand in your hoohah.'

'Sounds great,' Alex replied, snapping back to reality. 'Looking forward to it. Just let me know how I can make myself useful.'

'Hmm,' she replied, 'You can attack some salad vegetables with a knife if you like, apart from that not much.'

'Yep, I can do that.'

'Paul is in charge of the barbecue tonight, bless him. I hope he's up to it, he's still looking a little green around the gills. We're having surf 'n' turf: jumbo prawns, steak, some veggies, corn on the cob and I'm doing sweet potatoes in the oven.'

'This really is too much,' Alex replied, secretly delighted at the prospect of grilled prawns. 'I'm going to look like the size of a house when I leave, not that I don't already. I swear if I stand still long enough, Banksy will start drawing on me.'

Erin stopped loading the cranberry juice into the fridge. 'Alexandra Moran, are you really still making fun of your weight? Look at you in your little sundress, you're gorgeous altogether, I don't want to hear another word about it.'

'I know,' she replied. 'Force of habit. But back then, you lot were tiny wee women, all midriffs and peplums, while I was snapping on the Spanx. It was a challenging time for me.'

Alex clearly remembered how she envied her friends back then. She never felt like the fat friend exactly, she just owned more shapewear than anyone else. She had always been just that bit bigger than the others. According to her mother it was all down to her father's side of the family.

'Your granny Alexandra was a plump woman – big bosom,

huuuge arse but she carried it well. I expect you will be the same, given that you take after the eejit of a father of yours.'

Erin smirked. 'You have no idea how much I wanted your figure when we were younger. You reminded us all of Nigella Lawson, before she went all meecro-wavy.'

'You're kidding? I looked nothing like her.'

Erin opened the window and stuck her head out. 'Who did we think Alex looked like at uni?'

'Nigella,' the voices chorused back, including Paul.

'See,' Erin said, closing the window. 'We all thought it. You were all hair and boobs and effortless.'

'I can't believe it,' Alex replied. 'I wish you'd all told me back then; my ego could have used a boost. I might have even learned how to cook.'

'I'm pretty certain we did, but you probably didn't hear us over the sound of your own self-deprecation. I would have killed for your boobs. I still would to be fair, I've never been blessed up top. I swear when they were making me, they just whispered my tits on.'

'Now who's making fun of their body?' Alex laughed. 'What are we like? Your tits are perfectly fine by the way and I have no idea why I complained about my body back then, I was half the size I am now!'

Erin spooned some sundried tomatoes into a bowl. 'Half the size? Hardly,' she replied. 'But even if you were, what does it matter? You should see what we all see, and we're the only ones that matter. Now wash up and grab some lettuce.'

Alex obliged, cleaning her hands at the kitchen sink. *Nigella Lawson, eh?* she thought. *How did I not know this back then? Do I still resemble her? Even if I do, probably more like I'm more like Nutella Lawson.* She chuckled quietly at her own joke as she opened the salad drawers at the bottom of the fridge. Erin was right though. She was hard on herself and to what end? To be the butt of her own jokes?

She missed having someone around to give her a reality check. The friends she had back home didn't tend to do this; everything was purely superficial. She missed this. She missed friends who didn't coddle or bullshit. Friends who would champion her. She knew she would never have friends like this again and she'd almost ruined it all.

CHAPTER 32

'Did you have a nice drive?' Tara asked as they got ready for lunch. She sat down at the dressing table and grabbed a hairbrush. 'Not too boring, I hope. I should have come with you; I've never seen the Chaplin statue up close and—'

'Tara, can we talk?'

She laughed. 'Jeez, not a Chaplin fan then? I was never a fan of—'

'Tara. I'm serious. We need to talk. Shit, I don't even know how to say this.'

As she met Aiden's eyes, she didn't have to ask what he wanted to talk about. It was obvious.

'Oh. I see.' She paused brushing. 'So, you're done, right? Six months in and you've already had enough of me? Of us.'

Aiden's gaze shifted towards the floor. 'I'm sorry. You're really important to me, but this... it isn't working anymore.'

'Why?'

His face looked visibly pained. 'It isn't any one thing and it's not anything you've done, it's—'

She began brushing her hair again, trying to keep calm.

'Look, I know I kinda threw you in at the deep end here, with the reunion and all but surely we can—'

'It's not about that,' he replied. 'And I'm so sorry to do this now, the last thing I want to do is hurt you.'

'But what's changed? I thought we were having fun!' she implored. 'How long have you felt like this?'

'I dunno,' he replied. 'I just know that I shouldn't have agreed to come on this trip. It wasn't fair.'

She spun around on her stool. 'But you think it's fair to do it now?' she questioned, her voice almost a harsh whisper. 'Am I so unbearable that you couldn't have done this after we leave on Monday?'

'Of course not,' he insisted. 'Tara, you're an amazing woman, we're just not right for each other. You deserve someone else. Someone better. I am truly sorry.'

She threw her hairbrush on to the dressing table. 'So, what, we just ride out the rest of the weekend pretending everything's fine? Making everyone else feel uncomfortable? I don't think so. Pack your stuff. I need you to leave.'

Aiden rose to his feet, quietly accepting her request.

She felt her heart catch in her chest as he began gathering his clothes from the wardrobe. That dark blue shirt she liked so much, his movie T-shirts, his spare jogging trousers.

'This is bullshit!' she exclaimed. 'Who does this? Who breaks up with someone for no good reason in the middle of a holiday?'

'Tara, I'm so very—'

'Sorry? Yeah, so you keep saying. Ugh, screw this, I can't even look at you.'

Tara quickly made her way into the bathroom and locked the door, her mind spinning in disbelief. Worst of all she could hear her mother's voice in the back of her head.

You should have never told him about rehab, darling. Who wants to make a life with someone who's already ruined theirs.

And that awful, garish red hair? Really, Tara, I thought I taught you better than that.

She took a deep breath and stood in front of the mirror.

I am good enough. I am smart enough. People like me for me.

She repeated it four times before she could finally feel her heart rate returning to normal.

The confusion was overwhelming. What the hell had changed for him? Yes, the relationship was somewhat unconventional but that's what he said he wanted. *Just two people, hanging out, seeing where it goes.* He'd said that, in her bedroom, clear as... She paused as that memory suddenly became a little clearer. A little truer. He hadn't said that at all. She had. She had been the driving force behind their laid-back relationship... but she never forced him to be there. Christ, he wasn't even her type, but she liked him. He was a good man and she hadn't known too many of them. As she sank down on to the bathroom floor, she heard Aiden's footsteps walk across the hallway before disappearing down the stairs.

CHAPTER 33

'Aiden on his way?' Erin asked as Tara sat down at the patio table. Everyone else had been digging into lunch for the past ten minutes, picking at tapas style dishes with jugs of orange juice and ice being passed around to the overly warm guests. 'We're missing Christine too.'

'Christine's still out, roaming the hillsides,' Becky informed her. 'God knows how she does it in this heat. I want to pass out just thinking about it.'

Beth scooped some salad on to her plate. 'Is she in training for something?'

'Nope,' Becky replied, 'unless the Uptight Olympics are a thing.'

Alex couldn't help but laugh. It was nice to see a glimpse of the old Becky and one who appeared to be expressing what they'd all been too polite to say.

'No, Aiden's not out for a run as such,' Tara informed them, grabbing a handful of bread, 'Though he may have bolted out of here with his tail between his legs.'

'What do you mean?' Alex asked, watching Tara rip at the baguette. Her face was unusually flushed. 'Are you alright?'

'He's gone,' Tara announced. 'I told him to leave. He's probably halfway to Waterville by now.'

The group paused eating, watching Tara stab the butter dish like it had also somehow wronged her.

Aiden was gone? Alex felt her stomach backflip into her throat. 'What happened?' she asked cautiously. Her trainers were over beside her sun lounger. She'd need to escape barefoot if Tara knew the full story.

'We broke up,' Tara replied. 'That's what happened. He dumped me. I'm officially single again! Hide your husbands, ladies... ah shit. Sorry, Erin.'

'It's fine,' she replied, brushing it off.

'But why?' Beth asked, dumbfounded. 'Did he give you a reason? Did you fight? God, has he met someone else?'

Alex would have held her breath if it hadn't already left her body.

'Who the hell knows,' Tara replied. 'He just wasn't feeling it anymore apparently. He probably sends his thanks for your hospitality, Erin, I just didn't stick around long enough to find out. I had to hide in the bathroom until he left.'

Becky immediately threw her arms around Tara in solace. 'Oh, I'm so sorry! Are you alright?'

Tara squirmed her way out of Becky's grip. She wasn't in the mood for physical contact. 'I'll be fine,' she insisted. 'I'm a big girl and I refuse to let this ruin my weekend, *our weekend*, so let's just move on, shall we. Enjoy the sun. Eat some fucking bread.'

Tara took her bread to the furthest sun lounger, put on her sunglasses and didn't let anyone see just how hurt she felt. She'd never been dumped before. It absolutely sucked. She was a mixture of rage and self-pity and she didn't like it one bit.

By now, Alex (feeling close to death, but hanging in there) was convinced that Aiden hadn't said anything to Tara because she hadn't yet been battered to death by a redhead with half a buttered baguette.

Maybe it's for the best, she thought. *Clean break. Problem solved. Life can go back to normal. Still, he could have at least warned me he was leaving. Said goodbye.*

Two hours later, everyone was sprawled out in the garden, in various stages of undress, soaking up the sun. Tara had been particularly quiet, which was understandable, though she did eat the whole baguette and no one questioned her.

'We all still up for a beach picnic later?' Erin asked. 'I mean if you're not Tara, of course we can do something else, it's no problem.'

'Bring it on,' Tara insisted. 'Cocktails sounds ideal.'

'Fantastic,' Erin replied. 'Music playlist suggestions are always welcome, everyone.'

Bzz. Bzz.

Alex lifted her phone. Unknown number. She clicked on the message.

These seagulls really do have it in for me. Can we talk? In person. Same place?

Her heart racing, she closed her phone, wondering if anyone else had noticed the sudden look of surprise on her face. Thankfully they were all too busy replying to Erin's barbecue suggestion. Pulling her T-shirt on, she slipped her feet into her trainers.

'Think I'm going to go for a walk,' she announced. 'I'll fall asleep if I lie here any longer.'

'Want some company?' Erin asked.

'No, I'm good,' Alex replied quickly. 'I need to make a couple of work calls anyway.'

'On a Sunday?'

'Publishing never sleeps,' she heard herself reply. 'Barbie sounds amazing though. Won't be long!'

Really, Alex, she thought. *You make up shit for a living and that's the best you could come up with? Eejit.*

Once out of view from the house, Alex quickened her pace, down past the sandy part of the beach to the embankment where she'd previously met Aiden. She spotted him, perched on a rock, knocking sand out of one of his trainers.

'I thought you'd left,' Alex said as she approached him. 'Tara said you'd gone.'

'I did,' he replied, pulling his trainer back on. 'I had to. Despite what she and undoubtably everyone else thinks by now, I do have a heart, Alex, and right now it is pretty beaten up.'

As she saw his eyes glisten, she swallowed hard. He looked gutted.

'Anyway, I just wanted to say goodbye properly.' He sighed, staring down at his feet. 'How is she?'

Alex felt the weight of his question. 'She's pretty upset,' she informed him, a lump forming in her throat. 'She's not showing it, but we all know. The house feels a bit weird at the moment.'

'What a mess. Alex, I'm sorry. Maybe I—'

'It is a mess,' Alex said, doing her best to maintain composure. 'But now we can just forget this ever happened, move on—'

'But I don't want to forget this happened!' he exclaimed. 'Even if we never see each other again, I don't want to forget a single thing about you or our time together. Why would I? It's been the greatest three days of my life.' Aiden took her hand. 'And I know it's wrong, this whole thing has been doomed from day one, but I'm not sorry we met, I'm only sorry that this is all we get.'

Alex began to reply, but her words vanished as her lips met his. It was soft at first, gentle but then something more urgent took over. She felt one hand in her hair, the other moving down her back. Those few seconds felt like forever until she finally, reluctantly, moved away.

'I have to go,' she said softly. 'But I'm not sorry we met either. Believe me.'

He nodded. 'I know. I just couldn't leave Kerry without telling you how I felt.'

Alex turned and began walking back to the house, half floating on air, half determined not to fall apart and become a blubbering wreck. How would she explain it? How would she ever explain any of it?

'Publishing world still surviving without you?' Erin asked as she wandered back into the garden. 'Barnes & Noble still in business?'

'Yeah,' she replied, holding up her phone to imply that her business calls had definitely happened and she wasn't a dirty great liar.

'You look kinda beat,' Erin commented. 'Though I think we're all pretty wiped. It's been a hell of a day so far.'

Alex nodded. 'Yeah, I think I might take a nap before dinner, unless you need a hand with anything right now?'

'All good,' Erin replied. 'We'll start setting up about half seven.'

'Sounds grand. I'll see you in a bit.'

Alex made her way upstairs as quickly as she could, swiftly closing the bedroom door behind her. Then, face in a pillow to muffle any sounds, she finally allowed herself to cry.

CHAPTER 34

'There you are!' Becky exclaimed as Christine arrived back. 'I thought you'd been kidnapped.'

'No, there's just lots of good running spots around here,' Christine replied. 'It's a pleasure to run somewhere where the air is so clean and the sights you see are just extraordinary... How are you, Tara?'

Tara peered down her sunglasses at Christine. Why was she being singled out? Had she suddenly grown horns? 'Me? I'm grand.'

'That's good,' she replied. 'Just thought you looked a little glum.'

'Do you want a drink?' Becky asked, trying to draw Christine's attention away from the recently dumped. The last thing anyone needed was Christine poking around in Tara's emotional wound. 'There's some really nice juice in the kitchen.'

Christine smiled. 'Sure. That would be great. I might take it upstairs; I need to shower.'

'I'll bring it up,' Becky replied, pleased that Christine was being so amiable for once. Maybe the countryside was good for her. The stress of living and working in London could take its toll on anyone.

Pouring some fruit juice and ice into a glass, she made her way upstairs, hearing the shower running as she passed. Becky placed it on the dressing table and began looking for something to wear for the beach picnic.

At least I can get away with wearing a skirt, she thought. *No one in their right mind would wear smart trousers to muck around on the sand. Or shoes. God, I think this might be the best evening ever.*

She pulled out a long white cotton maxi dress, perfect for the occasion. Wide straps, with embroidered flowers and frills around the bottom of the skirt. She hadn't worn this particular dress yet and she couldn't wait to show it off.

'Is that new?' she heard Christine ask from behind her. She was tightly wrapped in a bath towel.

'It is! Thought I'd wear it this evening for our last night. Make a bit of an effort, you know?'

Christine pulled on her robe, before removing the towel from underneath. Becky used to find her particular brand of modesty cute, but now it was just strange. *I'm your girlfriend*, she thought. *Seeing you naked is kinda part of the deal.*

'Tara did look quite down,' Christine reiterated. 'Did I miss something?'

'Aiden left,' she informed Christine. 'Broke up with Tara. That's probably why you sensed she was a bit down. I guess anyone would be.'

'How unfortunate,' Christine replied. 'Though I'm not convinced they were particularly right for each other. I'm sure she'll be fine, she seems resourceful.'

'She's pretending she's alright, but it must be really tough for her.'

Christine pulled on her underwear, moving over beside Becky and her new dress.

'It's very girly,' Christine replied, inspecting it closely. 'It'll show quite a lot of your bare arms, won't it? Glad to see you're dealing with your body issues, well done. Very brave.'

As Christine turned to open the drawers, Becky found herself glowering at the back of her head. Body issues? She didn't have body issues! She didn't care that the tops of her arms were a little chunky, in fact she hadn't even noticed until Christine had pointed it out while comparing to her own.

'And what will you be wearing?' she asked Christine. 'Did you bring anything other than slacks and running shorts?'

'Hmm, I did bring some wide-legged, linen trousers,' she replied. 'I'm sure they'll be fine. No need to go overboard, it's just dinner.'

Becky realised that regardless of how amiable Christine tried to appear, deep down she didn't give two shits about anyone else except herself.

———

Alex, faced still mushed into her pillow, heard a knock at her door.

If I pretend I'm asleep, they'll go away, she thought. *I'm really not in the mood for company.*

'Moran! Unlock the door, please.'

Alex lifted the pillow off her face. It was Tara. Why was Tara suddenly at her door? *Oh God, this can't be good.* Her pulse began to race as she sat up in bed, wondering whether to open the door or escape out the window. Steeling herself, she reached over and opened her door.

'Look at the state of this,' Tara said, pointing to her hair as she invited herself into Alex's room. 'I look like I've been playing on the power lines.'

Alex quietly breathed a sigh of relief, wiping her damp eyes as Tara barged past.

'There's nothing wrong with you,' she insisted as Tara sat down at the dressing table.

'Nothing wrong? You're shitting me, right?'

Alex couldn't help but smirk. Tara's bright red hair hung limply around her shoulders, some strands plastered to her face, while a halo of static frizz held strong around the top of her head.

'And I swear the heat from the sun is fading this very expensive dye job,' she moaned. 'I should have stayed blonde. Blondes thrive in the sun! *This* is not thriving.'

'I mean, it'll be fine after you wash and blow dry it,' Alex reassured her. 'I have some anti-humidity stuff in my case if you want to use it.'

'I already borrowed it.'

Alex looked at the empty space where her Color Wow spray had once been. Some things never changed.

Tara exhaled loudly. 'UGH! No wonder he dumped me,' she said, peering into Alex's mirror. 'Imagine waking up to this every morning. I'd feckin' bolt too.'

'Stop that!' Alex insisted, 'I'm sure it had absolutely nothing to do with that. You could be ten years in the ground and you'd still look beautiful, now shut up.'

At once Alex felt like a horrible human being. Of course, it was nothing to do with her hair, *she* was the reason this was all happening, and here she was, acting like the dutiful friend. But what else could she do?

'Your eyes are all red,' Tara noted. 'Have you been crying? You look like I feel.'

'Allergies,' Alex replied quickly. 'I have allergies.'

'Since when? I don't remember you having allergies.'

'Yeah, they appeared in my late twenties. Adult onset. Weird.'

Is that even a real thing? she thought. *Please don't google that.*

'It must be the cat or hay fever or something. I'll see if Erin has any antihistamines. Now go and get a shower. You'll feel better.'

Tara slowly got up and took a moment to compose herself. 'Thanks, pal. You're right. Onwards and upwards.'

'Exactly,' she agreed. 'I'll see you at dinner.'

Adult-onset allergies, she repeated to herself as Tara left. *You couldn't have just said you were tired? Idiot.*

As Tara left the room, Alex held her head in her hands. All of this hiding, this pretence, it just made her feel grubby. She wanted to scream. All she did was meet a boy on a plane and now hearts were broken. Hers included. But as much as she tried to reason with her conscience, it was pointless. She'd fallen for Aiden and there wasn't a damn thing she could do to make any of it better.

CHAPTER 35

In her new dress, Becky felt like a million euros as she helped set up the beach picnic. She helped Erin carry the portable fire pit down to the beach and unravel the large tartan blanket onto the sand, while the others stayed behind, collecting chairs, food and two large Bluetooth speakers for the music.

'Are you and Christine alright?' Erin asked. 'You just seem a little...'

'Fed up?' Becky asked. 'Ugh, I'm sorry. I don't want my bullshit contaminating this lovely weekend. I'm alright, we're just in a bit of a rut at the moment.'

'It happens,' Erin replied, sliding the feet of the fire pit into some metal poles. She'd never assembled a firepit before and this didn't seem particularly sturdy. 'I just got the feeling maybe things weren't as grand as they could be. Is she, um, always like this...'

'What, judgemental? Stubborn? Annoying?' Becky laughed as she smoothed the rug on the sand. 'Sometimes.'

'I know it's been ten years since we all lived together, but you just seem so different now,' Erin remarked. 'I mean, it's like you're battling to be this version of you which none of us recognise!'

Becky grabbed the hair claw from her head and threw it on the ground, letting her hair fall on to her shoulders.

'Before Christine, I dated a guy called Stephen Fox and I absolutely adored him,' she began, running her hand through her hair. 'Followed him from one side of the UK to the other. He was a funny, sweet, quiet man, biggest blue eyes I've ever seen and he cheated on me so frequently, I think eventually we both lost count. I knew it was happening, but I stayed because while he messed around, I was the one he came back to. That was a win in my book. But eventually he didn't come back. When I asked him why, he said that he was fond of me but that he just couldn't be serious about someone that he couldn't *take* seriously. Ridiculous and embarrassing, I believe his words were. We'd dated for four years and I was a joke to him.'

'Oh, Becky, I'm so sorry. What an arsehole.'

'He was,' she agreed. 'I met Christine eight months later, self-esteem all shot to hell, and she was so beautiful and confident and interested in me, so I decided I'd be someone she could take seriously. Big-time businesswoman Becky! It hasn't quite gone to plan.'

'You know we all took you seriously, right? Weird rituals and all.'

Noticing the rest of the group coming down the path, Becky lowered her voice. 'I know,' she replied. 'And the more time I spend with you all, the more I remember just how happy I was being plain old ridiculous, embarrassing me. Fuck, I hate being an adult. It's too hard.'

Erin laughed. 'I hear you,' she said waving to the rest of the group. 'Hey, lads, just drop the stuff here and we'll sort it.'

'I'll work things out,' she told Erin. 'Don't worry.'

Dinner comprised of surf 'n' turf, rotisserie chicken, salad, bread, marinated olives (which Tara hated with a passion) and a wooden board with seven different types of cheese and crackers. For dessert Erin had made a huge fruit platter alongside shop-bought profiteroles and chocolate sauce.

'Beth, since your movements are somewhat limited, I'm trusting you with the music this evening,' Erin told her. 'Just nothing that will scare the lough life, please.'

Delighted, Beth embraced her new career as resident DJ, arranging songs that embodied their friendship. As 'I'll Be There for You' began playing, Beth felt a marinated olive bounce off her forehead.

'Hey!'

'And I'll keep going until you turn that shite off,' Tara yelled.

Beth quickly skipped to 'Bad Guy' by Billie Eilish and an olive ceasefire was declared.

'Aiden's staying at the Waterfront Hotel,' Paul announced, looking at his phone. 'He's asked me to drop off the rest of his stuff tomorrow.'

Tara bounded over towards him. 'He's texting you? Why?'

Paul took a step back from a rather irate-looking Tara. 'We exchanged numbers. He's a nice guy. Don't shoot the messenger.'

'Damn, I forgot the serving utensils,' Erin said, handing out some napkins as Tara scolded Paul for being a traitor. 'Alex, be a love and grab some from the kitchen island.'

'Aye aye, captain,' she replied, shooting off back up the path, while Erin got on with carving the chicken. Alex was having a lovely night and it had only begun. Good company, a gentle buzz from the wine and so far, some excellent musical choice from DJ Beth, well, eventually.

Picking up the serving spoons back at the house, Alex heard the patio door open with a *click*, *whoosh*, then footsteps.

'We forgot the ice too.'

Christine stood in the doorway, a weird little smile creeping over her face.

'Oh, no worries,' Alex replied. 'If you grab the cooler in the corner, I'll help load it up.'

As instructed, Christine retrieved the bright blue box, while Alex took out the large bag of ice.

'You look like you got a little sun today,' Alex remarked as she began to shake out the cubes. 'It suits you.'

'Hmm,' she replied. 'I did have quite a lengthy run earlier. It was busier than expected.'

'Really?' Alex replied, shaking the last of the bag in. 'Think that should do it. It'll be heavy, but let me just grab the spoons and—'

'You know, I was sure I saw a certain American at the beach on my way back,' Christine recounted, her voice almost taunting Alex. 'Such a shame he'll no longer be joining us.'

Alex swallowed hard. 'Really? Maybe you saw him heading towards his hotel.' She quickly turned to pick up her spoons, heart thumping.

'No,' Christine continued. 'I didn't see any luggage. I wasn't really paying attention to that though.'

'Thought you might need a hand with the cooler!'

Alex had never been so pleased to see Paul in her life. 'Definitely,' she replied. 'I'll be down in a sec if you want to give Christine a hand.'

They both took a handle each and left the kitchen, leaving Alex to quietly hyperventilate.

She saw us, she thought. *Oh, this is bad. This is very bad.*

By the time Alex returned to the beach, she felt sick. She was sure that at any moment Christine would whisper something to Becky, Becky would shriek in horror and it would be game over. However, everything appeared to be normal. Tara was picking at the salad, Beth and Paul sat chatting near the firepit and Becky was with Christine, who didn't appear to be whispering anything; in fact she looked like she was enjoying herself.

Did I get this wrong? she thought, placing the serving spoons on the table. *Maybe she saw Aiden while he was waiting for me, before I got there. I hope that regardless she keeps it to herself.*

CHAPTER 36

'Do you feel like getting a quiet spot...just me and you?'

Becky narrowed her eyes. 'Not if just you want to talk about my fat arms again.'

Christine smiled. 'Nothing of the kind, I just thought some time alone might be nice.'

Becky liked the way Christine's eyes twinkled. A few wines, nice food, music and now she wanted some alone time. Finally, Christine had relaxed enough to enjoy herself. They might be leaving tomorrow but Becky would take what she could get.

'Sure,' she replied, giggling. 'We can move up the beach a little.'

Lifting their drinks, they shuffled off to the side, allowing the rest of the group to continue partying. 'Dynamite' by BTS. *Damn, I love this song*, she thought, but she'd refrain from dancing if it meant some quality time with her girlfriend who'd probably disapprove of her gyrating around the beach anyway.

'Sláinte,' Becky said, raising her glass. 'Did I tell you how gorgeous you look tonight?'

'You did,' Christine responded. 'I really wanted to get you

on your own for a while. Be able to talk openly without everyone around.'

Becky ran her fingers along Christine's arm and over her hand. 'Well, I'm all yours...'

Christine smiled and brushed the hair from Becky's face. 'You know... I feel like you're regressing.'

Becky frowned. 'I'm sorry?'

'Regressing. I mean, it is understandable, that you'd slip back into old habits and patterns when you're around old friends. I'm just not sure how beneficial it is to —'

'You brought me over here for this?'

Christine nodded. 'I thought it was important you hear it.'

Becky removed her hand and ran it through her hair. 'Jesus wept, are you shitting me?'

'Sorry?'

'I though you wanted to move away to have a bit of a kiss and a cuddle, maybe feel me up, you know – show me some affection.'

'I hardly think being intimate in front of strangers is appropriate.'

'But instead, you brought me over here to give me a lecture like you're my mammie or something. I cannot believe this.'

'I think you're overreacting,' Christine informed her. 'All I was saying was that sometimes we—'

'Oh, for the love of fuck, will you just stop!'

Christine flinched as Becky sprang to her feet. 'I'm so sick of this. You just can't help yourself, can you? Jesus, it's like going out with a feckin' textbook.'

'Well, I'm sorry you feel that way.'

Becky brushed the sand off her skirt, absolutely fuming. 'I'm not regressing, Christine, I'm remembering what it's like to have fun. Do you remember what that's like?'

'Fun is subjective,' Christine replied as she watched the others fling themselves around.

'Perhaps you should try some regression therapy,' Becky insisted. 'Maybe back to when we first met because I have no fucking idea who you are anymore. I used to be dazzled by you – your face, your body, your intellect. Do you remember the sex we used to have?'

'Can you keep your voice—'

'It was intense. We'd be at it for hours and now? Now it's barely worth mentioning. I've forgotten what your mouth feels like on my—'

'Enough!' Christine yelled. 'I've tried so hard with you, Rebecca, but you have no capacity for change.'

'Change? I've done nothing but change for you! The hair, the clothes, my goddamn name, even my personality. See this dress? I love this dress,' she snarled. 'And I love my hair when it's wavy and wild and I love walking around barefoot, even though my feet get filthy, and I love my big fat arms.'

Christine looked around uncomfortably, aware that people could overhear them. 'Rebecca, I—'

'I'm not finished. I believe that we're all connected. Every living thing. I believe in energy work and magic and rituals.'

'What on earth are you talking about?'

Becky picked up some sand and let it run through her fingers. 'I'm talking about the parts of myself I hid to be with you.'

'I didn't ask you to do that.'

'I know,' Becky replied. 'I chose to. That was my first mistake.'

'And your second?'

Becky brushed her sand-covered hands against her skirt. 'Thinking I could be happy with you. That I could trust you.'

Christine exhaled loudly. 'For God's sake. You can trust me. I've done nothing but support you.'

Becky laughed. 'Are you serious? Even now, you're more

worried about people hearing us than what I'm saying to you. I wouldn't trust you if you told me my own name.'

Christine began to get up.

'The truth is we both chose to hide a part of ourselves in this relationship, only your choice was far, far more insidious than mine. You hid the fact that you're a manipulative, calculating excuse for a human being. We're done, Christine.'

Christine threw her hands in the air. The first true sign of emotion all evening. 'Fine! Run along to your band of merry misfits, Rebecca.'

'It's Becky,' she replied, kicking off her shoes. 'And these are my people and they know me better than you ever will.'

'Your people? My God, you're quite delusional. These women don't know you; these women don't even know themselves!'

'Jesus, you are so bloody arrogant. Two days and you have already got everyone figured out, huh?'

Christine cackled. It was a harsh, spiteful sound, unlike anything that Becky had heard before. 'I've been doing this job a long time and I have *never* met a more chaotic group of people, you included, my darling.'

'I'm done, Christine,' Becky said. 'We're done. Take your shit, take the car and go home. You don't know half as much as you think you do.'

'Oh, I know a lot. I can read you all like a book,' she sneered. 'You have Erin, who clearly has no one so she had to scramble together a band of oddballs from her past for comfort. Beth, who's obviously lying about what's wrong with her and doesn't trust any of you enough to be honest. Tara, who frankly doesn't have a clue what she wants and then you have Alex, who's been carrying on with Tara's boyfriend, Aiden, behind her back! I saw them earlier, at the beach. And you, Rebecca... you're just a—'

'You say one more word and you're going to see just how fucking chaotic we can really be.'

Becky spun around to see Erin, her face almost contorted in anger. 'You get your shit and you get out of my house and never so much as breathe this woman's name again.'

Christine laughed again, but it wasn't quite so cocky. 'My pleasure.'

As she walked back to the house, Becky turned to hug Erin, but it wasn't only Erin who'd heard everything.

'What did she say?' Tara asked, her wide eyes looking at Becky. 'Aiden and Alex? What is she talking about?'

CHAPTER 37

'Alex, what the fuck is going on?'

Alex felt like she was either going to pass out or throw up.

'Tara, I...' Alex felt her words fall away. The game was up. There was no point in lying anymore, not to Tara and not to herself. An entire weekend pretending that whatever was happening between her and Aiden wasn't actually happening. Fighting it. Rationalising it. Enough was enough.

'The guy I met on the plane. It was Aiden.'

'Whaaat!' Beth exclaimed, her jaw almost hitting the sand while there were audible gasps from the rest of the group.

'I had no idea you guys were together!' Alex insisted. 'Not until you both turned up here and—'

'But *he* knew we were together,' Tara hissed. 'He knew from the moment he met you. And when he turned up here with me, you didn't think to say, "Hey, lads, weirdest thing: we've just sat on the plane together! Isn't that a fun story?"'

Alex shifted uncomfortably. 'Not really. Not after I'd already announced that I'd met someone amazing and given him my number. That seemed worse, to be fair.'

Tara, hands on hips, began pacing back and forth beside the bonfire.

'So, let me get this straight; you've been sneaking around all weekend? Stealing moments together, kissing behind *my* back, but in full view of Sigmund fucking Freud over there! Gah, the whole thing is so grubby, I can't look at you.'

'Maybe I should go,' Alex suggested, standing up. 'We can chat when—'

'You're not going anywhere!' Tara barked. 'Not until I find out what in the hell has been going on here.'

And with that Tara grabbed Alex's shoes and threw them into the firepit, a smouldering end to a perfectly good pair of Christian Louboutins. Alex gasped.

Beth, Erin and Paul sat on the sand side by side, guarding their own shoes while transfixed by the whole situation. Christine could have been inside, robbing them blind, but that was a chance they were willing to take.

'Is this revenge?' Tara asked Alex.

'Revenge?'

'For me banging that guy in uni? Nigel Boyle or whatever his name was, because if it is, that's just pathetic.'

'Niall Doyle,' Alex reminded her. 'And of course it isn't.'

Tara paused for a moment, bracing herself for the next question. 'So have you slept together?'

'No!' Alex exclaimed. 'It was just a kiss. One kiss.'

'Did it mean anything?'

She wanted to tell Tara it was just a mistake. That it meant nothing. Anything to spare her feelings. But there had been too many lies already.

'Yes,' she replied. 'It did. It meant everything.'

Alex didn't feel the slap at first. She felt herself falling and hitting the sand after Tara lunged at her, but the sting on her face came later. And when it came, it burned like hell.

CHAPTER 38

'Tara, my love, you can't drive, you've had too much to drink!' Beth yelled as she hobbled behind a rather irate redhead looking for her car keys.

'Then I'll phone an Uber!' she insisted. 'I'll flag someone down, Christ, I'll walk if I have to, I don't care. I need to see him.'

Beth did her best to calm Tara down, but it was pointless. She was determined to have it out with Aiden. Face to face, or possibly fist to jaw, Beth wasn't exactly sure what Tara was planning. She watched her friend throw on a coat which didn't belong to her, but Beth thought it best not to mention that.

'Why don't you just sleep on it?' Erin suggested. 'Talk to him in the morning, yeah? You never know, you might feel—'

'I'll feel just as pissed as I am right now,' Tara responded. 'Only he might have checked out by then. It has to be now.'

'Fine, I'll take you,' Beth conceded, realising that Tara would hijack a passing horse to get where she needed to be.

'You sure?' Pete asked quietly.

She kissed his cheek. 'I've only had the one drink; I'll be alright to drive, lovely.'

'Perfect,' Tara replied. 'He's staying at the hotel on the beachfront. I've googled it. Let's go.'

Any plans to talk Tara out of her imminent confrontation were short-lived, as the moment they pulled up outside the hotel, Tara shot out of the car like a greyhound out of a trap. Beth could swear she saw dust trails. She immediately called Erin from her car.

'We're here. She has just gone in. Front desk might turn her away, she does look a bit mad. She's wearing Paul's waterproof jacket and a pair of flip-flops.'

'God help Aiden,' Erin replied. 'He'll be lucky to come out of this with his balls intact. I still can't believe this is happening.'

'Look, I'll wait here for her,' Beth insisted. 'If the Guards are called, she might need a quick getaway. Or to be bailed out.'

She heard Erin's soft laugh down the receiver. 'Seems fair.'

'How's Alex?' Beth asked. 'That was quite the smack.'

'Tearful,' Erin replied. 'Sore. I've given her a cold cloth for her face. What a mess. Keep in touch.'

As she hung up the phone, Beth put her head back on the seat and closed her eyes. Just for a moment. She might have been exhausted but that would have to wait. For this first time in a long time, she felt needed. She felt valuable. She wasn't giving that up for anything.

———

'Hi, Aiden Smith's room number, please. In my rush to get over, I've completely forgotten it.'

The desk clerk looked up from his screen and smiled politely at this somewhat unhinged-looking woman in front of him.

'Sorry, madam, but we can't give out that information. I could ring his room for you. Let him know you're here.'

'Sure. Tell him Alex is in reception.'

She watched as the ruddy-faced man made the call. A few seconds later he hung up the receiver.

'Room 31,' he replied. 'Mr Smith says just to go on up.'

Tara wished she could have taken a photo of Aiden's face as he answered the door. She'd never seen someone switch from excitement to confusion to horrified so quickly.

'Tara?'

'Surprise!' she said, flatly barging past Aiden. 'Thought I'd just pop by. See how you're settling in.' The hotel room was impressive. Fresh white walls, a large king-size bed and a stunning sea view.

'Jesus, nice digs,' she said, peering out of the large windows. 'If I'd known you could afford this, I'd have stayed here instead.'

He closed the door behind her. 'Tara, what are you doing here?'

She turned and sat on the arm of the easy chair near the window. 'What am I doing here?' she repeated. 'I mean, we could explore that, sure, but as your face has completely drained of all colour, I'm guessing you might have an inkling.'

'Alex,' he said quietly.

'Feckin' BINGO!' Tara exclaimed. 'It seems that Christine saw you both on her run this afternoon. Good old Christine, with her beady wee eyes, making sure she doesn't miss a trick.'

Aiden sighed, rubbing the back of his neck. 'Fuck. I'm so sorry. You have no idea how horrible I feel about this.'

'I was so confused,' Tara continued. 'Wondering why you'd suddenly upped and left but it's all starting to make sense now. You dumped me to make it easier to creep around with Alex behind my back, right? The pair of you make me sick.'

'No, it wasn't like that, I swear...'

'How was it then? You want to explain to me how the hell any of this happened?'

She watched him sit on the edge of the bed, his head bowed. 'I'm not even sure I can explain it,' he replied. 'One moment I was in the airport coming to meet you, the next she was there and we got talking and—'

'And what? You just couldn't control yourself? It was love at first sight?'

He hesitated for a second. 'No... I don't know. Maybe.'

She shrieked in disbelief. 'Ha! That is just brilliant. How lucky for you, how romantic! Don't let the part where you were supposed to be in love with me get in the way of this unexpected romance. Maybe she can write about it in her next feckin' book.'

Aiden waited for her to stop flailing her arms around in case he got caught in the crossfire.

'I'm really fond of you, Tara. But I don't think it's love.'

Tara rolled her eyes. 'Oh, thanks,' she sneered. 'Good to know.'

'And I don't believe you love me either. Not really.'

'Not anymore I don't!' she replied, childishly.

'I'm serious,' he said. 'Look, I know you're angry and you have every right to be, but please just sit down, take a moment and think about it. Really think about it.'

'Don't try and turn this shit around on me, I'm not the one who kissed someone else! This isn't about me.'

'Please.'

Tara huffed loudly and sunk into the easy chair; flailing arms now crossed defiantly.

'You've known her for three days!' she exclaimed. 'You're telling me that's more real than what we had?'

'Tara, you're the one who said you just wanted to hang out, see where it goes. I thought you only wanted a fling!'

'Why on earth would I want you to meet my friends if it was just a fling to me?'

He raised an eyebrow. 'Come on now. You asked me here so you wouldn't have to come alone. For moral support, right? I'm not stupid.'

She pushed her hair behind her ears, 'Yes... well, no, not exactly. I really did want everyone to meet you.'

'Can we just be honest?' he asked. 'You wanted me to keep you company because that's what we do. We keep each other company. We're more like friends than anything else.'

He was right about that. They'd only slept together twice since they'd met. She'd put it down to the fact that he worked most nights at the clinic, but the truth was, neither of them were that into it. It was fine, but it's hard to get excited about *fine*. While this was true, it still hurt.

'OK,' she replied. 'I'll admit that we weren't particularly hot and heavy, but some relationships aren't.'

'I need one that is,' he replied. 'Maybe I wasn't sure what I wanted either when we met, but I'm sure now. We're not in our eighties, Tara. You should want more too. Why would you settle for less?'

'Then why not break up with me?' she asked. 'If you thought this was passionless and temporary, then what's the point?'

He rubbed his hand through his hair. 'Because I didn't want to hurt you. I didn't want to be yet another thing you had to deal with. You've been going through a lot, you know? I didn't want to add to that.'

'So, you just felt sorry for me?' she scoffed. 'Poor little lost Tara, fresh out of rehab—'

'You know that's not the case!'

Aiden stood and walked over to the window, cranking it open. The air in the room was stifling.

'You know that my dad died the day after my brother told us he was sick, right? Eli couldn't help with the funeral, or travel back for it. A month later I sold my business and came to live in London to be nearer to him and his family. Are you only with me because you feel sorry for me?'

'Of course not.'

'Well, that isn't my motive either. You are greater than the sum of your parts, Tara.'

'OK, Aristotle.'

His futile attempt not to smile failed.

As they sat in silence, Tara felt empty. Of course, she'd known that Aiden wasn't forever, she just never expected it to end like this. Deep down, she'd thought that when the time came, she'd be the one to bow out first.

'Regardless of what I feel for Alex, I didn't... I *don't* want to lose you. I'm sorry I fucked this up.'

'Well, you did,' she replied. 'Christ, Aiden, you should have just been truthful with me.'

'You're right.'

'In fact, you shouldn't have come on this trip at all. Fuck being the good guy, Aiden, you should have been the honest guy.'

Aiden put his head in his hands. 'So, what happens now?'

'I'm leaving,' she replied. 'I'll go back to Erin's, tomorrow we'll all go our separate ways and then, I guess we just all move forward. One foot in front of the other. But first, I need to deal with Alex.'

CHAPTER 39

The firepit was still going strong as Paul, Becky, Erin and Alex gathered around it.

'I should leave, shouldn't I?' Alex suggested, nervously wringing her hands. 'I should just pack my bags and piss off. Maybe, when Beth comes back, she could run me into the village too.'

'Yeah, good idea,' Paul responded. 'Maybe you could check into the same hotel as Aiden. That'll be a good look.'

Alex saw Becky give Paul a little nudge to shut him up. She threw back her head and made a groaning noise.

Erin grabbed a bottle of wine and sat down cross-legged on a blanket. 'Now, tell me to mind my own business if you like,' she said, unscrewing the top. 'But what exactly went on with Aiden? Was it just a kiss? Just the once? Shit, were you guys going at it on the beach when Christine—'

'No!' Alex exclaimed. 'Not at all. He came to say goodbye and we kissed. It wasn't planned and that's as far as it went.'

Alex saw Erin sipping her wine, looking unconvinced, and so explained: 'God, this whole thing sounds ridiculous and I cannot properly explain it because even I don't understand it. I felt like I was hit by lightning. Like the universe suddenly opened up and *BAM*, there he was. As hard as I tried, I couldn't shake it off, and believe me, I tried.'

'Obviously not hard enough,' Erin remarked. 'Oh shit, they're back.'

Everyone grew silent as Tara and Beth joined their little pow-wow. 'We need to talk,' Tara said, her glare directed at Alex.

'Shall we leave?' Erin asked.

Tara shook her head. 'No point. Everyone knows what's been going on here.'

Beth sat down beside Paul. The tension was almost unbearable. Everyone quietly feared for their shoes.

'Wine. I need wine,' Tara said, her stress now getting the better of her. Erin obliged, handing over her plastic cup which Tara proceeded to down in one. While everyone sat, she remained standing, pacing back and forth.

'Did any of you know what was going on here?' she asked, holding her cup out for more. 'I mean apart from that arsehole Becky brought with her?'

Becky might have protested that comment if she didn't now agree wholeheartedly with it.

Everyone shook their heads while Erin filled up Tara's cup for a second time. The wine was warm, but Tara didn't care.

'Fine, so Alex is the only one I need to be mad with right now.'

'Tara, I'm really sorry,' Alex began, but Tara held her hand up.

'I'm actually stunned you're still here,' Tara began. 'The fecking audacity, it's astounding really. At least Aiden had the sense to leave.'

'I was going to leave,' Alex replied. 'I mean, I will. If you want me to.'

Tara placed one had on her hip. 'Probably best. Need a hand packing?'

'Hang on,' Beth interjected. 'It's late. Everyone's been drinking. I don't think anyone should be going anywhere.'

Tara raised her eyebrows. 'Oh really. Nice to know whose side you're on, Beth.'

'I'm not on anyone's side and this isn't my fight,' Beth replied. 'Also, it's Erin's home, not yours.'

'I don't want anyone to go,' Erin responded. 'I hope we can all work this out.'

'Jesus, it's like no one has my back here!' Tara exclaimed. 'This bitch threw away a lifelong friendship for someone she's known for three days!'

Paul coughed in a manner which indicated that he found that comment to be complete and utter bullshit. 'Are you serious?' he mumbled.

'Sorry, Paul,' Tara growled. 'I didn't quite catch that.'

Beth felt herself blush. 'No, I'm sure—'

'I mean, you're joking, right?' Paul continued.

Tara frowned. 'No. Not at all.'

He rolled his eyes. 'Lifelong friendship... give me a break. This bond you have. This bloody friendship I keep hearing so much about, where has it been for the past ten years? Where was this great camaraderie, this unwavering support, when your husband died, Erin, or when Beth...'

He paused as Beth's eyes locked onto his.

'When Beth what?' Erin asked.

He sighed. 'Nothing, that isn't the point. All I'm saying is, how can you claim to owe each other everything when, for the past decade, you've given each other nothing?'

The silence that fell over the group was deafening. He turned to Tara who was still as defensive as ever.

'You seem to forget that at uni, I knew all the same people

you did. I'm not defending what Alex did, but from where I'm sitting, you don't look so innocent yourself.'

Beth turned to Paul and placed her hand on his. 'Maybe that's enough. Why don't you go back to the house, love?'

Paul lifted his glass (and his shoes) and started to walk back, leaving everyone stunned by his outburst.

It took a few minutes, but finally Tara, looking marginally less hostile, broke the silence. 'Niall Doyle.'

'What about him?' Alex asked.

She sank down on to the sand. 'I knew exactly who he was and I did it anyway.'

She heard Erin give a little gasp and shuffle closer towards her.

'Fuck. And I wasn't even that drunk. Not really.'

Tara looked around the group, trying to gauge the response from the open-mouthed women. Astonishment seemed to be the general consensus.

'Damn, that's feckin' cold, Tara,' Becky said, pouring herself some wine.

'I know,' she mumbled in agreement. 'I know.'

'I don't understand,' Alex said, her cheek still sporting a bright red handprint. 'Why would you do that?'

'Because I was young and I was jealous,' Tara responded, bringing her knees up to her chest. She hugged her dress around her legs. 'I could never quite figure out why we pretty much came from the same background, yet our lives couldn't have been more different.'

Alex wasn't buying this. 'With the exception of Beth, everyone's childhood was far from perfect.'

'Maybe,' Tara replied. 'But our fathers left and our mothers are so similar in many ways, but the difference is, that my mother wanted me as a trophy, while yours didn't particularly want you at all. I always envied how well you carried herself.

How well you coped, while I was falling apart. I guess I wanted you to feel as shitty as I felt.'

'That's really messed up,' Alex said. 'What the hell is wrong with you?'

'A lot actually,' Tara replied. 'Did Aiden tell you that when we met, I'd only been out of rehab for six weeks?'

A hush came over the group. 'He never said a word. Rehab?'

Tara nodded. 'I'd been mentally unwell for a long time. Longer than I knew. You know that my mother was... *is* a difficult woman. I feel like I've either been fighting against her or running from her my entire life. She instilled in me a sense of insignificance. That my worth was entirely linked to my appearance, just as hers had been.'

The sadness on Tara's face made Beth tear up. Her friend had been in pain and she'd missed the signs. They'd all missed it.

'I was like a little doll to her,' Tara continued. 'Look pretty so someone will want to marry you. Your only value is in your face and your figure. Fuck, she even made sure I went to university so I could meet someone of *better stock*, not so I could be educated.'

Tara grabbed Erin's cup again and drank while the others stayed silent. Even the lough seemed quieter than usual.

'Anyway, rebellion, tattoos, piercings, yada, yada, I went to New York with absolutely no idea who I was and New York was the worst place to find that out. I worked hard, I took far too much cocaine, pills, whatever, and I latched on to every unsuitable dickhead I met. I was surrounded by people, but I had no real friends. On my thirty-first birthday I woke up in the ER with no idea how I got there or what had been done to me.'

'Tara, I—'

'Let me finish,' she told Alex. 'After that, I bought a ticket to Heathrow and I left. Didn't tell anyone I was going. Christ, I was so lost. Thankfully I'd made enough money to get help, which took eight months and a lot of crying.'

She paused, staring into her cup. 'Aiden was the first real connection I made after rehab. He used to drive me to therapy groups, hang out in my flat, take me to gigs when I felt low.'

'Tara, I'm—'

Her eyes met Alex's. 'Aiden said that when he met you it was love at first sight. Did you feel the same?'

Alex nodded. 'There was definitely something there, but when he arrived here, with you... We both tried to fight it but... ugh, what a disaster. I'm so sorry.'

'I'm sorry too,' Tara replied.

Alex squinted in confusion. 'For what?'

'Um, did you hear the Niall Doyle story?'

She heard Becky laugh.

'But I had no right to put my hands on you. I just felt like everything was falling apart again; I didn't mean to hurt you.'

Alex reached over and placed her hand over hers. 'I never meant to hurt you either."

The sea lapped gently against the shore as they held each other, while three feet away, a pair of perfectly good shoes continued to burn.

CHAPTER 40

Alex splashed water on her face and winced. Her cheek was still bright red and sore, and the mark showed no signs of fading any time soon. She'd do her best to cover it but knew that she'd be travelling home today looking like she either had slapped-cheek syndrome or was the type of woman who liked to have the odd scrap now and again.

With Aiden gone, she felt the pressure had lifted somewhat. No pretending. No running into him in the hallway, no stolen glances over breakfast.

No texts.

He had not been in touch since he left last night. Nothing. Not even a stupid emoji. Perhaps this whole fiasco was just too much for him to handle. Understandable, his showdown with Tara couldn't have been pretty; Alex wouldn't blame him if he'd just cut his losses and run. Maybe that was that and she'd never see him again. Over just as quickly as it had begun.

Everyone was already in the living room when she got downstairs. Erin had laid out some toast and pastries and was currently enquiring whether anyone wanted a boiled egg.

'Never,' Tara replied. 'Horrible wee bald things.'

'Morning,' Alex said, lifting a croissant. 'Is there any tea on the go?'

'Oh God, your face,' Erin exclaimed. 'In the light of day, it looks like a port-wine stain.'

'Yes, thank you, Erin. I'm hoping someone will have some decent concealer or foundation with them. Maybe a balaclava?'

Tara just sat there, looking horrified.

'You know, you really shouldn't have done that, Tara,' Becky said.

'I know. Thanks, Captain Obvious.'

'You should have challenged her to a duel or something,' Becky suggested. 'We don't see enough of them anymore.'

'It's alright,' Alex reassured her, grinning at Becky's suggestion. 'It's forgotten... no Paul this morning, Beth?'

'Aiden left some things. Paul's gone to drop them off at the hotel,' Beth replied. 'He'll probably have some breakfast there.'

'Since we're not leaving until three, I thought we'd do a little ceremony... vanquish some demons, affirm a new future?' Becky looked around the room.

'I thought you'd stopped all that,' Tara said to an unreasonably chipper Becky. It appeared her first night without Christine hadn't dampened her mood at all. 'I was quite enjoying the vanilla Rebecca with her sensible slacks.'

'I had,' Becky replied, 'But you never forget. It's like riding a broomstick.'

'I think it's great idea,' Beth agreed. 'It was the last thing we did on graduation weekend. Seems appropriate.'

'You've changed your tune,' Erin remarked. 'I seem to remember you having a panic attack in case everyone laughed at your wish thingy.'

'Affirmation,' Becky corrected.

'Well, sure, but that was then,' Beth replied. 'I think I'm safe now. You wouldn't laugh at a woman with a walking stick now, would you?'

Tara snorted. 'Nice try, Hop-a-Long, no special treatment here.'

Beth laughed loudly. 'Fair play, I wouldn't expect anything less... However, all jokes aside, I think the time has come for us to discuss something important, Tara, and I think I speak for all of us, when I ask – where on earth did those boobs come from?'

'Rude!' Tara replied.

'Beth!' Erin exclaimed. 'You can't say that! You cannot just suddenly ask someone about their bolt-ons, no matter how impressive they are.' She leaned in. 'I mean, are they silicone or saltwater?'

'I have no idea what either of you are talking about,' Tara responded, swiping away Erin's hands. 'I just happened to develop much later in life.'

'What, in your thirties?'

Alex began to laugh. 'Girls, that's quite enough. We're all adults here.'

'Thank you, Alex,' Tara replied.

'If she doesn't want to discuss those massive knockers, she doesn't have to.'

Tara began to laugh. 'Fine, OK. It was a spur-of-the-moment decision.'

Erin poured herself more tea. 'Spur of the moment? Boobs aren't an impulse purchase. You can't just pop out and get them in your lunchbreak. Those things take planning.'

'Fine! I had the cash and I went for it. Ten grand, not including the private hospital room and car ride home.'

'Ten thousand dollars?'

'Worth every penny,' she replied to a shocked-looking Beth. 'It's probably the only decision I made in New York that I don't regret.'

'Can you breastfeed with implants?' Beth asked. 'I've always wondered.'

'Yeah,' Tara responded. 'I made sure it wouldn't be a problem, you know. If the need ever arises.'

'I thought you never wanted kids,' Becky said. 'Or was that Alex?'

'Me,' Alex interjected, raising her hand. 'I'm fine just being the group auntie when you all pop one out. Or three in Beth's case...'

'So come on,' Tara said. 'I can't be the only one to have had some work done. It's 2022!'

'I've had a little Botox,' Erin confessed. 'Just once. My forehead looked like it had been polished, it was awful. And some liposuction. And maybe a chemical peel. Or six.'

Everyone started to laugh.

'And here you are telling me to stop worrying about how I look!' Alex said. 'The hypocrisy!'

'Completely different,' Erin exclaimed. 'You try looking at yourself on an IMAX screen. It's unsettling.'

'I haven't had anything done,' Beth admitted. 'I've never even been waxed.'

'Lies,' Tara replied, 'I clearly remember waxing your moustache before a night out. You were starting to look like Salvador Dali.'

'I've thought about getting my tits done,' Alex said, biting into some toast. 'Not implants but maybe a wee lift. Gravity is already dragging these puppies towards my knees, heaven only knows what they'll be like in my fifties.'

As breakfast continued, no one mentioned the previous evening. Nothing about Aiden or Christine or the absolute chaos that had unfolded. Perhaps there was nothing more to be said. It was all very calm, very civilised until Tara spotted the urn over the fireplace.

'Is that...?'

Erin nodded. 'Scott. Yes.'

'Right. OK... So, are you just keeping him in there, or...?'

Alex laughed and choked on her tea at the same time.

'Tara!' Beth exclaimed, shooting a disapproving look at Alex for laughing. 'You can't just—'

'What? Come on, we're all thinking it! I'm not even sure Catholics are allowed to keep ashes at home, are you trying to give the Pope a heart attack or what?'

'When have I ever been Catholic?' Erin asked, 'My parents are Protestant!'

Now Becky was laughing.

'Really?' Tara remarked. 'I honestly thought you'd done the whole communion and everything. You had little photos in an album.'

'Nope, that was me,' Beth interjected. 'My mammie still has the dress somewhere in the attic, on a mannequin like a haunted artifact.'

Tara grinned. 'Look, all I'm saying is, if it were me, and I was in there, I'd rather be part of the air or the sea or buried under a feckin' tree, than stood on a shelf reminding folk that I'm dead. If it was the other way around, would you want Scott feeling sad every time he passed your dusty arse on his way to make a sandwich?'

Erin began to laugh and she knew that if Scott was here, he'd be laughing too. She laughed so hard that her Yves Saint Laurent mascara began to run. *Waterproof, my arse.*

'I know,' she said, wiping her eyes. 'I feel like I should scatter him, but...'

'But what?'

'...but then he will be completely gone.'

The laughter quickly stopped and for a moment, each woman felt Erin's heartbreak as if it were their own. Beth reached over and took her hand.

'Oh, sweetheart, I'm sorry.'

'How do I let him go?' she asked, her voice breaking into a

sob. 'How do I live in a world that doesn't have even a tiny part of him in it?'

'You don't have to,' Tara said. 'I'm so sorry, I should never have said that.'

'I'm glad you did,' Erin replied, grabbing a tissue for her nose. 'Because I needed to laugh about this. I haven't worked, I've barely slept, I don't go out. I needed to feel something else other than sad. Other than hurt. Other than angry.'

'But it was thoughtless,' Tara acknowledged. 'I'm mean, what the hell do I know... about anything? My life is a mess and I'm out here questioning your choices.'

She looked over to Alex and sighed. 'I met a perfect guy, but not for me. He's perfect for you. Who am I to stand in the way of happiness, just because I don't know what that is?'

Alex leaned across and hugged Tara. 'You're more loved than you know,' she said. 'Remember that.'

'How did we let this go?' Beth asked. 'You know, Paul was right. Who are any of us to talk about our friendship when we let it fall apart so easily?'

She looked around the table, at each person displaying the look of disgrace that she felt. 'We should have done better; we have to *be* better.' The unspoken agreement was unanimous.

'I put Christine's face in the freezer.' Everyone turned to look at Becky who was currently buttering her toast. 'If you could just leave the photo in there for at least a week, I'd appreciate it. Maybe a month, I'm a bit rusty these days.'

Erin started to chuckle. 'No worries, she can keep Reese company.'

———

'What do you all thinks happens, you know, when you die?'

The walk to the beach with Scott's ashes had been a slow one, giving Erin the time to process her thoughts.

'Heaven, I guess,' Beth said. 'Big pearly gates and all that, knowing that you've lived a good life... that gives me comfort.'

Tara, though never one to bite her tongue, seemed reluctant to answer. 'I have no idea,' she finally replied, though everyone knew her answer would be, 'Nothing at all, lads. We just die. Worm food. Nothing more to it.'

Alex, normally good with words, found it difficult to find them. 'It doesn't matter what we all think. Whatever reassures you is all that matters.'

'Becks?' Erin asked. 'Any thoughts? Reincarnation? Floating around space? Ghosts?'

'For what it's worth, I don't believe that anything actually dies,' Becky replied as she held on to Erin's arm. 'We have such energy that burns within us, carries us, defines us. Energy never dies, it just changes form. Your Scott, your love, isn't in that jar. He isn't anywhere because he's everywhere. He's free. And you need to be too. Energy goes on just as life must.'

'Fuck. Forget what I said, I'd go with that,' Tara mumbled, and Erin smiled.

'But also ghosts,' Becky added. 'Definitely ghosts.'

As they stepped onto the sand and neared the shore, Erin stopped. 'Give me a moment?'

Becky let go of her arm. 'Love you, Erin.'

Erin walked towards the sea while the others stood behind, understanding that this moment was just for her. She walked until the cold water hit her ankles and she could firmly plant herself in the sand. Everything was so calm. So still. Hand on the lid, she felt her lip begin to wobble. 'You loved it here,' she said quietly. 'And I can't think of anywhere else I'd rather come to remember you.'

She opened the lid and felt her throat tighten. Her heart battered her chest slowly. 'I'm sorry you didn't have more time, my love... I'm sorry that we didn't have more time. I'm sorry this is where your story ends. Just know that I love you with every breath in my body and I know, in my soul, that somewhere, you're loving me even without the breath in yours.'

Her hand gripped the urn as Erin began scattering the ashes into the sea, never saying the word goodbye. Goodbye was too final.

When Erin finally joined the girls again, she noticed that someone had drawn a circle around them in the sand. Of course, it was Becky; no one else had the overwhelming urge to make sand shapes.

'Becky, I'm not sure this is the right time for this,' she said, her face still wet from her tears. 'Maybe we can just leave it for now?'

'I think this is exactly the right time,' Becky replied, firmly. 'I think we all need to come together. If the water wasn't so cold, I'd suggest some sort of cleansing ritual. Trust me on this.'

Erin knew it was pointless to protest further. She stood in between Alex and Tara.

'Do you remember what you all wrote last time we were here?' Becky asked as they joined hands.

'Were we meant to?' Tara asked. 'Was there homework I wasn't aware of?'

'No,' Becky replied as she felt Beth struggle to grasp her fingers. 'Beth, is your hand alright?'

Beth raised her hand which now resembled a weird claw. Her last three fingers trying to grip on to nothing while her first two pointed upwards in a powerful spasm.

'Fucking hell,' Tara exclaimed. 'What have you done?'

'It's alright.' Beth sighed. 'This happens a lot – my leg, my hand, sometimes my feet. Usually my meds control this but not today apparently... MS can be so unpredictable.'

They all stared at her. Then to her hand. Then back to her.

'I was going to tell you all... eventually. I just wanted a weekend without anyone feeling sorry for me... Christ, can we stop staring at the claw now, it'll go back to normal in a bit.'

'Multiple sclerosis?' Tara asked. 'That's what you have?'

Beth nodded. 'About ten years now but diagnosed two years ago. Remember all those stumbles I used to have? Turns out it wasn't just the booze.'

'MS? What is that?' Becky asked.

'It's basically your body attacking your brain and nerves. It eats away at the coating on the nerves so that the signals don't go through. I can tell my leg to lift up and walk until the cows come home, but the nerve is so damaged now, it simply cannot do it.'

'They can treat it, right? Is it bad?'

'It's bad, but it could be worse.' Beth replied. 'I'm on meds. Look, can we all just get on with Becky's little ritual before I start needing the loo!'

'But you're OK?' Tara asked. 'I'm so sorry that—'

'Yes. Honestly, I'm fine! I don't want sympathy, I just wanted you all to know! It felt like time.'

Becky took Beth's arm in hers, seemingly reluctant to carry on.

'No feeling sorry for me, remember? Let's just do this.'

Becky nodded, determined not to wobble.

'No affirmations this time,' she said. 'I just want us to close our eyes and speak to how we're feeling.'

Nobody said anything at first, not even Tara who was usually this first to break a silence with some smart-arse remark. But as each one closed their eyes; it didn't take long for them to feel the weight of the past ten years press down on them.

'Success, homes and Andrew Scott.'

Becky looked at Erin who still had her eyes closed.

'That's what I affirmed last time. An ego boost, material wealth and a handsome face. That was the bullshit I wanted at twenty-two because what the hell did I know about life at twenty-two? Becky had the right idea, asking for happiness, health and love. That's all that matters, not my work or my house in Marbella.'

She noticed everyone's jaws drop in surprise. 'Obviously I didn't buy it. Scott did. He was very successful, you know. Loaded, in fact.'

There was a collective mumble of acknowledgement.

'But I will take my hurt and my loss and I will make my life matter again.'

No one responded, but everyone held hands just a little tighter.

'You know, I didn't even buy a lottery ticket,' Tara said next. 'To buy my imaginary island. I mean, at least buying a lottery ticket would have shown that I hoped my life might be different one day. Nobody buys one in the hope that life will remain the same, do they? After graduation, I ran from here, but I never got anywhere. Not really. It's hard to get to where you're going when you don't know where that is. Over the past ten years, I've learned what it's like to broken and now I need to learn what it's like to heal.'

'I'm going to do this sitting down,' Beth said, lowering herself towards the sand with Becky's help. She sat, one leg tucked under and the other stretched straight out.

'I didn't want a money or success or an island, I wanted a husband and two kids,' she began. 'Paul and I were already engaged, so that was a foregone conclusion and I thought having children would be too. Even if I'd had more or less than two, it wouldn't have mattered. But then...'

She stopped and took a deep breath, determined to get through this.

'Look, I know that pregnancy is entirely possible with MS,' she said. 'But I also know how unfair and unpredictable this disease is. Will I have enough energy to play with my kids? Will I even be able to walk them to school? Will they be left to look after me in the future if I decline? Because I could not bear that.'

She wiped her eyes on her sleeve. 'I came here this weekend to feel normal again. To be with the people who knew me before I had any idea I was ill. The people who loved me before any of this consumed every moment of my life. I just wanted to feel like myself again. Even Aiden kept it to himself. Did you know his brother has MS?'

Tara nodded, but everyone else stayed still.

'Well, there you go. Life is a messy, unfair little shithead to everyone. That's all I've learned in the last ten years.'

As Becky sat down beside Beth, one by one they all did the same.

'Successful author, wealthy, with someone who loves the bones of me. I think that's what I wrote.'

Becky nodded to confirm.

'Which I actually feel is a reasonable request,' Alex said, 'because even one of them alone would be enough but I got two. Success means I keep writing; money means I have a roof over my head and love means that I get to experience what's it's like to be adored by another human being.'

She paused, wiping the sand from her legs.

'I don't think I've ever been adored,' she continued. 'Not really. Not properly. And I've spent years dating the wrong men for the right reasons, just hoping that one day, someone will adore me, and then it happened. Finally, it happened. And the best part was, I adored them too, even if it was only for four days.'

She looked at Tara. 'I'm sorry.'

'Don't be,' she replied. 'I'm just sorry it took so long.'

A loud sniff from Becky made everyone turn.

'You're all killing me here,' she managed to say, in between sobs. 'You're all such amazing, strong women. I've been listening, thinking about what I've learned since we were all last together and the truth is, well, nothing. My problem was that I forgot what I already knew, what I already affirmed: that I am happy, I am healthy and I am loved. All by myself. I don't need a romantic partner to give me that.'

The sat together, appreciating how far they'd come as friends. As women. In just one weekend.

'Actually, I did forget one thing,' Tara said, as usual the first to break the silence. 'And it's been bugging me for a few minutes now. I have to ask... your kids' names. What were they?

'Willy and Nelly?' Becky answered. 'No... wait... Willy and Tilly.'

'Billy and Hilly?' Tara suggested. 'Millie and Haribo?

'*William and Lily*,' Beth informed them, 'As well you know. Honestly, sometimes I wonder if—'

'Guys,' Alex interrupted, 'before you start squabbling, can I just ask one thing?'

'Sure.'

'Promise me we'll keep in touch, this time. No matter what.'

As they all agreed, this time Alex thought it felt different. That this promise hit a little differently.

CHAPTER 41

'Really was wonderful to see you, I wish we had longer. Next time we all get together, we'll make it a week.'

'In Marbella of course,' Tara added, leaning in to hug Erin.

She laughed. 'Of course.'

Paul grinned. 'Was quite the weekend, Erin. Best time ever, even when I honestly thought there would be a double murder at one point.'

Beth nudged him disapprovingly, opening the car door. 'We had a brilliant time.' She leaned in to hug Erin too. 'I'm proud of you,' she said softly. 'Keep going at your own pace, eh? Onwards and upwards.'

Erin squeezed back. Beth's hugs were always firm and with purpose. 'You too. And if you need to get away, you're welcome here anytime.'

'Here? But you're still selling the house? Right?'

Erin shrugged. 'Maybe that's something I'll have to give some more thought to. Besides, I hear that the beach is very healing for people with MS.'

'Really? Where did you hear that?'

'From my own mouth. About three seconds ago.'

Beth snickered. 'I'll hold you to that. Now, come here, you three, before I start getting maudlin.'

Alex, Tara and Becky all stepped forward to join Erin in the hug. It was time for them all to leave, but no one wanted to let go.

'Beth, you need anything, you call me,' Alex said. 'And if you eventually need somewhere ground-floor to live, I will kick my ex out and give you that granny flat in a heartbeat. Are we clear?'

Beth nodded, unable to stop the tears flowing down her face. 'Thank you,' she said, 'God, now I'll never stop.'

'You sure you want to do this?' Alex asked Tara as Paul loaded her cases into his car. 'I mean, I understand not wanting to go back to London right away, but it's already been a stressful weekend, totally my fault of course.'

Tara smiled. 'I'm sure. It's about time I visited my mum in Cork and these lovely folk can drop me on their way to the ferry. There are things that need to be said... but if it goes horribly wrong, I have your number.'

'Absolutely.'

'You can wait on me hand and foot for stealing my boyfriend...'

Alex grimaced. 'Oh God, I'm sorry! It wasn't planned I just—'

'I'm kidding, Moran. Dry your eyes.'

'Are you sure you don't want me to drive you guys to the airport?' Erin asked. 'Save you a cab fare.'

Alex shook her head. 'We're good. Go and cuddle that cat, I'm sure he's feeling neglected.'

'He's fine actually,' Becky replied. 'He's glad we came, although someone put ham in his dish and he doesn't eat ham. It gives him the runs.'

Erin gasped. 'How did—'

Becky smiled as their cab pulled up the driveway.

———

Alex missed the click-clacky sound of her Christian Louboutin summer sandals as she strode through Kerry Airport. Her old Skechers didn't make her feel quite so sophisticated, but it was a small price to pay for keeping Tara's friendship.

'They've just called my flight,' Becky said, 'When's yours, Alex?'

'Not for another hour,' she replied. 'It'll give me time to catch up on some *Married at First Sight*, I'm so behind. Now, hug me and get going!'

'Do let me know how you get on with a certain someone,' Becky said.

Alex smiled weakly. 'After all that, I'm not sure I'll ever hear from him again,' she replied. 'If I were him, I'd have cut my losses and run.'

'You never know,' she replied. 'Actually, do me a favour. Watch my stuff, I need to nip to the loo.'

She ran off, leaving Alex to stand with the bags. She felt like a porter... a porter who was also a master criminal, slipping past security and now able to move freely throughout the airport, undetect—

Bzz. Bzz.

Alex opened her phone.

Did you pack those bags yourself madam? Also, nice trainers.

Risking whiplash with the speed she turned around, Alex saw Aiden walking towards her.

'What are you doing here?' she asked, attempting to pick her jaw up off the floor. 'I thought you'd be long gone.'

'Oh, a certain someone texted me your flight time.' He motioned towards Becky on her way back from the bathrooms.

'Better run,' she said, taking her trolley. 'Gosh, what a surprise seeing you here, Aiden. Byeeee!'

Alex laughed as Becky made her exit.

'You alright?' he asked, looking at her face. She nodded. 'Everything's good. I think.'

'So, I'm single now,' he said. 'You might be aware.'

'Yeah, I heard,' she replied, pointing to her face.

'Damn! Tara?'

'Who else? I'm surprised you got off so lightly.'

'We talked things through. For a moment there, I did think I wasn't going to make it to check out alive. But there's something I've been meaning to ask you for a few days now,' he said tentatively. 'And your answer might determine where we go from here.'

Alex felt her heart bungee. 'OK. Shoot.'

'Your dog that hates everyone. It isn't a Chihuahua, is it?'

She laughed. 'No, he's a sausage dog. You're safe.'

He exhaled. 'Phew, good to know! And listen, I know that this whole thing is probably still a mindfuck for you, so there's no pressure from me. I'm happy to take things slowly, or even—'

'Fast,' Alex requested, letting go of her case. 'I'd like to take this fast.'

He grinned. 'Yes, ma'am.'

As his hands held her face, Alex felt herself rise up in her old blue Skechers to meet his lips. Maybe she didn't need those Louboutin shoes after all. Sure, it wasn't quite *l'amour dans un aéroport*, she thought, *but I'll take it.*

CHAPTER 42

2032

'You're not wearing those shoes for driving, are you?' Pete stared at Alex's feet with both curiosity and concern. 'It's very hard to gauge pedal pressure with a heel, especially one of that size. What are they, six inches? Also—'

'Will you stop going on, Peter, she's a grown woman and one with fantastic taste in shoes, might I add.'

When Pete moved out of the granny flat eight years ago, Florence had virtually changed overnight. No more suspicious looks, no more snide remarks and although they bought a house ten miles away, Pete still looked after Winston and took him for weekends and holidays. The couple even adopted a Labrador, Walter, who although much younger than Winston quickly became his best friend. Darren the postman, however, was still enemy number one.

'No, actually,' Alex replied, mouthing "thank you" to Florence. 'My trainers are in the car. I just wanted to show my new sandals off and you almost ruined the moment. Thankfully, your wife has excellent taste and I feel sufficiently admired.'

Her new shoes didn't click-clack quite as impressively as her now deceased Louboutins, but they had a much springier step to them. She felt bouncy as she walked, like one of those cheerleader types she'd seen at sporting events, with perky boobs, a high swinging ponytail and a genuine zest for life. Sadly for Alex, at forty-two, in reality things had begun to swing a lot lower than she'd have liked.

Her case was already packed, this time without the help of Winston who, although still intent on sniffing everything on earth at least twice, had decided to fall asleep on her bed. With Walter. Belly up.

She pulled her case to the front door before returning to the living room. 'Those two are out for the count. They're so cute.'

'We might just hang out here for a bit until they wake up,' Pete said, 'If that's alright?'

She smiled. 'Mi casa es su casa,' she replied, noticing that Florence already had her shoes off and her feet up on the couch. 'Make yourselves at home. But if Winston has a farting attack in his sleep, can you open my window a crack before you go?'

Once outside, she loaded up her new Toyota, which according to Pete was one of the safest models to drive. This time she listened.

She connected her phone and clicked on the driving playlist she'd made specifically for the three-and-a-half-hour trip to Kerry. It consisted mostly of the *Hamilton* soundtrack, but she'd also thrown in some Lana Del Rey, some Fleetwood Mac, some Interpol and even some Lewis Capaldi which she knew she'd skip past when his voice made her eyes mist over and she couldn't see the road ahead properly.

Bzz. Bzz.

We're going to get food then head off in a couple of hours. Might give the best man time to sober the fuck up.

And this is why we didn't have the hen-do the night before the
wedding. I'll be there around twelve x

———

When she arrived at Loughview House, she was immediately
greeted by a team of people, carrying what looked like unlit tiki
torches and rolls of white ribbon down the path towards the
beach. She waved over at Paul, who was talking with two men
she didn't recognise before heading through the open front
door.

Once inside, she left her case in the first bedroom, which
already contained two open suitcases, a half-eaten packet of
Jaffa Cakes and a folded-up wheelchair.

'Thank God you're here,' she heard a voice say behind her.
'The whole place is a riot. I just heard Erin shriek a moment
ago, but I'm pretending I didn't in case she tries to make me an
accomplice to whatever's going on.'

Alex flung her arms around Beth, nearly knocking her over.
'Good to see you! Is it already that bad? Why is it so busy
outside? I thought we all agreed this would be low key?'

'Erin caved and got someone in to organise everything,' she
replied. 'I think she's regretting it. Honestly, even my wedding
wasn't this hectic and we did the whole dress, bridesmaids, the
church, and several thousand family members who all hated
each other thing. This should've been a breeze.'

'Well, you look well,' Alex told Beth, which was true. She
looked healthy. Glowing.

'I'll look a lot better when I finish my makeup,' she replied.
'I've piled on the weight with these new meds, so I've had to
bring a backup dress. My first choice was red and slinky and I
could not get it over my backside. If this one cuts off the circula-
tion, I'm sticking on some sweatpants, I don't even care.'

'Are you managing?' Alex asked. 'I saw the wheelchair...'

Beth nodded. 'I'm still upright most of the time; I just came prepared. I plan to walk along the beach with everyone else, even if I have to wheel myself along some of the way. Now, please go and see Erin and calm her down before she murders someone.'

'That bad?'

'The worst. You'd think she was the one getting married.'

Alex braced herself as she cautiously entered the living room.

'Hey, Lily!'

'Hi, Auntie Alex.'

Eight-year-old Lily Cooper sat cross-legged on the floor, her eyes glued to the television.

'How are you, sweetheart?' Alex asked.

'Good, thanks.'

'What are you watching?'

'*Return to Oz*. The best Oz.'

Lily appeared to be the only person so far who was dressed, hair done and ready to go, even if her black pinafore and red tights didn't exactly scream 'summer wedding'.

'*Return to Oz?* That's an ancient film,' Alex responded. 'I remember watching that as a kid. It was really creepy! Those things on wheels gave me nightmares.'

'It's my favourite film,' she gushed. 'Princess Mombi... she just takes... her head... off.'

Alex grinned. She was certain that when Beth gave birth to Lily eight years ago, she never envisaged her kid being this delightfully ghoulish. Alex adored her. They all did.

'Have you seen your Aunt Erin?'

'There's shouting coming from that way.' Lily pointed towards the kitchen. 'I think she's cross at Aunt Becky.'

'Really?' she replied. Erin was rarely cross with anyone, what on earth could Becky have done?

'Rebecca Murphy, I love you, but I swear if you don't stop putting tiny heads in my freezer, I will never invite you back.'

Alex popped her head around the side of the kitchen door to see Erin, holding up a frozen photo of Ryan Reynolds. 'Why is he in here?' Erin asked. 'The man's a treasure, he hasn't done a thing to you!'

'Exactly,' Becky replied. 'Imagine if I hadn't put him in there last year.' She shuddered. 'It doesn't even bear thinking about.'

'I have twelve heads in here,' Erin said, acknowledging Alex by the door as Becky flitted back into the living room. 'Graeme thinks it's hilarious, but it's starting to give me the bloody creeps. Last year I lifted some frozen veg and found Tom Hanks underneath.'

Four years after she scattered Scott's ashes on the beach, Erin became friends with a photographer named Graeme Hall. Graeme was good for Erin. He made her laugh, gave her space, and understood that he would need to take it slow and while she didn't fall in love quickly, when she did, she fell hard. She wasn't sure if she'd ever marry again, but for now, Graeme was enough. More than enough.

'Would you happen to be a little stressed?' Alex asked, looking at Erin's hair half in heated rollers and the other half in dire need of a comb through. Makeup smeared the front of her pink dressing gown.

'Of course I am,' she barked. 'There's a wedding here in two hours, everyone is running late and Ryan bloody Reynolds is sitting atop my ice trays.'

'Can I do anything?'

'Oh, let me think... are you wedding ready?' Erin asked, her brows furrowing as far as her Botox would allow.

Alex looked down at her trusty Skechers. 'Um, no.'

She tapped her imaginary watch. 'Two. Hours. Just get

ready in my room and the downstairs bathroom has the best lighting for makeup.'

Alex retreated to the living room where she found Becky painting her toenails bright blue. 'Bit nuts around here,' she remarked. 'Where's Julianne?'

Becky motioned to the patio. 'She's outside with the others, being sociable.'

Alex liked Julianne immensely. She had been dating Becky for two years and, unlike *she who shall not be spoken about*, thought Becky was the greatest woman ever to walk the earth.

'Any sign of Tara?' Becky asked. 'If she doesn't show soon, Erin is likely to hyperventilate.'

'Well, Ben was out front talking with Paul and Beth a while ago so she must be around somewhere. If she doesn't turn up, I say we just adopt him in her place.'

'Fair enough. Can you blow on my toes?'

'Jeez, Becky. Buy a girl dinner first.'

'Please?'

'Can't, sorry,' Alex replied. 'I've been ordered to get my arse in gear and I have no intention of facing the wrath of Erin today.'

Becky laughed. 'She's just worried that this wedding is going to be a disaster. Which it might be. I can smell rain approaching.'

'You can smell rain?' Alex glanced outside. Bright sunny day, not one cloud in the sky.

'Mm-hmm,' she replied. 'It's either that or death. I'm not sure, these nail polish fumes are really strong, it's throwing me off.'

Reluctant to press Becky any further, Alex grabbed her case from Beth's room and made her way to Erin's bedroom at the back of the house. Her jaw dropped. It looked like a boutique had exploded. Outfits tried on and discarded on top of eccentric hats and fascinators which would have been quite at home in the Moulin Rouge.

'You made it then... Holy shit ,what happened in here?'

Alex turned to see Aiden standing in the doorway, in his jeans and T-shirt. Yet another person still not even close to being ready.

'A wedding,' Alex replied. 'That's what happened. Choices were made here, and not all of them happy ones.'

Aiden moved behind her, wrapping his arms around her waist. 'Missed you,' he said, nuzzling her neck. 'God, you smell good.'

'And you smell surprisingly well for someone who was at a stag do last night,' she said, leaning into him. 'Everyone all in one piece?'

'Just about,' he replied. 'Nothing that a strong coffee and some electroshock therapy won't fix.'

'Did you see Erin? She's on the warpath.'

He sighed. 'I asked how she was and she shouted that she was *up to ninety* and before I could ask her what that meant, she called someone *a wee shite* so I made a quick exit.'

Alex laughed. 'Getting people in to help is supposed to make things easier... Aiden Smith, are you sniffing me like a big creep?'

'Me? No, I just happened to be inhaling the air around your neck.'

'I need to get ready and—'

'You do need to take some clothes off, yes.'

Alex grinned and pushed a reluctant Aiden out of the room.

CHAPTER 43

'I'm here!' Tara yelled from the patio. 'Can someone tell me why there's a tiki torch display on the beach? Are we having a luau?'

'Seagull deterrent,' Paul informed her. 'They're out in force and last thing we need is everyone getting shat on.'

'Where have you been?' Erin snapped as she flew to the patio doors. 'How can you be the last one to arrive when you stayed here last night? Even the boys made it back from Cork before you!'

Tara kicked her boots off and walked into the living room. 'One of life's great mysteries I guess... Hey, Lily, I like your dress. Very emo.'

Lily had no idea what that meant but thanked her aunt Tara anyway.

'It'll take me fifteen minutes to get ready,' Tara said. 'It's a no-fuss-no-frills kinda wedding. Remember?'

'Though I have opted for frills,' Becky interjected, showing the swishy, frilly nature of her skirt. 'Julianne bought it for me and how could I not wear this? It's perfection.'

'Things still hot and heavy then?' Tara asked, her eyes darting towards Lily to make sure she wasn't listening. 'No more love bites to show off?'

Becky blushed. 'Things are going very well, thank you. And no. At least not where anyone can see them.'

'Alex is in my room getting ready if you want to join her?' Erin suggested in a tone which indicated it was more of a demand. Tara jumped up from the couch and obediently skulked through. She arrived just in time to help Alex zip her dress up.

'Do they make these clothes for fucking orangutans?' Alex asked. 'No normal person has arms that long. King of the swingers isn't the look I'm going for.'

With a little effort, Tara managed to fasten her in. 'Done... I think.'

Alex picked and pulled at her dress making sure it sat correctly.

'It's nice,' Tara said as Alex gave her a customary twirl. 'Understated. And we did say no fuss or frills.'

Alex frowned as she preened in the mirror. She'd liked this dress when she'd tried it on in the shop; a simple full-length gown, high in the back, low cut in the front but nothing too revealing. The saleswoman had told her it was perfect for a wedding. Now she wasn't so sure. 'Jesus, I look like a middle-aged teacher who's been forced to chaperone the school prom.'

Tara was already stripping out of her clothes. 'No, I wouldn't say that. It's probably just more suited to an evening event. Maybe one held by the prison service.'

Alex started to laugh and cry at the same time, much to Tara's amusement

'Look, there's at least four hundred dresses on the floor here. Rummage around. Find something more fun!

'And is your dress fun?' she asked, digging around on the

floor. She picked up a simple pale pink gown and held it against her.

Tara unzipped the large clothes bag that hung on the back of door.

'I'm the bride. Of course it is.'

———————

'Hey, Wednesday Addams, are you good to go?'

Lily nodded, turning off the television. As she turned to leave, she paused and looked Tara up and down.

'Well?' Tara asked. 'Verdict.'

'You don't really look like a bride,' she informed her.

Tara looked down at her dress. 'I don't? What do I look like then?'

Lily grinned. It was the first time she had seen a blue wedding dress, not to mention one which wasn't particularly fancy. 'You kind of look a fairy princess.'

Tara laughed. Maybe not quite the look she was going for but she'd take it. Her (something blue) maxi dress was not only pretty but the most comfortable thing she owned. It was paired with a daisy crown made by Becky (new), a silver necklace her mother had given her years ago (old) and Alex's earrings (borrowed) which they'd decided looked better on Tara ten minutes earlier. On her feet, she wore pale silver heels.

Beth, in a fuchsia-pink dress, complete with puffball skirt, entered the room.

'Now, I know we said nothing fussy, but this is the only dress that will contain my fat arse. I wore it to a Eurovision party and I'm never throwing it away. Hang on, Alex, is that my dress?'

Erin was the last to come down, both sides of her hair now matching.

'Well, don't you look like an absolute treat!' Becky said. In fairness, Becky and her purple frilly skirt looked as delightful, but Erin's peach, A-line dress was just as elegant as she was.

As Tara looked around the living room, she felt completely blessed despite that being a phrase she'd never normally use, because *yuck*. Her friends had done her proud.

'Right lads, shall we go and have a wedding?'

CHAPTER 44

Despite Erin's initial worries, the beach wedding crew had done an amazing job. It was beautiful. Tasteful. White chairs sat on either side of the makeshift aisle which reached a simple wooden arch, with flowers climbing either side and draped white, gauzy cloth.

At the couple's request, the guest list was small – around twenty-five in all: Tara's close friends and their partners; Ben's friends; his parents, Anton and Geraldine; his best man, John; and John's daughter, Harriet, a year older than Lily.

When the music began, everyone turned to see Tara standing alone at the end of the aisle. *Here we go*, she thought. *Time to get married.*

Although they'd planned a small wedding, those faces staring back her made Tara nervous. It reminded her of group therapy, only everyone was better dressed. Their faces were full of hope, full of expectation and (unlike group therapy) full of champagne on empty stomachs.

'I mean, sure, love is great and all, but once you get to know everything about the other person, then what? You just sit there, never being surprised again until one of you dies?

Really, Tara? she thought. *You haven't thought like that in years, but now is the perfect time? What is wrong with you?*

Her heart raced. Her stomach flipped into her throat and back down again into her feet. Little beads of sweat were forming around her hairline and beginning their slow descent down her face and back. As her eyes fixed on Ben at the other end, beaming from ear to ear, she froze. Literally froze. All she could feel was her heart beating rapidly in her chest.

Stop it, she thought. *You can do this. Walk up there, say I do, walk back with some free jewellery. People do this every day.*

She hadn't considered how overwhelmed she'd feel at this moment, or how, even at forty-two, walking herself up the aisle might unlock some deep-rooted daddy issues she hadn't considered until now. Or even the reality of walking in the sand in high heels, an absolute error in judgement Whatever it was her feet and legs were completely numb.

She wasn't sure how long she stood there for, how long she kept smiling as the music played, but she saw a look on Beth's face that told her it was longer than any of them expected.

'Ma'am?'

She felt an arm link into hers. A familiar warmth she'd once known.

'I've got you,' Aiden said quietly. 'Just one foot in front of the other, right?'

She nodded, gripped his arm, and took her first step towards the rest of her life.

———

'As many of you know, many moons ago, Aiden and I once dated,' Tara began. A nervous laughter rumbled across the room. The wedding speeches had gone swimmingly until now. Tara felt that with no father of the bride, she'd speak on her own behalf.

'But a simple twist of fate determined that Aiden and I were absolutely, one million percent not meant to be. That twist of fate being him meeting one of my best friends, Alex.'

Alex felt her arse tighten. *Please do not let this be some weird long-game revenge arc*, she thought. *I cannot run in these heels.*

'However, if I hadn't met Aiden, then he wouldn't have been able to introduce me to his boss, Ben – the man that I was and am one million percent meant to be with. The absolute love of my life.'

As Tara leaned down to kiss her new husband, Alex unclenched. Maybe this wasn't going to end in her getting slapped again.

'I guess what I'm trying to say is that life is really fucking weird – oops, sorry, Lily and Harriet – and in the blink of an eye, everything can change. We get so wrapped up in the small things, that sometimes we forget that these small things are actually springboards to much bigger, better, life-changing experiences.' She picked up her glass and took a sip. 'Twenty years ago, when I left university, I never expected to find myself back here in Kerry, newly married and pregnant at forty-two.' Tara laughed, raising her glass. 'Surprise, lads! It's apple juice.'

Gasps rang out, Ben's mother's loudest of all.

'But deep down, I knew that wherever I was, whatever I was doing, no matter how many mistakes I made, there would always be four girls beside me – for better or worse, for richer or poorer, in sickness and in health.' She watched as her friends all linked hands and Tara held her own to her heart. 'I love you all and thank you, everyone, for coming.'

———

The wedding reception ran from Erin's patio, all the way down the path and onto a gazebo on the beach. Tara thought it was nothing like she'd pictured for her wedding; it was better than she could have ever dreamed of.

Her original surf 'n' turf menu stayed the same, alongside cheeseburger sliders and veggie options for the three guests who preferred not to eat anything that once had a face. There was also an array of mini desserts: brownie bites, old school pudding cupcakes and a selection of bitesize tarts. The wedding cake, already cut and half demolished by the kids, was a three-tier, raspberry-and-champagne-infused sponge with white chocolate buttercream and a layer of raspberry conserve.

They ate dinner on the patio and took dessert in the gazebo, six tables, with white linen covers, everyone floating from group to group, commenting on the food and sharing stories of the happy couple. John's daughter, Harriet, ate herself into a heightened state of silliness while Lily managed to go from indifference to vaguely interested when the evening dancing began.

'Ladies and gentlemen, please welcome Ben and Tara to the floor for their first dance as husband and wife.'

Beth applauded wildly as they walked hand in hand to the floor. Fully expecting something unconventional for their first dance song, Beth was surprised when she heard 'I Do' by Aloe Blacc and LeAnn Rimes begin to play. A song about love choosing you when you thought you were through with it. It was just perfect.

'Shall we dance?' Paul asked, noticing his wife's expression. Although she wasn't particularly romantic by nature, on occasion he'd catch her looking starry-eyed, like now, and it melted his heart.

'I'm not sure I could, love. My leg's—'

'I don't care,' he said, holding out his hand. 'We'll make it work. I'll hold you up if I have to. Just dance with me.'

Beth took his hand and slowly made her way to the floor. Erin spotted her and smiled. 'She's amazing,' she said to Graeme. 'I'm not sure how I'd cope if something like that happened to me. Having to wake up every day, knowing that it's going to be a struggle. Not being able to walk properly or dance—'

'I know. And yet she does it. Millions of people struggle.'

'Yes, but millions of people are not my friend.'

He kissed her on the cheek. 'I didn't mean to sound dismissive. I meant that it's inspiring. And you'd cope because life is worth more than our struggles. And because I would be with you every step of the way.'

'Do you think they'll ever get married?' Alex asked Aiden as she spotted Graeme kiss Erin on the cheek. 'They practically live together anyway.'

'Who knows,' he replied. 'It's 2032. He's divorced, she's widowed, maybe they're done with the whole marriage thing.'

'I think they should,' Alex said. 'Maybe it's old-fashioned, but I personally think it's a beautiful thing.'

'So can we tell everyone that we got married last week, then?'

Alex quickly scanned the room and shushed Aiden, who laughed. 'No,' she mouthed. Not yet!'

After a three-day holiday in Las Vegas, the S in Alexandra's name no longer only stood for Siobhan. It also stood for Smith. Alexandra Smith Moran. She got butterflies every time she said it to herself.

She knew that Aiden understood why she wanted to keep things quiet. Getting hitched abroad during the run-up to one of your best friend's wedding? Tara's wedding? First you steal her boyfriend, then you steal her thunder. *Fuck no*, Alex thought. Today wasn't about them. This was Tara's time; God knows she deserved it.

CHAPTER 45

'Has anyone seen my husband?'

Tara watched five grown men look around the immediate area and shake their heads. She could likewise tell he was not within three feet of everyone, given that she also had eyes.

'OK, any idea where he might be?'

They paused and surveyed exactly the same area once again.

'You know what, it's fine, it's not urgent. When he shows up can you just tell him we're going further down the beach for some girl time.'

Three hours after Tara had become *Mrs married woman keeping exactly the same name, thanks,* she encouraged Beth, Erin, Becky and Alex to ditch their significant others and take a walk with her. No partners, no family, no outside noise, just them.

The beach wasn't any different that evening, Erin thought as she pushed Beth along in her wheelchair. The beach had been the same for probably thousands of years... hundreds of thousands maybe. She knew it was something to do with tides and landforms and if she had paid more attention to geography at high school, she would likely have a more accurate answer; however, tonight the sea looked different. Calmer. Clearer. The waters felt entirely at peace. Erin, however, did not.

'You've been swanning around my house for three days and not a word about that baby,' she exclaimed in disbelief. 'I can't believe it. Quite frankly, I'm offended and we still know nothing! How far gone are you? Have you thought of names? Was this an accident or were you—'

'Slow down!' Tara insisted 'I'm only fourteen weeks! Besides, we wanted to tell everyone, together at the wedding; it wasn't some grand conspiracy. Anyway, you would only have gotten ahead of yourself. You'd have been organising gender reveal balloons before I'd even gotten down the aisle.'

Erin continued to be offended. 'Me? Away you go, I'd have done nothing of the sort.'

Becky snickered. 'You so would have. Five minutes after Tara announced her engagement, you were on the phone to some baker asking about wedding cakes.'

'Some baker? *Greggs* are a baker. Hilary Powell-Brown is a world famous pâtissier who is booked months, sometimes years in advance,' Erin clarified. 'I didn't see you objecting when you were stuffing your face with cake ten minutes ago.'

Becky grinned. 'Hell no, it was delicious. Julianne has been ordered to squirrel away as much as possible while I'm gone.'

Alex noticed that Becky's eyes always lit up at the mention of her girlfriend's name. Exactly as it should be.

'No wedding bells for you two?' Alex asked, pulling her dress out of the sand. 'I can see you and the good carpenter getting hitched.'

Beth agreed. 'Maybe in a forest somewhere. She could hollow out a tree and the imps could ordain the ceremony.'

'It's a bit early for all that,' Becky replied, grinning. 'Besides, imps live in boglands and most of them are arseholes. I'd rather be married by a leprechaun.'

'Do you think Ben's parents are having a good time?' Alex asked, her head turned towards a group gathered at the top of the beach. 'I get the feeling this is all a bit alternative for them. I think they're still looking for the vicar.'

'Maybe,' Tara replied, the water slowly lapping over her toes. 'It's hard to tell with parents sometimes.'

The group fell silent as Tara's hand reached for her necklace.

'We're all so sorry about your ma,' Becky said. 'I'm sure she would have loved this.'

'Love's a bit strong,' Tara remarked with a slight smirk. 'But she would have *liked* this. Definitely liked. I mean, of course she would have bitched and moaned the whole way through, but she'd have been happy about the wedding and the baby. I hope so, anyway.'

Despite her best efforts, Tara had never managed to completely reconcile her differences with her mother. They'd continued their relationship on a superficial level until former Miss Ireland, Louise Landry, slipped and fell on ice last December and passed away three days later from a bleed to the brain.

They continued further along the beach, until Alex decided that she couldn't walk any further.

'Beth, I really feel like you should let me have a wee shot of your chair,' Alex announced. 'Aiden stood on my foot while we were dancing and—'

'What the fuck is it with men and your feet?' Erin asked.

'I know!' she exclaimed. 'It's like I'm cursed.'

'It's not a toy, Alex,' Beth informed her. 'Besides, I let you put your shoes in my bag on the back there, so you could carry your mimosa. I'm already helping you.'

'True,' Alex replied, giving her a small cheers with her glass. 'However, my shoes are not the problem here, it's—'

'You know I'm really unsteady on my feet, don't you?' Beth responded. 'You were there when we had the MS talk, yeah?'

'I was, yes, but... oh! Maybe you could hold on to it for stability and push me like you're going shoppin' or something? Pretend we're at Waitrose.'

'Why would we be at Waitrose?'

At this point, they were all in stitches.

'Do you know how much I love you all?' Erin asked as Beth conceded, letting Alex sit in her chair. 'Like real, true love. The kind that grabs your heart and refuses to let go. That's the love I feel for all you all.'

'Jesus, fine, you can have a shot of my chair too.'

'No, I'm serious!' Erin insisted as Tara declared she might pee herself laughing. 'You're all amazing and I love you.'

'Do you realise that it's been twenty years since we first all stood over there and declared our intentions?' Becky asked, pointing towards the gazebo. 'God, we really thought we were so grown, didn't we? That we had it all worked out.'

'We had no idea,' Beth said softly.

Erin took Beth's hand. 'No idea at all.'

They all lingered, reflecting on just how quickly twenty years had passed. The heartbreak, the mistakes, the people they'd lost.

'Way to bring the mood down, witchy-woo,' Tara muttered. 'Remind me to keep you away from the baby's christening.'

As they all stood there in glum silence (except Alex who had continued to commandeer Beth's chair.) Alex slipped her phone from her pocket.

'She's not wrong though,' Becky said watching Alex tap rapidly. 'We knew nothing back then, but we weren't supposed to. And right now, we know less than we'll know in another twenty years—'

Bzz. Bzz.

'Are you seriously texting right now? We're trying to have a beautiful moment.'

Alex smiled and put her phone away. 'Apologies,' she said, 'and you're right, Becks. We're at a wedding, for God's sake. An excellent wedding by the way...'

Tara grinned. 'It really is.'

'And we're all lamenting over lives that haven't even been fully lived yet. Jesus, we might have been naïve back then but at least we weren't so bloody pessimistic.'

Alex hesitated for a moment as she heard 'Anything Could Happen' by Ellie Goulding begin playing.

'This song!' Becky exclaimed, absolutely delighted that the universe was obviously listening. 'Remember, it was playing the night we made our affirmations!'

Alex would never tell her that she'd just texted Aiden to put it on the sound system.

'Everyone, gather round,' Becky insisted.

'Seriously?' Beth whined. 'Not again.'

Tara groaned. 'I swear if you make us—'

'Nothing like that,' she replied, smiling. She raised her glass. 'To the next ten years. To us.'

And there on the beach, five girls from Dublin University toasted the women they once were and the women they continued to be.

A LETTER FROM JOANNA

A huge thank you for choosing to read *The Weekend Trip*! If you enjoyed it and want to keep up to date with my latest releases just sign up using the following link. Your email address will never be shared and you can unsubscribe at any time.

www.bookouture.com/joanna-bolouri

The idea for *The Weekend Trip* initially came after a conversation with a friend I hadn't seen for a long time. Neither of us are living the lives we planned in our early twenties – in fact I'm not sure anyone I know actually is. Despite all your hopes and dreams, life can knock you sideways when you least expect it, whether it's health or loss or just finally meeting the right person at the wrong time...

We all make and lose friends throughout our lives, but sometimes those friends aren't actually lost, and as I recently discovered, sometimes they're just a Facebook message away.

I hope you loved *The Weekend Trip,* and if you did, I would be very grateful if you could write a review. I'd love to hear what you think, and it makes such a difference helping new readers to discover one of my books for the first time.

I also love hearing from my readers – you can get in touch via Twitter, Facebook or Instagram.

Joanna x

KEEP IN TOUCH WITH JOANNA

 facebook.com/jbolouri

 twitter.com/scribbles78

instagram.com/joannabolouri

ACKNOWLEDGEMENTS

Firstly, I'd like to thank everyone at Bookouture for their help and support, especially my amazing editor, Lucy, who has the patience of a saint. I'd also like to thank the team at Susanna Lea Associates for being as wonderful as ever. Finally, a huge thanks to my friends and family. I love you all.

Milton Keynes UK
Ingram Content Group UK Ltd.
UKHW012250270324
440206UK00005B/292

9 781837 901005